I0823809

Advance Praise for

BEST BOY

"Richly layered and elegantly told, *Best Boy* is a twisty thriller that dives deep into questions of memory, identity, and the ties that bind. Weaving classic mystery elements with the best of modern psychological suspense, the talented Deborah Goodrich Royce deftly draws her reader in, and turns up the tension page by gripping page. This is a breathless and engrossing must-read about the lies we tell each other—and ourselves. Don't miss it!"

—**Lisa Unger**, *New York Times* Bestselling Author of *Close Your Eyes and Count to 10*

"Deborah Goodrich Royce writes with the cutting clarity of a glittering diamond. Bringing readers deep into the mind and voice of leading lady Viveca Anders, Royce delivers a nuanced drama over multiple timelines and wrestles with the weight of secrets—those we keep from others, but especially those we keep from ourselves.

At times dark, at times laugh-out-loud funny, this is a dishy and deeply textured read that will have you racing through the pages to figure out what happened, and what happens next."

—**Allison Pataki**, *New York Times* Bestselling Author of *Finding Margaret Fuller*

"Once again, Deborah Goodrich Royce hits a home run with a suspenseful novel that flip-flops seamlessly as the story unwinds. Ingrid Lind has escaped the past and her humble Detroit origins by transforming herself (literally) into a Hollywood actress, wife, and mother. But while trying to escape what happened one long ago, horrible night she is blind to the present dangers lurking all around. This latest read from the mistress of suspense deftly peels back the onion until the final truth is revealed."

—**Lee Woodruff**, #1 *New York Times* Bestselling Author of *In an Instant*

"This novel is electric—a low pulse that builds and builds, then explodes in a devastating lightning strike. I felt this way right from the beginning, all the way through—I could NOT stop turning the pages."

—**Luanne Rice**, *New York Times* Bestselling Author

"Can you outrun, overcome, outlive a tragic mistake of youth? In Deborah Goodrich Royce's novel *Best Boy*, Ingrid/Viveca tries, but the past lives inside her and haunts her and ultimately manifests in a chilling confrontation, spinning *Best Boy* into another Deborah Goodrich Royce intelligent psychological thriller that the reader is compelled to keep turning pages to finish."

—**Joanne Leedom-Ackerman**, Author of *The Far Side of the Desert* and *Burning Distance*

"From the very first page of *Best Boy* by Deborah Goodrich Royce, I was captivated by the story of the young woman who becomes Viveca Stevenson. Driven by a traumatic event in high school, Viveca reinvents herself—new face, new voice, new life. But just as she settles into her picture-perfect world in suburban Connecticut with her husband and son, someone emerges from her past carrying a ghost of a memory she can't quite recall.

From there, Royce took me on an emotional roller coaster, expertly weaving together three timelines, each more riveting than the last. With a gripping narrative and masterful control of suspense, she explores the truth that we can never fully outrun our past.

Best Boy is a haunting, propulsive novel about the cost of secrets and the past's refusal to stay buried. I'll be thinking—and talking—about this book for a very long time."

—**Victoria Christopher Murray**, *New York Times* Bestselling Author of *Harlem Rhapsody*

"A new Deborah Goodrich Royce novel is always reason to celebrate. And *Best Boy* is a delicious read, full of Royce's wonderfully wicked plot twists and engaging characters. I can't say more because I don't want to spoil the gasp-inducing surprises that keep the reader turning the pages fast!"

—**Ann Hood**, Author of *The Stolen Child*

"*Best Boy* is a beautifully written psychological thriller that delves into the cost of burying secrets to preserve a carefully constructed life. With poignant prose and a keen emotional intelligence, Deborah Goodrich Royce introduces us to Viveca Stephenson—a woman whose seemingly flawless world teeters on the brink of collapse. As Royce masterfully blends past and present, she unearths the trauma Viveca has long tried to forget, crafting a haunting narrative of love, loss, and the fragile truths we hide. Gripping and emotionally resonant, this is a novel that will stay with you long after the final page."

—**Elise Hart Kipness**, Bestselling Author of *Close Call*

"Deborah Goodrich Royce's *Best Boy* is a beautifully layered, deeply introspective, and courageous mystery. While building a deliberate storyline full of twists and unanticipated revelations, Goodrich Royce does not shy away from reflecting on the emotional price of personal tragedies, complicated personal choices, and problematic historical social issues. *Best Boy* is a treasure for both mystery lovers and those who love meaningful literature. Personally, I love a great mystery that comes with a genuine heart and a deep soul and that's *Best Boy*."

—**Jeffrey Blount**, Author of *Mr. Jimmy From Around the Way*

"Deborah Goodrich Royce is the new queen of bladed psychological thrillers. *Best Boy* proves her immense talent. A propulsive novel that had me laughing even while nervously gripping the pages. Royce expertly balances readers' emotions on the tipping point of terror and delight all while extracting her characters' innermost secrets. It reminds me of my favorite cult classic films. As soon as I finished, I wanted to rewind/reread, and so will you!"

—**Sarah McCoy**, *New York Times*, *USA Today*, and International Bestselling Author of *Whatever Happened to Lori Lovely?*

"Deborah Goodrich Royce has outdone herself with her latest, a gripping psychological thrill ride that explores the power of the stories we tell ourselves, the ones we build our lives on, and that we feverishly seek to uphold so as to not fall apart. Best Boy is the kind of novel you can't put down and that you desperately don't want to end!"

—**Christa Carmen**, Author of *The Daughters of Block Island* and *Beneath the Poet's House*

Also by Deborah Goodrich Royce

Reef Road

Ruby Falls

Finding Mrs. Ford

BEST BOY

BEST BOY

A Novel

DEBORAH GOODRICH ROYCE

A POST HILL PRESS BOOK

Best Boy

ISBN: 979-8-89565-334-0
ISBN (eBook): 979-8-89565-335-7

Cover design by Conroy Accord
Interior design and composition by Greg Johnson, Textbook Perfect

This book is a work of fiction. People, places, events, and situations are the product of the author's imagination. Any resemblance to actual persons, living or dead, or historical events, is purely coincidental.

Post Hill Press
New York • Nashville
posthillpress.com
Published in the United States of America
1 2 3 4 5 6 7 8 9 10

Printed in Canada

To Luanne…
Always inspiring, ever generous,
and forever a friend.

"No man has a good enough memory to be a successful liar."

—ABRAHAM LINCOLN

Prologue

INGRID 1998

Feeling returned in stages. Ingrid was asked to describe all of it to the nurses, the doctors, the female officer from the Special Victims Unit. The searing between her legs. The ache in her back and neck. The pulsing throb of her nose and the acid sting in her throat. It hurt to warm up. As cold as she was, the air felt like knives as she thawed in the hospital bed. They finally gave her a sedative.

"You might've died out there," said the nurse as she tapped the needle. "Can't believe it's Halloween. Feels more like Christmas! If that boy hadn't have… Well."

The nurse did not say any more about it. She left that conversation to the cop. And converse they did. Like everything Ingrid was asked to talk about, she was asked to talk about it more than once. It was thoughtful to give her a woman detective. Ingrid didn't know if it was policy or happenstance, but it definitely made sense. It would soften the shame she might feel in recounting the events of the evening. If she could remember the events of the evening.

But nothing came.

Ingrid's memories stopped about an hour after she'd left her friend Emilia's house—dressed up as Posh Spice with Em tricked out as Sporty—and before she came to on the cold hard ground.

She remembered walking through the streets, the leaves mostly gone from the trees, big piles of them placed at the curb.

"Take that!" Em had laughed as she kicked with her fake Doc Martens, sending arcs of leaves flying, unleashing their powdery smell of decay.

Ingrid might have joined her if she hadn't been wearing sandals that laced all the way up to her knees. She didn't want to get leaves stuck between her toes, freshly polished as they were in a burgundy shade that was almost black. Chanel's *Vamp* was what she'd wanted. Instead she'd made do with *Wine Not,* Sally Hansen's knockoff version. Either way, she wasn't about to ruin the pedicure that had taken her two hours to apply.

She remembered arriving at Kelly Roush's house where all the lights were blazing. It looked like a stage set in the middle of a dark theater, like *The Streets of Old Detroit*—the place she'd always loved at the Detroit Historical Museum. The place that had drawn her in when she was little and made her feel safe. The place that had inspired her to start making shadow boxes when she was nine years old.

She remembered flagging at that moment, standing outside the unfamiliar house. Kelly Roush's house did not make her feel safe. Kelly Roush was popular. She was part of a crowd that Ingrid and Em were not.

"Hey," Em had said, grabbing her arm and propelling her forward. "*Boldness be my friend*."

"Shakespeare?"

"Who else to face the Kelly Roushes of the world! And Ing…" Em had paused and turned to her. "How many fucking Halloween parties have we been to in our lives? It's no big deal."

She remembered Em had laughed. And she'd laughed too.

Then they had plunged into the foyer, with its blast of heat and smell of sweat and beer. Kids stood everywhere: in the entry hall, in doorways, on the stairs leading up to the bedrooms. The entire school—it felt like the entire town—was there. Ingrid remembered finding it odd that there were so many people she did not know. Or maybe she just hadn't recognized them in costume.

Ingrid had paused to observe them. Talking and laughing with each other, looming at her like reflections in a funhouse mirror. Leering versions of sexy nurses and naughty nuns. Ridiculous versions of Elvis in the white jumpsuit and Prince from *Purple Rain*.

She remembered a guy handing her a drink, the red Solo cup sticky and wet. And maybe she remembered drinking it. But the block of hours after—hours in which she'd remained at the party and then somehow left Kelly Roush's house to make her way to the high school parking lot—she struggled to retrieve.

And it was those hours in question—four and a quarter of them to be precise—that would be debated by the citizens of her town as they aligned themselves on one side or the other. Those who were inclined to sympathize and those who chose to cast stones.

That night—really it was early morning—in the hospital, Ingrid was asked over and over again to describe what had happened. The detective tried different phrasing. She offered coffee, water, tea. But Ingrid could not imagine drinking anything with the ice pack attached to her nose and the agony in her throat. And none of it helped her remember. She could have saved the detective the trouble—had she had the courage—and told her this had happened before. These voids in her mental landscape. Not often but enough to scare her. The ocular migraines she got began with a blurred-out field in the center of her vision, before moving on to prisms of colored lights that shimmered at its periphery, signaling the onset of the migraine itself. Sometimes—not always—Ingrid would pass out and be left with blanks. Windows of time in which she'd suffered excruciating pain that she simply could not recall.

But never had those blanks lasted hours.

Until tonight. Until sometime after she and Em walked through the door of that party. Until waking up in the parking lot of their school.

At last the drugs administered by the nurse kicked in, and Ingrid found relief—temporary though it was—from torments both physical and mental. The physical subsided in time. The mental was only just starting.

The breaking of Ingrid's nose, in the end, was not the worst thing that could have happened. Her nose, which had been crooked since birth in a way her mother found endearing but other kids made fun of, had made her recognizable in a quirky—imperfect—way. But everything changed that night. All it took was a rhinoplasty specialist to break it again and set it straight. And that forced introduction to plastic surgery—violent though it was—was a key that would unlock a series of useful doors.

From the pain of what happened that night—she knew what it was even if she could not remember it—Ingrid gained her eventual status as a great beauty, which became one of her calling cards. That combined with her voice which, like her nose, would be forever altered in a way that would play a part in her destiny.

In the aftermath of Halloween 1998, some argued that sixteen-year-old Ingrid Lind—already in her senior year of high school and young for her grade—had been raped, beaten, and strangled by a sexual predator. Others demurred. They believed she had engaged in a consensual act of erotic asphyxiation. Her assailant—or partner, depending on which side you fell—had used the long pleather straps of her Posh Spice gladiator sandals, which she'd bought at Party City earlier that day, that much she remembered, to tighten around her throat.

The broken nose—for which he'd used his fist, according to forensics, which found traces of foreign human tissue mixed in with a little makeup—was harder for them to justify. Either way, the first irony was that whatever occurred that night—willing or unwilling—had left Ingrid with damaged vocal cords. Her voice would be forever husky, unable to achieve any volume. It made her sound vulnerable. It made men crazy with desire and aroused in them a longing to protect her. Which brought the next level of irony—the fact that Ingrid elicited this protective response from men after what had occurred in an utterly unprotected moment at the hands of a man. But it was her voice, combined with her beauty, that would make her a star.

But all that would come later.

Ingrid never went back to high school. She stayed home with her mother, who abandoned her career in the same way her daughter abandoned her studies. Her father went one step better and, in fairly short order, abandoned the two of them.

Ingrid submitted to one round of surgery to fix her nose and a second to improve a few other flaws in her face. Dr. Wolensky had liked her.

"Ingrid," he said, peering closely at her nose with the aid of a small ruler. "You could be a beauty. You are very close, really, to having a classically perfect face."

"That's funny," Ingrid said, and would have laughed if she could. "The kids at school call me Woodstock. Like the bird in *Peanuts*."

"I'm quite serious. And I would," he said, turning to Mrs. Lind, "be honored to perform another surgery or two on your daughter. There's not much that needs to be done. A few tweaks, if you will. And the results, I think, will surprise you."

Ingrid looked to her mother, but her mom just smiled distractedly.

"There will be no charge," he added.

That was enough for Ingrid. What did she have to lose? Her mother couldn't say no, not after everything her daughter had been through.

Luckily, it turned out he knew what he was doing. Ingrid soon became unrecognizable as the girl she once had been. Both inside and—thanks to Dr. Wolensky—out.

Not that anyone saw her. Other than her medical appointments and sitting for the GED, she did not venture beyond the four walls of her house. But when it was over, when she turned eighteen, when she felt like she could escape without leaving a trace, she got out of that nowhere town and took her newly perfect face and her newly imperfect voice along with her. She headed west and changed her name and erased her history, in that age-old American tradition. All she'd had to endure was a little pain and humiliation along the way. She'd dealt with worse. And she would have to deal with it again.

But that would be foreshadowing.

1

VIVECA 2018

Viveca Stephenson slipped out the door, shutting it gently behind her. The sun was low to the east and hit her in the face as she turned. She squinted and put on her sunglasses. Just then a herd of deer took off, spooked by her arrival. She counted five of them and followed them down the driveway to the road.

It was a perfect day in September. Which was the perfect month in Greenwich. And Greenwich was a practically perfect town—a geographical version of Mary Poppins. The air was crisp, the humidity of summer gone, but it was still warm and sunny.

Viveca didn't technically live in Greenwich. She lived in Riverside, a peninsula off the mainland, flanked by the Mianus River to the west and Greenwich Cove to the east. It was a part of Greenwich, to be sure, but a less rarified part. If you told someone you lived in Greenwich, it had the ring of Palm Beach or Beverly Hills. Riverside was more ordinary and that was its appeal.

The front of the house faced marshy woods to the east. But the back of the house was what had won her heart when they'd bought it a decade before. Looking west to the river, it caught sunsets 365 days a year. It was where they gathered in summer and fall on the terrace. No matter the season, the view was magical. Boats bobbing on their moorings, and—in the distance—the steeple of the Second Congregational Church peeking above the tree line. *That's the highest point in Greenwich*, Viveca often said, pointing it out to her ten-year-old son. So often, in fact, in the course of Theo's life that it had become an inside joke. Driving through town, he would tease from the back seat, *Hey, look Mom, it's the highest point in Greenwich.*

Just wait, Theo, she would laugh, *I'll get even more repetitive as I get older.*

A mist skimmed along the road as she walked. The temperature was shifting, as if making up its mind which way to go. The grass had lost its spring luster and settled into a deeper green before it browned for winter. Patches of purple asters dotted flower beds, yellow and burgundy chrysanthemums filled pots on front porches, and the occasional crepe myrtle tree was still in bloom.

Viveca continued to the end of the peninsula. She stood on the jutting seawall that always made her feel like the main character in *The French Lieutenant's Woman*, beaten by the wind as she waited for her man to return. There she paused, cast her eyes at the distant horizon of New York, then turned to make her way home.

Her morning walks were her way to start the day consciously. She had learned long ago that grabbing her phone to check the news or—worse—social media immediately upon waking ruined the tone of the day. And she was all about setting her own tone and not letting the world set it for her. Her walks were less about exercise than they were about awareness. She would exercise harder later. After she had driven Theo to school, she would go to Club Sweat where the workout was as intense as the name implied. She was already wearing her Lululemons.

At thirty-six, Viveca felt great. Migraines were still a problem. Her headaches often followed a monthly cycle that corresponded with her periods, but really anything could trigger one: stress, humidity, hunger, even lights that were too bright or pinpointed. But other than this one persistent issue, she had no complaints.

She still looked pretty good too, though she had to work harder for it every year. Since the birth of Theo, she kept her blond hair chin length in a blunt cut that added body to its flyaway quality. Most women her age had long hair these days. Maybe it started with the Kardashians. Maybe the royals, Kate and Meghan. But everyone now had stick-straight hair to the middle of their backs. Or they curled it at the ends and didn't brush out the results, so it hung in adult-aged ringlets. But Viveca had always loved the badass style of the old Hollywood stars like Joan Crawford and Bette Davis. Women like that could not be bothered with long hair.

Her husband was in great shape too. At fifty-six, the silver threading through Henry's wavy brown hair set off his ice-blue eyes. His jawline hadn't yet sagged and he hadn't put on an ounce. There was no denying the unfairness of the male/female aging process.

Viveca stooped to pick a few straggler daylilies in front of her friend Devon's house, knowing she wouldn't mind. She would put them in a vase on the breakfast table this morning as a little surprise for Henry and Theo. She loved to stage the setting, just like she had with her shadow boxes as a little girl.

Later, after the gym and a hot shower at home, she threw on a tan linen shift and flats and hustled out the door, headed for Greenwich Avenue. Once she got to the top of the Avenue, she had to creep along at a snail's pace scanning for a parking spot. It was always a game, though, if you were having lunch at the bottom of the Avenue—at Mediterraneo, say, where Viveca was meeting friends today—as to exactly when you should grab a spot. Greenwich Avenue was long—more than a mile from top to bottom—so if you parked too soon, you'd end up with a hike. But if you waited until you got to your destination, you may have missed your chance and you'd have to circle around. The process could take half an hour.

Viveca was running early as usual. Her friends laughed about her Midwestern habit of thinking she was late if she didn't arrive fifteen minutes early. Well, the early bird and the worm and all that.

A spot!

She wheeled her white G-Wagon to the left in front of Betteridge Jewelry store, just as a woman in a black-on-black Escalade tried to edge in from the right. Viveca held her ground and the Escalade moved on. Once parked with time to kill, she closed her eyes for a moment and allowed the autumn sun to stream through the windshield onto her face. Mostly she kept her skin protected and saw her dermatologist monthly for laser and peel. She and her friends had even toyed with the idea of Botox. At her age, though, she worried it might just make her look startled. Still, there were two lines of uneven length forming between her brows that needed attention. Who was she kidding all alone in this car? She had already made the Botox appointment.

Locking the car and programming the meter, she looked forward to being the first to arrive. Devon Terry, Greta DiNardo, and Max Weinstein were power women of Greenwich. All three of them had worked in PR before "taking some time" to raise their kids, of which they each had three. Three seemed to be the magic Greenwich number. Some people had two or four, a few had singletons like Theo, but that was rare. Occasionally, there were the women who just loved being pregnant, like fertility goddesses, who had five or six. But these were not the large Catholic families of Viveca's childhood. These were families making raw statements of virility and power. *We're-so-rich-we-can-birth-a-team-and-pay-for-it* kind of statements.

Theo was such a perfect boy that Viveca and Henry felt satisfied. Plus Henry already had John and Margo, the children from his first marriage. Though his kids hadn't grown up in Viveca's house—they were already in middle school when she and Henry had married—Viveca had kept rooms for each of them. Now they were out of college and on their own in New York. Theo adored them and they'd always been sweet with him.

Viveca crossed to the sunny side of the street. Her luncheon today was all about the upcoming school fundraiser. Theo attended the all-boys school in town. She and Henry had debated each choice available—everything from public, to Montessori, to single-sex, to country day (as opposed to country boarding, she guessed). And each one had its adherents. They were all well-rated and Viveca would have been happy to place Theo in any one of them. But Henry had wanted to toughen up his gentle son, so the all-boys school was the one they'd picked.

Theo was the best of her. He was the best of Henry, too. He was sweet and shy and not at all like most boys at his school. Those boys had a kinetic energy—an almost electrified need to run and punch and horse around—that Theo just did not. His eyes were green like his mother's. His hair fell in soft brown waves like his father's and Viveca cut it far less than was expected. She couldn't bear to see Theo's curls drop to the barbershop floor as though, like a child version of Samson, his strength resided in them. His nose was crooked like his mother's. Not the nose she had now and had lived with for half her life. Theo had the nose that Viveca had been born with. The nose she'd had until she was sixteen. The nose that was broken and fixed to look better than it ever had. Before she was, in fact, Viveca. When she had still been just plain Ingrid. But on her son, this nose was perfect. It humanized his handsomeness. And everybody loved Theo. He was kind and gentle and bright. He had no real athletic talent—a handicap that could have derailed him at a school like his—but he was smart enough to be funny and to make others laugh along with him. Theo was a beautiful boy in every sense of the word. He was, as Viveca often told him, her best boy.

"Viveca Stephenson," she said, giving her name to the maître d' at Mediterraneo. "Oh wait. It's probably under DiNardo. Greta DiNardo?"

"Right this way," he said as he took up a large menu to lead her to the back room. Viveca checked her watch—it was only 12:15. She'd have time to pull up her auction donations from her phone. She was pleased she had secured some high-ticket items that would do well for the school. She had even managed to get a puppy.

"Viv!" A cry went up from all three ladies who were already seated around the table.

"You're fifteen minutes late! That's not like you." Greta gestured to the bottle of Whispering Angel that was floating in an ice bucket. "We got started."

"Wait, what? I'm distinctly early for our twelve-thirty meeting!"

"'Fraid not, kiddo," Greta said. "Check your emails. The meeting was moved to noon. Remember school gets out early today? Professional development, whatever that is."

"Shoot." Viveca exhaled, plopping down on the remaining chair. "When did you send it?"

"I dunno," said Devon. "Maybe nine?"

Viveca had been at the gym by nine and hadn't checked in.

"Don't worry," added Max, ever the peacemaker. "We've only had some wine and you don't drink anyway. We took the liberty of ordering everyone the chicken paillard. Grilled not fried!"

"Thanks," Viveca muttered, feeling off.

"All right," Devon said, refocusing the group. "We need to top last year's auction so we need big-ticket items. Who has a plane?"

Viveca found herself studying her friends. They were all gorgeous, each a shining model of American womanhood, and all in their mid-to-late forties, a little bit older than Viveca. They had each been in a different aspect of PR. Greta in fashion, Devon in entertainment, and Max in publishing. Each one of them had worked her ass off and then married and had kids fast when her warning bells went off.

Greta did not look like a Greta. She also did not look like a DiNardo. In fact, her ancestry was 100 percent Korean. Her parents had simply liked the name Greta and her husband's family was Italian. She wore Chanel suits as comfortably as pajamas. Maybe it was from her years of organizing runway shows. Viveca, who had tried on Chanel at Saks and found it itchy and restraining, was in awe of her. There was something armor-like about the way Greta dressed and carried herself. A toughness that would deter anyone from messing with her. Max was the opposite: long, loose curls paired with caftans and flowing shawls in bold block colors. Pieces of jewelry that came from exotic places and were large and tribal. Also a little like armor. Her style was formed in the literary salons downtown and it suited her as well as Chanel suited Greta.

Devon, whose milieu had been the entertainment industry and who remembered crossing paths with Viveca back in the day, was the prettiest of them all. She simply shone with her dark curls worn short, golden-brown skin, and amber eyes. Together with the Brunello Cucinelli camel-colored cashmere dress she was wearing, suede boots, and gold earrings, she looked like she should be boarding the private plane she wanted to score for the auction. All she needed was a vintage Louis Vuitton bag to complete the picture. That and a tiny dog.

"How about a puppy?" Viveca remembered.

"Brilliant," said Devon. "Do you have a breeder who'd donate?"

"Not without the winner committing to a full-body cavity search!" whooped Max. "Breeders don't fuck around. They don't relinquish their pups to just anyone."

"Forget about a dog," Greta said. "The last time they had one at the gala, it shat on the dance floor. Then I think it died. Which traumatized the kid whose family bought it."

Devon and Max exchanged raised-eyebrow glances at the use of the word "shat."

"It died?" Viveca was disappointed. "I actually did get someone to pledge a puppy."

"Forget it," Greta repeated. "We can't."

"I have a plane," Max said, changing the subject. "Jonathan's colleague belongs to this ski club in Montana and goes every weekend. He'll donate five hours."

"That's great," Devon said.

"What about the ski club?" asked Greta. "Can he add some nights there?"

"I can ask," Max said. "Hey, Viveca. How about an item from your old acting agent again? People always love those walk-on parts in a movie."

"Sure," Viveca said. "I'll call Rachel."

And on it went. At exactly 1:10, having split the check four ways and agreeing on a 22 percent tip, the ladies all fled to their cars to pick up their boys by 1:30. Viveca had to run in order to accomplish it, having parked, she now realized, way too far.

2

INGRID 1990–94

The thing that first struck Ingrid about *The Streets of Old Detroit* was the fact that they existed in perpetual night, situated as they were on an underground floor of the Detroit Historical Museum. The surprise came when you walked down the steps and found yourself—all at once—leaving the modern era to enter what felt like a life-sized dollhouse. She had already been to Greenfield Village, where old houses had been recreated in the open air. There, you walked down dirt paths to get to them. The sun would shine or it would rain, just like it was doing all around you where freeways buzzed and the River Rouge plant still belched out Fords. As much as Greenfield Village was a world apart, you were still aware of the regular world it sat in. All you had to do was look around you.

But *The Streets of Old Detroit* existed in a basement. It had a sealed-off feeling, like a bubble was surrounding it. As you traversed its bricked pavement—uneven and bumpy—a yellow glow spilled from old-fashioned lampposts and the windows of pretend storefronts. Ingrid's favorites were Sanders Confections and Kresge & Wilson Big 5 & 10 Cent Store, nostalgic renditions of stores that still existed. Not only could you look at these shops from the outside—examining window displays of reproduced old-fashioned merchandise—but you could walk inside and touch such items as plastic ice-cream sundaes and almost real bolts of cloth.

But it was the darkness she found most appealing. It was the darkness that made the yellow light stand out, popping from the shadows and illuminating the various scenes like they were stage sets. It made Ingrid think that—artificial as it all clearly was—the scene could magically come to life. At any moment, those streets might fill with people in period clothes in horse-drawn carts or on those giant-wheeled bicycles that nobody rode anymore. It was the darkness that made her feel safe, like she, herself, was hidden in a cloak where she could watch the world pass by. It was the darkness, in contrast with those yellow lights, that made the space feel warm, no matter how chilly the thermostat read. And it was that juxtaposition of light to dark, onstage to off, player to audience, that she tried to recreate with the shadow boxes she started making when she was nine years old.

Her tools were simple and at hand: old shoe boxes, remnants of fabric, wallpaper, buttons, spools—anything her mom or a neighbor was throwing away. And dolls. Barbies or cheaper knock-offs became the characters in her made-up worlds—shifting from one shadow box to another, changing costumes, becoming whatever Ingrid wanted them to be. At night, she would turn off the lights in her room and shine a flashlight into one of the boxes, propped up on books so she could orchestrate the action with both hands. And, again, it gave her that feeling of an illuminated *seen* world that she could choose to enter or not. She could just as easily remain unseen in the safety of the dark.

The first time Ingrid visited *The Streets of Old Detroit* was with Miss Haney's fourth-grade class from Keller Elementary in suburban Royal Oak. Ingrid's parents, Nils and Betsy Lind, had full-time jobs in the small factories that surrounded Detroit. Her dad was a tool and die maker; her mother was a bookkeeper. They did not have time to take their only daughter to museums.

Fourth-grade social studies had a section called "Your Home State." Miss Haney hailed from old Detroit stock, unlike most of her students whose families were composed of incoming hordes of automobile workers. Miss Haney loved showing off her city, which had been laid out just like Paris, she informed them, after the Great Fire of 1805 had leveled it to the ground. Accordingly, in place of Paris's Place de l'Étoile, Campus Martius became the center from which a series of boulevards radiated out like spokes in an oversized wheel. "Perhaps predicting Detroit's automotive future," Miss Haney had said with a laugh. Miss Haney's favorite day in all of fourth grade was the day they boarded the bus for the Detroit Historical Museum and *The Streets of Old Detroit*.

Ingrid's parents were hardworking, God-fearing people. They took their Lutheran religion as seriously as they took their life. Ingrid's dad was a second-generation Detroiter, his parents having come over from rural Sweden in the 1920s. For reasons that weren't clear, her grandparents had skipped the great settlements of Swedes in Minnesota and Wisconsin and started life in Michigan instead. While Detroit was filled with Poles, Italians, and even a wide variety of Arabs, it was short on Swedes. There were fancy design-minded Scandinavians involved with the art school, Cranbrook, up in Bloomfield Hills. But in Royal Oak, the Linds were an oddity. Ingrid's mother, on the other hand, was garden-variety American, with the maiden name of Stanhope, and she had converted to the Lutheran faith when she'd married Ingrid's father. There were other Lutherans in Royal Oak but they were descended from Germans who had come after World War Two.

By the time Ingrid was in Miss Haney's class, her parents seemed so unhappy with each other that Ingrid could not imagine her mother changing something as substantial as her religion to please him. She couldn't imagine her mom doing much of anything to please her father—other than cook Swedish meatballs, which Ingrid's dad grudgingly allowed were better than his mother's. Ingrid's family was probably not the unhappiest of the entire fourth grade, although Ingrid had no real insight into other families' levels of happiness. Children did not tend to divulge such secrets. Ingrid certainly would not have known whom to tell about her father's drinking. She did not know what was normal when it came to alcohol consumption. She just knew that her stomach tied up in knots most evenings when her dad came home and only relaxed after he went out the door again after dinner. She did not know where he went.

But Ingrid had her boxes. They weren't fancy like dollhouses with battery-operated lights and furniture that looked like miniature antiques. They were just shoeboxes tricked out with whatever Ingrid could cobble together to create a world to her liking. She didn't really show them to anyone except Emilia, her next-door neighbor and closest friend. Em would sometimes play with the boxes with Ingrid, but Em's nature was more analytical. She preferred to stand back and advise Ingrid on what to add or subtract. The highest praise from Em was a cryptic "Sweet!" when Ingrid had made a good one.

Mostly the girls spent time at Em's house instead of Ingrid's. Ingrid's parents worked all day. Em's parents were both teachers—Anne taught high school English and Julius, community college chemistry—so they were more often at home. Em's mom was usually around after school and could be counted on to bake. Molasses and Toll House cookies were her specialties, probably because they were her own favorites. Mrs. Waldron said baking took her mind off the teenagers at school.

"*I would there were no age between ten and three-and-twenty*," she would say, letting the girls know it came from *The Winter's Tale* by Shakespeare.

Em and Ingrid were the tallest girls in their grade. Emilia was a year older but they both had November birthdays. As educators—a word that Ingrid's parents would not have used—Em's parents believed in the benefits of holding back. So Em had started kindergarten at age five-going-on-six, while Ingrid had started at four-nearly-five. In addition to being tall, Em was what Ingrid's mother called "big-boned." Even at practically the same height, she seemed twice the size of Ingrid. With Ingrid's crooked nose, skinny legs, and wispy blond hair that her mom crudely chopped at home, it had been no surprise that the other kids had taken to calling her Woodstock.

Emilia was with Ingrid on the fourth-grade trip to the Detroit Historical Museum. She'd been there several times already because her parents *did* make time for educational outings. As a result, she was not as mesmerized by *The Streets of Old Detroit* as Ingrid was. Maybe because Emilia's household—in spite of her annoying younger brother, Sebastian—was a good deal happier than Ingrid's own, she had no need for that type of fantasy. Or maybe it just wasn't her thing.

Later, as Ingrid moved from elementary to middle school, she added theater to her fan deck of escape routes. It wasn't so different from shadow boxes. Those she had filled with dolls that she used to act out scenes. In theater, she just inserted *herself*—or a self-selected version of herself—into playing the scenes. It didn't even feel like her when she was onstage acting. Plus, there was that continuum of darkness. The same darkness that surrounded the vignettes of *The Streets of Old Detroit* surrounded the players on the stage of the theater.

The knowledge of theater—the impetus to try out for a play in seventh grade—had come entirely from Em's family. Mrs. Waldron—who went by Nan instead of Anne for its Elizabethan ring—was always quoting Shakespeare. She'd often drop his words into her own in an effort to engage the children.

"*Wherefore art thou, Romeo?*" Mrs. Waldron would say, taking time to explain that this was a reference to his name and its abhorrence to the family of Juliet. "If he'd had a different name, would Juliet have been able to love him openly?"

Em would roll her eyes and drag Ingrid upstairs to whatever it was they were doing that had little to do with Capulets and Montagues. Or maybe it did, after all, and they were just too naive to see it. The Waldrons happened to have been Black while the Linds—indeed the majority of the town of Royal Oak—were not. Ingrid understood the comparison but, when she and Em were in elementary school, that kind of prejudice seemed—to Ingrid anyway—remote.

Names held symbolic importance for the Waldrons. Emilia's was taken from four plays by Shakespeare: *The Comedy of Errors*, *The Winter's Tale*, *Othello*, and *The Two Noble Kinsmen*. Sebastian was a name used in three of Shakespeare's works: *The Tempest*, *Twelfth Night*, and *The Two Gentlemen of Verona*.

Once—when the girls were in eighth grade—Ingrid carried a shadow box through the gate in the fence that separated her backyard from Emilia's. Since Mrs. Waldron had given her the Payless shoebox and the piece of gold fabric she'd used, Ingrid wanted her to see the end result. It was a depiction of the child King Tut, complete with relics placed in his tomb (pilfered playing pieces from an old Monopoly game). She had used a Black Barbie, twisted the doll's hair into a turban made with the fabric, and used gauze bandages for the linen wrappings.

When she didn't find anyone in the kitchen, Ingrid brought the box up to Emilia's room to wait for her. Lying on her friend's purple bedspread and staring at the popcorn ceiling, Ingrid heard a heated conversation down the hall. It was coming from Sebastian's room and sounded like an argument between him and his mother. She could not make out the words.

Sebastian was the kid who did not go with the flow of his family. They all loved Shakespeare and Sebastian could quote him as easily as his mother, but he resisted going to plays. They all loved jazz and Sebastian had more musical talent than the rest of them, but he wouldn't show up for band practice. They read, they bantered, they quoted, they embodied the kind of family Ingrid wished she were a part of. But Sebastian withheld his participation. It was as though he was stingy with his superior intellect and refused to share it unless it was on his own terms. He certainly did not even when his family compelled him. His parents were progressive enough to endeavor to accept him as he was. They made a show of not *pathologizing* him, as Ingrid had once heard Mrs. Waldron say to another mother on the phone. This was after Sebastian had done something to that woman's kid, likely talking in circles in a way in which the other kid couldn't keep up. No one could keep up with Sebastian and no one really liked him because of it. He was prone to shifting moods, dark to light but not much in between. Ingrid's tactic was to avoid him.

"Hello!" Ingrid heard Em shout as she stomped through the back door. She hopped up from the bed and ran downstairs to meet her.

"Ingrid!" said Mrs. Waldron, who must have just entered the kitchen herself. "I didn't know you were here. And how was your day, Emilia dear?"

"Ugh." Emilia grabbed a handful of cookies from the tin. "I stink at flute."

"*Our doubts are traitors and make us lose the good we oft might win by fearing to attempt*," Mrs. Waldron quoted. "*Measure for Measure*."

"Mom?" Em took another cookie and turned to face her mother. "I suck at flute."

"Emilia. You may not yet play the flute as well as you someday will—if you persevere—but there is no excuse for using that kind of language."

"We can't all be Shakespeare," Em mumbled through a mouthful.

"Well now, I don't know about that. Even Shakespeare's origins were humble. But he studied hard—education is key, girls—and eventually became the person we think of as Shakespeare." Mrs. Waldron picked up the cookie tin and turned to Ingrid, "Would you like one?"

Ingrid took two. They were molasses cookies—sweet, spicy, and sticky. She could see from the window that the February sky had become inky with just a thin line of orange at the horizon, and realized her mother would already be home cooking.

"I should go," she said and scooted upstairs to retrieve her shadow box.

"Hey." Sebastian's voice in the unlit hall made her jump. He was Ingrid's age—thirteen, a year younger than his sister. But he was still in seventh grade due to the holding-back policy of their parents, which was a fairly catastrophic policy as far as Ingrid could tell. His age, his height, his intelligence just made him more of a misfit. Plus, he was extremely handsome. He looked a lot like Em with curly black hair and finely arched eyebrows that gave them both ironic expressions even when they were at their most serious. On Sebastian though, these features came together in the kind of good looks that made him seem stuck up.

"Hey," Ingrid responded, trying to scoot around him.

"You look older," he said, feinting slightly to his left, which blocked her passage.

"I'm the same age as you, Sebastian."

"That means we can date."

"You're practically my brother."

"JK Ingrid. I don't date girls."

"Well…" She struggled for a response. Was he saying he was gay?

And just like that, Sebastian turned and walked away, effectively dismissing Ingrid and whatever little game he'd been playing. Ingrid moved quickly into Emilia's room, grabbed the shadow box, and headed downstairs to get her coat.

"G'night Mrs. Waldron! G'night Em!" she called out. She didn't add Sebastian's name to the mix.

She was halfway across the yard before she realized she'd never shown Mrs. Waldron her shadow box. Letting herself in the back door, she hung her coat on a peg and lined up her boots next to her parents' shoes. Her father was a stickler for order.

"Dad home?" she asked, kissing her mom on the cheek as she passed her, sitting at the kitchen table. "You look tired. Want me to help with dinner?"

"He took a second shift so it's just the two of us," her mom said and Ingrid breathed a sigh of relief. "Popcorn and movie for dinner?"

"Yes!" Ingrid pumped her fist and went to the cupboard to grab the kernels. Even when there was little that Ingrid shared with her parents, she and her mom could always share movies.

They settled on the sofa for a viewing of *My Fair Lady.* It was one of their favorites and they watched the whole thing. Afterward, a sleepy Ingrid carried the new shadow box upstairs, placed it next to the others, and dived into bed without brushing her teeth. It was not until the next day that she noticed that the King Tut doll was missing.

3

VIVECA 2018

Viveca made it to the school in time but was last in the pick-up line. Once again later than her comfort zone. Theo was his good-natured self and did not complain that he had to sprint to get to her. He was just starting to greet her when he dropped a bunch of papers outside the car door. Viveca put her G-Wagon in park and hopped out to help him gather up his work. Together, they stomped on the skittering pages and snatched them up in their hands.

"Hang on." Viveca stopped Theo from scooting under the car. "Let me grab that last one. My arm is longer."

Standing up, she handed him the final soiled sheet.

"Thanks Mom," he said and gave her an awkward boy hug before getting into the car.

"What's all that?" Viveca asked as she pulled onto the road. "A report?"

"Yep," Theo beamed. "Tutankhamun probably died of a broken leg, did you know that? They used to think he died from a blow to the head but they've scanned his mummy and now they think it was a broken leg that did it. What's that bone? Femur?"

"The thigh?"

"Yeah. National Geographic called it 'one of history's oldest cold cases.' And now it's solved. I mean, too bad for him. He was king and all. Pharaoh. But they couldn't save him from a thigh fracture. But how do you fracture your thigh at nineteen? Isn't that like an old-person thing?"

Viveca laughed. "Well, maybe a horse fell on him? Or he fell off his chariot, or some huge impact like that?" Viveca offered. "I mean, you're right. He wouldn't break his femur from tripping."

She loved how passionate Theo became when he discovered a subject that interested him. He was oldest in his fourth-grade class because of his October 30 birthday. Of course, all his birthday parties had a Halloween theme. This was complicated for Viveca but Theo was such a sweet soul that—over the years—the taint of that holiday was replaced by his shine of innocence.

"Hey, you know I did a King Tut shadow box when I was around your age? One of our neighbors had some gold fabric and she gave me a piece of it."

"Did you save those boxes?"

"No I…no. I grew up and moved out and they got lost or something." Viveca had been open with Theo about her interests as a girl. She was less open about why she lost touch with everyone in her hometown, and why she never went back. "Anyway," she added, "the dollhouse I have in my office is like my old shadow boxes only much better."

"Yeah," he said. "But that's like commercial stuff. Stuff you buy at that dollhouse store in town. I wish I could have seen the ones you made. From twigs and nests."

Viveca let out a guffaw. "Well, they weren't that rustic! I used nice wallpapers and fabrics. How'd you pick King Tut?"

"You know he became king at age eight? Two years younger than I am."

"Don't get any ideas, Theo."

"Have you heard of the curse of Tut?"

"You mean all those people who died when they opened the tomb?"

"Yeah! Howard Carter."

"Right, but I don't remember much of it."

"Wait 'til you read my report."

Viveca felt a surge of love and pride. "I can't wait, sweetie."

She swung up the driveway and pulled into her spot on the forecourt, surprised to see Henry's Porsche missing. She thought he was working from home today. She walked around her car to see if Theo needed any assistance, but he was already bolting up the front steps. She followed him with her housekey in hand and let them both in.

"Aya?" Viveca called from the foyer. It wasn't as though her housekeeper would hear her. No one ever heard her if they weren't in the same room.

"Did you have lunch at school even with early dismissal?" she asked her son.

"Yeah," he called over his shoulder as he was already mounting the stairs, eager—she was sure—to tear off his school uniform and throw on some sweats.

"Well come down to the kitchen for a snack, okay?"

"I will, Mom." And with that he was gone.

Viveca pushed through the swinging doors and blinked at the brightness of the kitchen, where all the lights were blazing. Aya stood at the stove with a wooden spoon suspended above a large pot, one of Viveca's favorite Le Creusets in the original orange color. Daphne, the old French bulldog that had been with Viveca since her acting days, was snoring at Aya's feet.

"Hey Aya," she said as she walked over to the Nespresso machine and rifled through the coffee pods. "Where are the regular pods? The Kazaar I like? This is all decaf."

"I told you to order them last week, remember?"

"No." Viveca faltered. Why didn't she remember that? "Can you order some now?"

"Sure." Aya picked up her phone from the counter. "No problem. I should have done it myself to begin with."

Aya was tall with a ballerina's posture, which was extraordinary because she had to be in her seventies by now. Though she lied about her age so Viveca would never really know. Her life had followed a circuitous path from her childhood in Marrakesh to her young married life in Montreal, to some years later in LA where they had first met.

"Thanks," Viveca said as she scooped grounds into the basket of the drip coffee maker. "Mmm. That smells amazing."

"Harira," Aya said. It was one of her specialties. "And bread."

"Theo will be thrilled," Viveca said. He was a surprisingly good eater for an American kid and relished the delicacies Aya made. He especially liked harira, a soothing wintry soup. And Aya's bread was delicious. Round and thin, it was chewy and grainy at the same time from the addition of coarse semolina flour, Aya always reminded her. It had a consistency halfway between a French baguette and American corn bread. With butter it was one of the seven wonders of the world.

"Oh wait," Viveca said, interrupting her own thoughts. "There's no school tomorrow so Theo's going to sleep at Dixon's. And Dixon's mom wants him there for dinner."

"Will you be having dinner at home?"

"Henry will be in the city tonight. He has his board dinner. He asked me about the shirt he likes with his tux. I almost forgot."

"Yes, I gave it to him earlier."

"Oh. Well good. I'm going to step out for a bit."

Viveca intended to go to a meeting tonight since she hadn't been in a few days. Along with her morning walks and workouts, AA kept her on track, as she knew very well by now. In all the years since she'd been going, she had only slipped once.

"I'll probably eat when I get home," she said. "Just leave it on the stove. Thanks."

"Very good," Aya said. "I'll wrap up the bread."

Viveca poured the coffee and added her favorite oat milk. "Want some?"

"Too much caffeine from tea." Aya picked up her spoon and went back to stirring. "Now my doctor says I need to cut back on sugar."

"You could try it without?"

"It makes me gag."

Viveca laughed. "Hey, I almost forgot. Where's Henry's car? I thought he was here."

"Maybe it was stolen?"

"What?"

"Just kidding. Don't you remember the guy was coming to take it away for detailing? It's on its way back now."

"Oh. Right." Why didn't she remember that? "I'm heading upstairs. Let me know when you're leaving, okay?"

"Sure," Aya said. "Are you all right?"

"I'm fine. Why?"

"You seem preoccupied."

"Nope. All good here." Viveca took her coffee and started toward the back stairs before turning back to Aya. "Did you get the mail?"

"Not yet."

"No problem," Viveca said, changing course. "I'll get it."

* * *

Viveca went outside, cradling the hot coffee in both hands against the afternoon chill. By this time of day, the sun was on the far side of the house, leaving the front in shadow. She walked down the flagstone steps of the porch, flanked by massive Tuscan columns, and crossed the checkerboard of red brick and flagstone of the forecourt.

The scent of cut grass mixed with that of the coffee, all of it overwhelming her with thanks for this place, this family, this life. Gratitude was a practice. Something she *did*, not just something she had. Years in a twelve-step program had taught her this. She looked around and noticed how tall the bank of rhododendrons had grown, dwarfing the short stone wall that separated their property from the road.

She should have them trimmed. They were almost obscuring the stone wall now. All of Connecticut—all of New England—was crisscrossed by these walls. Here, where generations of farmers pulled stones out of the ground, more plentiful than potatoes. What else was there to do with them but build a network of walls that separated neighbor from neighbor?

Everything about her house was different from where she had grown up. For starters, it was Georgian, which was a word she would not have used as a child. A two-story house in Royal Oak would have been called Colonial. And it would not have been clad in gray stone. It may have had bricks on the lower story and clapboard on the second. And it would have been smaller than the houses that surrounded her now.

Then there was this forecourt. No house back in Royal Oak had a forecourt, a word Viveca hadn't even heard before she'd moved here.

She worried about raising Theo amidst such wealth, though he showed no signs of being spoiled. He and his friends were always doing community service in a way she'd never done as a kid. But the sheer abundance of their lives had to have some effect. Though she couldn't really say what advantages she'd had from the scarcity of her own early years. Ambition, she guessed. She was definitely ambitious. But had that been a factor of the simplicity of her origins or the shock of that Halloween night?

She walked on, enjoying the satisfying crunch of gravel beneath her shoes. Henry had redone the driveway when they'd bought the house nine years earlier, declaring it all wrong. The curve of it had been too wide, he said, swinging all the way out to the front edges of the property and making the house look large. To be clear, at six thousand square feet, their house *was* large—even if it was small by Greenwich standards. But, as Henry said, the goal was to make it look less so. Which he promptly did by tightening its circle, piling rhododendrons along the stone wall, and clustering holly trees at the corners of the house to make it appear narrower. Now, when you pointed the nose of your car through the gates, the full width of the house was masked.

And that was another item on Viveca's to-do list. A lightning strike had suspended the gates in an open position about a month ago and she had been meaning to call the electrician. But she kind of liked the way they now gaped wide. Like this, they lent a friendly feel to their property. *Come in*, they seemed to say, *welcome to our humble home*. Even if it wasn't.

Passing through the gates, Viveca flipped open the mailbox. She grabbed a pile of letters and one small Amazon box, wedged in so tightly that she had to set her coffee on the grass to extract it. She paused for a moment, as was her way, to scan through the stack. A car whizzed by, tapping the horn a few times and making Viveca jump.

"Yoo hoo!" shouted the driver. Devon.

"Hey," Viveca said. "Slow down a little!"

"Sorry!" Devon slowed. "See you tomorrow."

"See you!" Viveca tried to raise her voice but Devon was already gone.

4

VIVECA EARLY 2000s

"Viveca!" Lane yelled as she banged open the bathroom door and unleashed a blast of steam. It made their unairconditioned apartment even more unbearable.

Viveca looked up from the annotated copy of *An Actor Prepares* that she had bought used. She didn't know why Lane shouted. They were never very far from one another in this apartment. Lane stood in the doorway, magnificent in nothing but two white towels, one wrapped around her head and one around her torso. She made Viveca think of that actress in a sarong in the Bob Hope road movies.

"Dorothy Lamour," Viveca said.

"What?"

"That's who you remind me of."

"I don't know who she is," Lane said. "But I forgot to tell you my car is on the fritz. Can I borrow yours for my audition?"

"Actually I'll drive you," Viveca offered. "Do I have time to shower?"

"I'm kind of late," Lane said as she bent over to shake out her long dark hair. "Plus I think I used all the hot water."

"Let me get my keys." Viveca stood up. It was smart to drive Lane. As new as Lane was to LA, she wasn't as new as Viveca. She had an agent and got an occasional audition. Viveca hadn't cracked any of those codes. Not yet. "Do you plan to get dressed?"

"Haha. I'll just be a sec."

Viveca ran a brush through her hair, slipped into a dress and applied some lipstick, and grabbed her purse. She scanned the kitchen cupboards for a granola bar to take with her since she hadn't had breakfast. Naturally there was nothing. Neither she nor Lane was gifted at household management.

"Tada!" Lane appeared in a wrap dress and heels. "How do I look?"

"Gorgeous, as usual. But I'm starving."

"I'll take you out for brunch afterward," Lane said. "I promise."

"Good," Viveca said as they trooped down the stairs.

Viveca found two parking tickets tucked under the windshield wipers of the Honda Civic. "I don't know why they give you one after the other. I mean, I live here. It's not my fault I don't have a parking space."

"Yeah," Lane said. "Why don't we have parking spaces?"

"The guy I sublet the apartment from told me I had to park on the street," Viveca said as she started the car. "Which means you, too. Even if he doesn't know you're here."

"What a pain in the ass."

Viveca could not argue with that.

"Can I put on the radio?"

"Sure," Viveca said, pulling forward. "Where are we going?"

"Head east to San Vicente Boulevard. Number 12800."

Viveca turned left onto Olympic Boulevard and cranked up the AC. At least they'd be cooler in the car than they were in their apartment.

She had met Lane at the mall. Right after she'd taken a Greyhound bus from Detroit, right after she'd unofficially changed her name, right after she'd sublet the tiny apartment in The Flats of Beverly Hills from a guy who threw in this old Honda. Still, it was an apartment that—modest as it was—she couldn't afford on her own.

Her first priority had been headshots. She'd been prepared to pay for them—as little as she could get away with—but she wasn't going to pay someone to do her hair and makeup. Her hair was long and blond and didn't require much improvement. Makeup was another story. She figured if she went to a department store and bought lipstick, one of the counter girls would do her makeup for free.

The Beverly Center was a behemoth of an enclosed mall perched above a parking garage. And there at the cosmetics counter in Nordstrom, she had introduced herself as Viveca Anders to a pretty salesgirl named Lane Feldon. Ingrid—or Viveca, as she had to get used to saying—suspected Lane Feldon was not the girl's real name either. It sounded made up. Lane was beautiful in a dark and lustrous way that contrasted with Viveca's blondness. Lane was also a recent transplant to the City of Angels, having taken her own Greyhound bus from New Jersey. She spoke with a slight Jersey accent that Viveca could hear but suspected Lane could not. Lane had sold Viveca a tube of red lip rouge—Lane's affected name for it—and had moved in to share the rent.

Lane burst into song along with Britney Spears, who had just come on the car radio. Viveca joined in and the girls belted out "Oops!...I Did It Again."

They sang the whole song, then Lane got busy finding a new station to avoid commercials.

"Hey Lane?" Viveca said. "I've driven up and down San Vicente three times and I can't find the address you gave me. It doesn't seem to exist."

"What?" Lane looked around. "Wait, let me call my agent."

She promptly flipped open her Nokia and reported back to Viveca that there were two San Vicente Boulevards and they were on the wrong one.

"Shit!" Lane moaned. "I was already late, now we've gotta drive all the way to Brentwood. Why don't they tell you there are two roads with the same name?"

Viveca had no answer.

"Can you drive a little faster?"

"Lane, there's traffic everywhere. There's no *way* to go any faster."

Lane sat back and sulked for the rest of the drive. When Viveca finally pulled up to the two-story building, Lane practically jumped out of the moving car. She started to run toward the stairs and, just as quickly, turned back.

"Forgot my headshot!" she said as she grabbed it from the dash. "You okay here?"

"Mm-hmm," Viveca said. "Hey, good luck."

"You're not supposed to say that, you know. It's bad luck. You're supposed to say, 'break a leg.'"

"Well. You'd better hurry."

Lane turned and ran up the exterior stairs that led to the second floor.

Viveca sat back and closed her eyes. She hadn't wanted to alarm Lane, but a migraine was coming on. For the last five minutes of the drive, she had struggled to see. Normally, whenever that happened while driving, she would have immediately pulled to the side of the road.

And now, the light prisms started. She had no water bottle with her, but she reached into her purse to find a couple Excedrin Migraines to swallow dry. She had to let the ocular portion play out and hope it wouldn't be followed by full-blown pain. There was no way of knowing how long it would last. She should have had breakfast. She shouldn't have let Lane drag her out the door. She should have—

She suddenly felt like she was going to throw up. She opened the car door and was hit with the heat of an LA day. It made her feel even sicker. She closed the door and leaned her head back to combat the nausea. Then she felt herself slipping away.

"Viveca?"

"Viveca?"

"Viveca!"

She opened her eyes and looked around. Who was Viveca? And who was speaking?

"Here," the person said. A girl. "I brought you some water."

She blinked and saw she was in a car. She took the paper cone and drank. Her head was a dull ache.

"Lane?" she finally said.

"Jesus, you scared me!"

"Sorry. I get these, um…migraines. Where I sometimes pass out."

"You should tell a person that, Viveca. I thought you were dead!"

Viveca leaned forward to place her head on the steering wheel and flinched from the heat of it.

"How did your audition go?"

"Well, they'd left for lunch already because I was so late," Lane answered. "There was a note on the door to come back later. But when I got to the car I couldn't wake you. I went to some office to get you this water."

Viveca rubbed the back of her neck, pressing hard at a knot on the left. Her migraines often lodged on one side or another. Thank God this hadn't been a bad one. A bad one could last days. "So you're still not finished?"

"Actually, I just saw them and they asked if you can read with me."

"Me? I feel like hell. I *look* like hell!"

"C'mon Viveca. I'd do it for you."

So Viveca did it. She swiped on a little more lipstick and powdered her clammy face. Sometimes when she'd had a migraine it made her coloring more striking, her skin paler as a doll-like blush bloomed on her cheeks. This was one of those times. When the two of them marched up the stairs, Viveca stood in the doorway with the sun streaming behind her, making her hair glow like an angel's halo. She saw the two men notice.

"You're late," the taller guy—the one who would turn out to be the producer—said, looking straight at Viveca.

Viveca looked around the room to make sure he was talking to her.

Lane spoke before Viveca could. "I'm Lane Feldon," she said as she charged in their direction, her right hand stretched in front of her. Viveca saw both of the men recoil slightly. Not because Lane wasn't beautiful. But because she was heading toward them like a linebacker about to tackle.

"I'll just..." Viveca hesitated, realizing she was stealing the spotlight. "I can wait downstairs."

"No!" the second one—the director—practically shouted. "Our casting director isn't back yet and it'd be easier if you read with your friend."

Lane would later say that she regretted inviting Viveca upstairs with her. She should have, she realized too late, left Viveca in the car and made do without a scene partner. But hindsight is twenty-twenty and fate is cast in the stars. Viveca was meant to be one—a star, that is—and Lane was simply not. Or so Viveca secretly suspected but would not say to Lane before Lane stopped speaking to her.

To be clear, the role Viveca won that day was not a rocket to stardom. It gave her only one word to say in the movie—"awesome"—a word she had always despised. Still, she put some spirit into it and was able to parley it into a contract with a bona fide agent. Awesome, indeed. For her anyway. Not so much for Lane.

The roles came fast. *Awesomely* fast. Viveca Anders was born not so much when Ingrid Lind made up that name and spoke it aloud at the cosmetic counter at Nordstrom. Viveca Anders came into being when she had strung together enough small parts in *Law and Order*, *NYPD Blue*, and *CSI* to be able to claim her seat at the Hollywood table. Even if it was a small one.

She cast herself afloat in that bubble as she untethered from the past. She had not intended to completely sever ties. At least she hadn't consciously planned it. One thing had led to another. She'd arrived in Hollywood with a new name and face—not to mention voice—so the possibilities of anyone from high school recognizing her were slim. Her green eyes might have outed her. Cat eyes, her father had called them, both his and hers. But she didn't think too much about that.

To connect with home, the burden of communication would have been on her. Ingrid. Viveca. In the end, there was no real action she took. It was rather a lack of action. A lack of reaching out to anyone from her old life. Even if it hadn't been intended, there was still a perfection to it. A clean-slate kind of feeling that appealed.

Her parents had separated in the year after the incident. She had never been close with her father. But there was no defining moment of estrangement. It ended *not with a bang, but a whimper*, to quote Mrs. Waldron, who had occasionally branched out from Shakespeare to writers like T.S. Eliot. Ingrid's dad had simply left and Ingrid had remained at home with her mom. He called here and there after he'd gone, but those calls eventually dried up. She believed she had caused his abandonment of their family. She believed it was because of what happened that night. She did not know if she could find him now, let alone if she would want to.

Her mother had not done well. In many ways, the trauma of that Halloween night ate at her even more than it had Ingrid. Her mom was stuck in a loop of guilt and grief. She turned the wheels of her brain around and around in a maddening effort to pinpoint the moment when she could have intervened and saved her daughter. Ingrid had sealed off her own examination of that night and its repercussions into a tight box. She didn't want to dwell in its ugly aftermath with her mom. She also didn't have the tools to help *her* when she was trying to help herself. Between studying for the GEDs and enduring multiple rounds of plastic surgery, Ingrid was so focused on her own recovery she missed the danger signs in her mother.

Their movie nights that had been such a joy when her father was away from the house for an evening ceased to occur once her father had left for good.

Her mom's ability to work diminished and, in time, disappeared. She was seized with a terror of leaving Ingrid alone. She hovered and fussed and Ingrid regretted later that she did not have more compassion for the state of anxiety her mother was living in. Mostly Ingrid was annoyed with her, trying to carve out a little space for herself in that house which was closing in on them both.

In the end, Ingrid got on that bus and got out of town and her mother did not last the year. As the last remaining Lind, Ingrid's mom made her final exit by way of a surprise heart attack. Except Ingrid was not surprised. She knew how fragile her mother had become and she knew she should not have left her. But it was all too much to bear. So into a carefully sealed compartment in her mind went that bit of heartache along with the rest of it. Ingrid—now Viveca—just could not face it all. What happened that night. What happened after. The loss of her father. The much more painful loss of her mother. So face it she did not.

Viveca had not spoken with Em since shortly after that Halloween night. That tie could not be saved. Their lifetime of friendship came to a precipitous halt and there was nothing anyone could do about it. No more Emilia. No more Mrs. Waldron's cookies. No more walking through the gate in the fence between their yards. No more Shakespeare. No more Sebastian. All of it was finished and that finishing was final. There was no way back from where they had gone after that night.

But now, as Viveca in Hollywood, the world opened up before her. She moved out of her ratty apartment with Lane and rented a little house in the hills above Sunset Plaza. She bought a used Chrysler—a Sebring convertible in a shimmering baby blue—in a nod to her Detroit roots. She drove with the top down blasting music and heat. She carefully shared her story with people she met, revealing only preselected highlights of truth mixed with larger slices of fiction.

Viveca curated the life of a Hollywood actress like those she'd read about in the past. She drove out to the Pacific Ocean to read scripts, following along Mulholland and ending up on remote beaches peopled only by surfers. There she would sit wrapped in striped pool towels she'd "borrowed" from the Beverly Hills Hotel, eating cheese and sweet pickle sandwiches and drinking rosé from a jelly jar.

It turned out she liked to drink. The habit for which she had judged her father so harshly was becoming her own. But the bottle wrapped itself around Viveca differently than it had around her dad, and that was the dangerous seduction. It made denial plausible. She was not an ugly drinker in the way her father had been. She did not become critical or abusive. She was the kind of drinker who became more fun with a few pops in her. Freer, flirtier, less hobbled by thoughts of the past. So how could she be like him?

And she always functioned. She got herself to work every morning no matter how much she had imbibed the night before. In that way she was more like her father than she cared to admit. He had never taken a day off work in his life. So she couldn't consider herself superior to him in that respect. But she did not connect those dots. She had friends and boyfriends and jobs and life seemed to be good. In fact, she didn't know how it could get any better.

Then came a life-changing call.

While Viveca was on location in British Columbia, the assistant to Rachel Geller—a known star-maker agent—rang to say that her boss wanted to meet her. That she'd heard good things about Viveca and had seen one of her screen tests. Viveca could have missed the call because cell phone reception was so bad in the woods where they were shooting. But the assistant had caught Viveca when she was still in the motel before boarding the van for the set. Since the movie was only days from wrapping, Viveca was able to schedule an appointment right away. She would fly home on Sunday and meet Ms. Geller the following day.

5

VIVECA EARLY 2000s

"Sit down." Rachel Geller got right to the point as Viveca hovered at the entrance to the office. She was a large woman who owned her size in a sweeping black dress and chunky jewelry. Viveca guessed her to be about forty.

"Don't lurk in doorways," Ms. Geller went on. "It's inelegant. And close the door while you're at it."

"Hi," Viveca said and did as she was told, shutting the door and crossing over to a big tapestry chair. "This is pretty."

"George Smith. Costs a fucking arm and a leg but I'm worth it."

"Should I…?" Viveca backpedaled from the expensive chair and looked around for an alternative.

"Sit. It's tough as nails. Kilim." In all of Viveca's forays into shadow box decorating as a child, she had not encountered that word.

"That's the kind of tapestry?" she asked.

"They make it in villages in Turkey. It's for rugs so you couldn't destroy it if you tried. Well, maybe if you tried." She pivoted. "So, tell me about yourself."

"Well," Viveca began as she perched on edge of the George Smith Kilim chair. She would file that design information in her brain for future use. “There’s not much to tell. I grew up in rural Michigan. My parents were farmers and I was homeschooled. I’m an only child. Both my parents are dead.”

“Ha!” Rachel Geller whooped. “Bullshit! That’s the biggest turd anyone has ever dropped on my desk.”

“I…” Viveca lost her bearings. She had created a life history for herself, just like she’d learned to do in acting class for a character, and she thought it was rather good. She wasn’t sure how to continue.

“Homeschooled? What the fuck is that?”

“It’s when your mom…”

“Christ! I know *what* it is but what kind of *story* is that for you to be telling me right to my face?”

“The truth?” It came out much weaker than Viveca intended.

“And I was raised in a convent!”

Viveca’s mind went blank.

“Which I wasn’t! Because I’m Jewish! And because I’m from New York, where I went to Stuyvesant and then Brown! Because I’m smart! And you, Miss Whatever-Your-Name-Is-That-Sounds-Made-Up, should cut the crap right now or you can get your little ass off my George Smith chair and go back to your little agent and have yourself a little career.”

And that was how they became business partners. And, in time, friends. Viveca told her real story to Rachel Geller—most of it anyway—because the alternative held no appeal. She did not wish to have a little career or a little life. Big was what she wanted and Rachel Geller was big. Her person. Her jewelry. Her furniture. Her vision for her clients and her ability to deliver on that vision. Viveca wanted what Rachel had to give.

Once Rachel had smacked Viveca down on her made-up story, she proceeded to make one up for her that was remarkably similar. In fact it was the same. Raised on a farm on the Upper Peninsula. Swedish immigrant parents. Both dead in a car accident after homeschooling Viveca through high school.

“Nope. Wait,” Rachel interrupted herself. “Not a car accident. Too much chance of newspaper coverage. Cancer. They died of cancer. Not some environmental wipe-out like the fucking Love Canal, though. Just regular cancer. In fact, go with something down there." Rachel indicated her nether regions. "Like prostate. Cervix. People even die of cancer of the ass!"

"It sounds ridiculous," Viveca said.

"It *is* ridiculous." Rachel laughed. "That's why it'll work. You'll be like a modern Laura Ingalls Wilder. But tragic. People will love it."

People did love it. And her. Viveca, the orphaned farm girl with the angelic face and the devilish voice. There wasn't much anyone could find on Viveca on the internet so it was good to have a backstory that fit with that blank slate. Hay, cattle, sheep, oats, potatoes, barley. If you did the research, that was what they farmed on the Upper Peninsula of Michigan.

"Go with hay," Rachel counseled. "I mean, we're all familiar with grass. Which is hay-like. Hell! Maybe it *is* hay that we just cut short. Who the fuck knows. Don't go with cattle. You may get asked tricky questions and get backed into a corner. And read up on hay farming so you're ready for anything."

"Okay."

"Do you know any Swedish words?"

"Um, my dad was Swedish, not my mom. So, no, not really. He didn't even say much in English."

"Well. *Skol. Skål. Skull,*" Rachel said as she clinked her wine glass against Viveca's. They had gone out for dinner at Musso and Frank because Rachel was trying to school her in old Hollywood traditions. "Here's to making you the hottest Swede since Ingrid Bergman. You know who she was, right? You're not one of those starlets who doesn't know anything about film history?"

"Play it again, Sam!" Viveca practically yelled, proud that she could show off a little. Being with Rachel gave her precious few opportunities to shine intellectually.

"That's not what she said. She said, 'Play it, Sam.'"

Figured.

"I'm working on something that'll happen soon," Rachel continued. "A chance to meet Richard Curtis. Did you see *Notting Hill*? *Four Weddings and a Funeral*?"

"I loved those movies!"

"Well, he's got a new project in the works and I want you to meet him. But I want to wait until he's met everyone else first. It's *all* about timing, my dear. All of it."

It turned out that Rachel was right about timing. But it also turned out that timing was the thing Viveca got wrong instead of right. She met Richard Curtis and he liked her a lot. Rachel's timing had been spot-on in that way and Curtis immediately offered Viveca the lead in his as-yet-unnamed film. It was going to be a big production funded by a big studio.

But the truth was that Viveca—through her old agent, the little agent that Rachel had belittled—had already signed the contract on *A Dangerous Game*, a little film. It was not a great moment in the annals of their relationship when Viveca had to confess to Rachel that she needed to do that other movie first. Rachel did not take it well. But, being the resilient adapter that she was, Rachel began to spin straw into gold. She rationalized that it would be quick, that it would be over before the Curtis film began, and that it would hardly count as a feature since it would go straight to video anyway. No one would even know that Viveca had done it. Plus it might be good for her to cut her teeth on one more negligible film before tackling what was sure to be a noticeable role in a big-studio picture.

Some of those things turned out to be true and some turned out to be false. Back in LA, Rachel worked out the details of the deal on Viveca's breakout role in Richard Curtis's next film. And up in Carmel, Viveca did her action movie and it all seemed to go off without a hitch. They finished up and they all gathered at a local restaurant for the wrap party.

And maybe Viveca had been tired or maybe she had her period or maybe she'd just gotten over a migraine or maybe all of the above. But what was certain was that she drank too much. She had been pushing that envelope for a while and the night of the party she pushed it right off the edge of the proverbial table. She got in a car she had no business getting into—it belonged to the director—and crashed it off the edge of some corkscrew road. The director was in the passenger seat of his own car because he was actually drunker than Viveca. Viveca broke her collarbone from the impact of the seat belt, her left arm from she knew not what, and had a nasty black eye that lasted weeks. Miraculously, the rest of her face remained unscathed. The director was banged up but decided to let it drop so his wife and kids wouldn't ask too many questions. Rachel stepped in and settled things down with the producer. Viveca flew home to LA to recuperate. And Rachel made one demand.

"Get your ass into AA or your work with me is over."

And that—as Porky Pig would have said—was all folks. It was really what it took to force Viveca to get hold of herself. She had enough raw ambition to do what it would take to succeed. But it was too late to save the Richard Curtis film. With her injuries, she was unable to begin rehearsals on schedule and the role went to another actress. It would take Rachel another year to get Viveca back on track, but—by then—both Viveca and Rachel hoped to put the incident behind them.

6

VIVECA 2018

Viveca had a pretty good imagination. She could see the murderer, for example, lurking behind the pleasant facade of the white-haired librarian. Or the terrorist in the shifty-eyed man with a too-large bag on the subway. The sort of reveries people catch themselves having then laugh, saying to themselves—or the friend sitting next to them—"You won't believe what I just thought about that librarian. I imagined her chopping her colleague into tiny cubes to feed to her cat!"

She also thought of herself as cautious. If someone said, "Your money or your life!" with a gun to her head, she was certain she would comply. If she saw trouble brewing in a dark alley, she knew she would take an alternate route. This is what she believed, anyway, in spite of the obviously flawed choices she'd made in the past.

But the mind often seeks normality, no matter how abnormal a situation is. The mind, in fact, will go to great lengths to maintain a sense of order. Or, more accurately, to impose a perception of order on chaos. More often than not, a false perception.

After Viveca dropped Theo at Dixon's house in backcountry Greenwich, she hopped on the Merritt Parkway to attend a meeting at a church in New Canaan. She always felt better after a meeting. Less alone, less isolated within the confinement of her head.

She took I-95 home and stopped at Taco Bell. Tacos were Viveca's guilty pleasure. She never ate fast food in front of Theo. Or Henry. But, considering her bigger demons, a taco seemed a pretty tepid indulgence from time to time. The seductive smell of the greasy meal reminded her that it had been hours since her lunch with friends. She wolfed down all three tacos in the car by the time she pulled into her driveway.

On the porch, Viveca encountered a tableau that was distinctly out of the ordinary. On the left rested a pile of white fabric bunched up and dropped in a heap. On the doormat was a small piece of what looked like torn paper. The screen door stood wide open. Odd elements, to be sure, but not of themselves alarming. True, it was not how she'd left the house. When she'd gone out earlier, the screen door had been closed, like the heavy wooden door itself, and—except for the neatly placed doormat—the surface of the porch had been empty.

Viveca's mind briefly alit on the scrap of paper on the doormat, reminded of a novel in which a character was warned to keep a piece of paper wedged into the doorjamb. In this way she would know—if she returned home to find it had fallen—that her stalker was inside, waiting to kill her. Then her mind leapt over that thought as it worked to normalize the scene. And since Viveca had not, in fact, intentionally left a piece of paper in the doorjamb, it did not seem to apply.

Did I call the painter? she wondered, staring at the bundle of fabric that looked like it might be a drop cloth.

What was in need of painting? she further thought, turning her glance to the open screen door. *Wait…Aya must have called the painter to varnish the wooden door sill, which had been scratched by people's shoes.*

Viveca stared at the door sill. She could see that it was badly scuffed and had not been varnished recently. Clinging to the narrative, however—despite all evidence to the contrary—she entered the house, careful not to step on the door sill.

Locking the door behind her, Viveca dropped her bag on the hall table. She turned toward the stairs, and—confronted with the next bizarre picture in what was turning out to be a long string of them—froze. The staircase in front of her was shattered, its spindles and banister smashed and scattered across the floor. It was such an odd visual—something as massive as a staircase broken—that her mind still refused to process it.

And then Viveca heard the dog. Daphne was incessantly barking from somewhere in the direction of the kitchen. Viveca needed to get to her but the detritus from the stairs blocked her path. The absolute absurdity of finding her staircase destroyed in this way again prompted Viveca to seek an explanation that was *normal.* She grabbed her cell phone and called Aya.

"Did you fall down the stairs?" she asked. It was a ridiculous question. If Aya had fallen with enough force to shatter the banister, she would be dead or unconscious on the floor.

"What?"

"I said…" And then the normalizing stopped. It came to Viveca—in one bright burst—the meaning of what she was seeing. Someone had been in her house. Someone had thrown or dropped something down her stairs—an extremely heavy something—with enough violence that it had crashed through the railings where the stairs made a ninety-degree turn. She could now see that whatever had come down her stairs with such force had broken several stair treads as well. And then it came to her what that object must have been. It could only have been a safe. Their five-hundred-pound safe that was safely—or so she'd believed—bolted to the floor of Henry's closet. And then she realized that whoever did this thing could still be upstairs.

"Aya! Don't hang up! Please! I'm grabbing Daphne and getting out! I'm leaving!" she directed that last line upstairs for the benefit of anyone who might be listening. She wanted them to know—if they were still there—that she was getting out. That she posed no threat to them. But would they be able to hear her? No one could *ever* hear her.

"Are you okay?" Aya asked. "What's going on?"

"Listen!" Viveca implored. "If you hear something happen to me call 911!"

Why she didn't just disconnect from Aya and call the cops herself immediately she could not later explain.

Passage into the kitchen was impossible. Even if Viveca would have been able to move the splintered railings, she was sure the police would want to investigate the crime scene untouched. Crime scene! The words brought her back to that Halloween night and her hands reflexively rose to her throat.

She moved quickly into the dining room to access a second door to the kitchen. Inside, another explanation became clear. There on the floor, below a wide-open window—just the way Viveca had left it—was a sliced and bent screen.

Daphne was not in her usual bed near the kitchen table. Viveca quickly followed the sound of her barks to find her cowering in a corner of the laundry room. She shuddered as she picked up the dog and made her way out of the house, reversing the path she'd just followed and grabbing her purse along the way. She ran to the car, placing Daphne, her purse, and the phone—still connected to Aya on an open line, she prayed—on the passenger seat. She locked the doors before starting the engine and speeding down the circular driveway. When she was finally out on the road, in potential view of the neighbors, she disconnected with Aya and dialed 911.

Within minutes, a string of police cars arrived silently. Equally silent, two cops emerged from each vehicle—shield in one hand, drawn gun in the other. Viveca got out of her car to greet them.

"Thank you!" she began. "I came home and I..."

"Shhh!" the officer closest to her commanded. A woman. "Please be quiet."

The meaning of the shields and the guns became vivid.

"Is the house locked?" the same cop asked her.

Viveca tried to remember whether she'd locked the door behind her. She looked toward the front of her house. The view was blocked by the overgrown rhododendrons along the stone wall. Even with the gates wide open, you couldn't see Viveca's front door from the road, which may have been part of its attraction to burglars. "Yes, I think so," she answered.

"Can I have the key?"

Viveca went to her car to retrieve it. She handed the key to the officer, who paused and looked hard at her.

"Aren't you..."

"Yes," Viveca said. "I am. I mean, I was. I don't act anymore."

"I see," the cop said, as though there was something to be understood in the fact that Viveca had left her film career. An explanation of the night's events. Then she abruptly turned toward her comrades and nodded. They moved beyond Viveca as one, lifting their shields and leaving her standing in the middle of the road. *They looked medieval*, she thought, *like soldiers going into combat. All they were missing was chain mail.*

She needed to call Henry. She squinted at her watch and was startled to see it wasn't even ten. Whoever had broken into her house had done it in the early evening. Had it even been dark? And how had they known she hadn't just dashed out to the market and wouldn't return and surprise them? Viveca usually set the alarm when she was home alone at night, but she only did it when she was going to bed, after letting Daphne out one last time. Had she set the alarm when she'd taken Theo to Dixon's? No. Aya was still in the kitchen at the time and would have been the last to leave. And she wouldn't have set the alarm because Viveca had made such a point of keeping the windows open for the crisp fall air. The alarm would not have worked with all the windows open.

Viveca got back into her car and pulled Daphne onto her lap. The dog snuffled and settled and the warmth of her made Viveca feel better. Should she call Dixon's mother? What would she say to her? She couldn't very well go pick up Theo now, with the police still here. And why bring her son back to a house that had just been invaded? A house that no longer felt like their family's safe haven.

The brazenness of the incursion stunned her.

It was time to tell Henry. Viveca picked up her phone to dial him, but the call went straight to voicemail.

7

VIVECA 2018

As she waited, Viveca repeatedly tried to reach her husband. She shouldn't have been surprised he didn't pick up. It was the middle of his board dinner and he may have turned off his phone. Yet she felt unsettled.

It took nearly half an hour for a detective to reappear.

"Ma'am?" A cop leaned into the open car window, startling Viveca. "I'm Detective Kopple. Can you come with me?"

"Yes," she said. "Of course."

"Bring your car," he added.

Viveca pulled up the gravel drive.

Inside, she kept Daphne in her arms. Two cops—Kopple and the woman who identified herself as Gleason—led Viveca through her own house following the path of the robbers.

"They came in here," Gleason said, pointing to the kitchen window. "Then they went this way," Gleason continued, leading her down the back hall where some pictures had crashed to the tile floor. Glass crunched beneath their feet.

"Why would they go this way?" Viveca asked.

"They may have been trying to avoid the main staircase with its windows facing the street," said Kopple.

The cops did not turn on any lights as they walked, using the flashlight app on their cellphones instead. *Were they trying not to touch anything?*

"See here?" Kopple aimed his light around the bedroom at the top of the stairs, illuminating its blue hydrangea wallpaper in lurid streaks. Viveca tried to remember who made this wallpaper. Was it Colefax and Fowler? Something English but she wasn't sure.

"Ma'am?" Detective Gleason pointed her light at various spots. A closet door stood open, along with several dresser drawers. This was a room that doubled as Aya's when she slept at the house and was sometimes used for guests. "Looks like there was minor searching here unless you left the room like this?"

"No," Viveca said. "I'm sure it wasn't left like this."

On to the next bedroom, normally so cheery in a yellow floral wallpaper. There was the same evidence of the thieves' work in here: drawers hanging open, closet doors gaping. A pillow—stripped of its case—had been tossed to the floor.

"Why did they take a pillowcase?" she asked.

"To stuff with whatever they're taking," responded Gleason. "Take your time in the coming weeks to look around your house for anything that might be missing. Sometimes it takes a while to notice what isn't where it should be."

No one knew that particular fact better than Viveca herself.

"So, we think they moved quickly once they noticed the, um, primary bedroom at the far end," added Kopple. "You can see it from here."

Viveca looked up to see her bedroom at the end of the corridor, past the central staircase so recently trashed.

They continued on, peeking into Theo's room as they passed. Again they swept their flashlights in circles. It was such a perfect little boy's room she hoped he wouldn't grow out of too soon. Red-and-white-striped lower walls separated by a chair rail from blue walls with stars above. Toy horses clustered around a corral on a table by the window, reminiscent of the setups of her long-ago shadow boxes. Stuffed animals at the foot of the bed. Lacrosse sticks standing straight in an old umbrella stand. Books in their shelves and Theo's King Tut papers stacked on his desk. A place for everything and everything in its place.

"They don't usually expect to find anything of value in children's rooms," Gleason explained.

The thought of strangers' hands rummaging through Theo's childhood treasures made Viveca sick to her stomach.

Still continuing by way of flashlight—though a soft glow now rose up from the lamps in the foyer below—they made their way into her bedroom.

What she saw made Viveca grab onto the wall. The room had been ransacked. Not only were drawers left open and hanging at precarious angles, but the contents of those drawers were strewn about the floor. Underwear, scarves, and jewelry boxes were everywhere. Viveca knew these boxes had all been empty. She'd removed the jewelry to store in cases in the safe and kept the pretty boxes in a dresser. Now, a rainbow of Cartier red, Mish purple, and Tiffany blue covered the floor like spin art. It was clear from how far they had thrown them that the robbers had been annoyed by the empty boxes.

For reasons Viveca found less clear, her bed was disheveled and the matelassé coverlet was missing. In a flash, she realized that what she had seen on the porch must not have been a drop cloth at all. It must have been her bed linens. Why, she had no idea.

Following Kopple and Gleason into her dressing room—all aqua-lacquered woodwork and striped silk cushions—she saw more of the same. Orange Hermès and black Chanel boxes were torn open and tossed to the floor. Like the jewelry, Viveca had removed these purses to store in cubbies in their felt dust bags. The vestiges of the violent sacking of her possessions continued for about five feet into the dressing room and then abruptly stopped. Everything after that point remained intact and neat as if nothing had happened at all.

"We think this is when one of them found the safe and called off the search," Gleason said.

"This way," Kopple piped in, though Viveca did not need them to lead her to the safe. She knew where it was—where it *had* been—in her husband's closet. But she trooped behind them like a good little soldier anyway. And there, in Henry's equally well-appointed dressing room, finished in mahogany paneling and dark blue velvet curtains, the safe that held her jewelry and their family documents was gone. Only a large and rough-edged hole was visible in the floor, next to a deep row of splintered grooves.

"They crowbarred it out," said Kopple, pointing to the chunks missing from the floor. "They pulled the bolt right out. See that?"

Viveca did see it but was too stunned to speak.

"These gouges are from the crowbars they used to jimmy it up. Had to have been at least two of them. Maybe three. They had to put some muscle into it. And then,"—he walked over to the doorway and pointed his flashlight at the bed—"they would have taken a blanket or whatever from the bed and flipped the safe onto it and dragged it down the hall. Until they let it fly down your stairs."

The magnitude of the crime—and its attendant violence—was plain. These men, and they had to have been men to have had the "muscle" the detective referenced, were nothing like John Robie ("The Cat"), the jewel thief played by Cary Grant in Hitchcock's *To Catch a Thief,* her mother's favorite movie. That character robbed your house wearing espadrilles. That character practically left a rose on your pillow when he took your necklace. That was a character you would want to date. These guys were not that guy. These guys had ravaged Viveca's room, had wrenched a five-hundred-pound safe out of its bolting to the floor, had sent the entire thing careening down her staircase with such force that it had splintered like a game of jacks.

"Ma'am?" said Gleason. "We'd like to ask you some questions. Why don't we go downstairs?"

Viveca looked from one cop to the other, as they looked impassively back at her. It suddenly crossed her mind that they might think she had something to do with this.

"Viveca?"

Viveca spun at the sound of Henry's voice. Suddenly his face was fogged out by the scrim that was closing over her eyes, signaling the start of a migraine. A shadow was forming in the center of her vision. Next would come the brilliant slices of color that would dance in an arc above one eye—electric blue, canary yellow, Kelly green, candy apple red—and it all would last about fifteen minutes. Nothing could speed it up. Nothing could slow it down. Whether or not it was followed by searing pain was anyone's guess.

"Are you all right?" Henry continued. "What the hell's going on?"

"I need to sit for a minute. I'm having an ocular migraine," Viveca said to the crowd she could no longer see as she groped along the wall, meaning to sit on the bed. But the evidence of the bed's recent ravaging by strangers made her recoil as she neared it. She sat on the floor beside the bed instead, resting her head in her hands.

8

VIVECA 2002

"Can you make me a skinny margarita?" Viveca leaned over the bar as far as she could toward the hunky bartender in the tight black T-shirt. The noise level at the wrap party for *A Dangerous Game* was on depth charge.

"Poof," he said, raising both hands in her direction and wiggling his fingers, abracadabra style. "You're a skinny margarita. And I'm Bartender Ben."

"You're funny," she said, sizing him up. She could do worse tonight.

"And you're gorgeous." He smiled and winked before turning to his work. "One skinny margarita coming up."

"Number four? You might want to rein it in there, cowgirl."

Viveca turned to look into the crinkled, smiling eyes of Sidney Cassin. Sidney had played her father in the film they were now celebrating the end of. The merciful end. She prayed it went straight to video and died a quiet death.

"But who's counting, right, Sidney?" she asked.

"Right. Hey Bartender Ben?" Sidney turned, letting both Ben and Viveca know he'd just witnessed their flirtation. "Another Diet Coke for me."

"Coming right up," said Ben. If that was even his name.

Sidney Cassin was a movie star, the first Viveca had ever met. He had even been nominated for an Oscar. His star had eclipsed, however—when he'd risked everything a decade earlier in service of a drug habit—which was why he was making this low-budget action film with her now. His downfall had come when he'd had the bright idea to mail cocaine across state lines with the (unwitting) help of the United States Postal Service. The escapade had landed him in Folsom State Prison and, in the end, gotten him clean and sober.

He came out ready to act in movies again. But respectable movies weren't quite ready for him. Not just yet. So he took the part of Viveca's father in this low-budget film as a stepping stone in rebuilding the career he'd destroyed. Viveca knew he was in AA. He was very open about where he went on the nights they weren't shooting. She also suspected he thought she should join him there, although he hadn't said it like that. He'd said it in other ways—like his comment just now about her fourth drink.

Sidney was gregarious and charming and—Viveca believed—used his ability to make people laugh as a replacement drug for those he'd left behind. Somehow his years in prison hadn't broken him. Maybe his hold on happiness was a little white-knuckled. Maybe his gaiety was somewhat forced. But he demonstrated such an ebullient nature that it rubbed off on others.

"One skinny margarita for the lady." Bartender Ben returned with drinks in hand. "And a Diet Coke for the gentleman."

"Well..." Viveca clinked her glass against Sidney's. "Here's to number whatever."

"Viveca!" called a voice behind her.

Viveca turned—too fast, she realized, when the room spun around her—and looked into the face of the director. Liam Boyle was tall and lanky, the kind of guy she was attracted to. He was leaning down very close, a lock of unruly hair falling over one eye, and clutching a margarita that matched her own.

"Viveca Anders," he said in his Irish accent. "Great name."

"Thanks," she said. Did he suspect it was made up? Even though they had been working together for five weeks, they hadn't really connected. Most of the time his family was on the set—his pretty actress wife and their little kids—and he spent all his time when he wasn't working with them.

"You're most welcome." He laughed and took a big swig of his drink. Viveca did the same. She looked over and met Sidney's eyes. He was now talking with a group of people, the wardrobe mistress, a couple of grips, and—naturally—making them laugh. He winked at Viveca and held up his Coke, which annoyed her.

She wished she hadn't made this movie. Not only was it low-budget schlock that Rachel would never have *allowed* her to make had she arrived in time to stop it, but it was also an action film starring the son of a martial arts star who wanted to become a star himself. Viveca being cast as the female lead in this type of movie was debatable. The mere fact of her vocal impairment, which left her unable to shout with any real force, rendered some of her scenes laughable.

She should put the drink down. Switch to water. Go back to the hotel.

"I need some air," she said to Liam. "I'm going to step outside."

"Here, I'll walk you." He grabbed onto her elbow in an effort to steady himself. Or maybe to steady her? It wasn't clear who needed it more. They stumbled out into the glare of the neon night. It was brighter outside at ten p.m. than it had been inside the restaurant.

They were in a strip mall in the commercial stretch of Seaside, California. It was near where the production had set up offices in an abandoned grocery store, separated into cubicles with the use of old food racks. It was also near to where the actors were housed at The Seaside Inn. The inn offered about as basic a room as you could get while still being reasonably clean. What had probably cinched the deal for the producers was the fact that the inn had agreed to serve a predawn breakfast, thereby alleviating them of having to deliver that meal on the set.

The town of Seaside was not as rarified as Carmel, or as historic as Monterey, but it was a short drive to both of those locations and it was nice enough. On their Sundays off, the actors could walk down to the beach and eat at one of the local clam shacks.

"So where's your wife?" Viveca asked as she plopped onto the lone bench in front of the restaurant. Next to it was one of those cigarette things where you stubbed out the butts into sand. It reeked of rancid tobacco.

"She's taken the kiddos to Dublin to see the family."

"Sweet," said Viveca. "So what's a nice Irish guy like you doing making action films?"

"Life took a direction. I came here to make the Great Irish Movie. And one thing led to another."

"I would think a better place to make the Great Irish Movie would be in Ireland?"

"Yeah, well. I was misinformed."

She liked his wry humor.

"When did you get married?" she asked.

"To Sheila?"

Viveca let out a guffaw. "Isn't Sheila your wife?"

"Well, yeah. I just meant…" He drained his margarita. He put the glass under the bench and the motion set off a new wave of the foul odor from the cigarette container. "I dunno what I meant. I'm pissed."

"By that you mean drunk?" she asked.

"Yeah."

"Me too," Viveca said. "I'm pissed."

For some reason, her use of the Irish slang struck Liam as hysterically funny. His laugh made her laugh.

"Wanna take a ride?" He stopped laughing and asked.

"In a car?"

This tripped a new gale of laughter from both of them.

"Sure. Let me just finish this drink." Viveca downed her margarita and placed the glass under the bench too. "Where's your car?"

"C'mon. We can drive along the coast. It never gets old."

"No," she agreed. "It never gets old."

Liam had trouble at every stage of the operation. First he couldn't find his car—a little red vintage MG. Then he wasn't able to open the door once he'd found it. He had trouble getting into the driver's seat even though the top was down. Then he struggled to find his keys and had to get out of the car to pat down his pockets, which started the process all over again.

Viveca had a realization as she watched him, drunk as she was herself, that here was a man with a drinking problem. And that drinking problem was probably the reason Liam had not made the Great Irish Movie and was making a martial arts film with her instead.

Still, she did not think of her own drinking as a problem. Not yet.

"Lemme drive," she suddenly blurted.

"Nah, I can drive," Liam said, dropping the key and patting the floor to retrieve it. "Wait. I gotta piss."

This time he meant the word in the same way Americans mean it. He climbed out of the car once more and stumbled over to a pathetic little oleander bush decorating the asphalt. Viveca took this opportunity to move over to the driver's seat.

"Hey!" she said brightly when he returned. "Hop in."

Liam either forgot he had wanted to drive or surrendered to Viveca's stronger will. He stumbled into the passenger seat.

"Okay, we're off!" Viveca trilled as she started the car. One good thing her dad had done was teach her to drive a stick. The car lurched dramatically as she reversed out of the space. Well, she could kind of drive a stick. Enough for their nighttime adventure anyway.

The air was cool and the sky was starry. Not that you could really tell on this commercial strip. She made one right turn and then another—worried she might stall in a left—and soon entered a residential neighborhood. She started to feel cold. And lonely. Liam hadn't spoken in some time.

"Can you put the heat on?" she asked. "I'm getting cold."

He did not respond. She turned to look at him and saw that he was dead asleep.

"Hey," she said a little louder. "I don't really know where we are!"

It was beginning to dawn on Viveca that this outing had been a poor idea. It might have been the brace of cold air that was sobering her up. It may have been the presence of the man next to her, passed out and practically a stranger. But she wanted to get back to her hotel and she wanted to get there now. Liam's breathing deepened, developing into a snore and increasing her sense of concern. She was not in a full-blown panic, but she was growing more uncomfortable by the minute.

The road had risen into some hills. Viveca was working to stay in the appropriate gear for the incline. She didn't want to go too fast, but she also didn't want to slow down to the point of stalling. She had no idea where they were or how far they had gone. There was no ocean in sight and she was growing colder by the minute. Liam's snores had gone into some cartoonish zone where he stopped beathing for intervals before he would gasp, choke, and resume like a bellows.

"Hey!" She slugged him hard on the arm. "Can you wake up? I need some help here."

He sputtered and made an attempt to turn over, a move that was not possible in this miniscule car. But his arm flung out and hit Viveca on the right cheekbone. It startled her and brought home the fact of her predicament. The cold, the dark, this sleeping director, the fact that she was utterly lost—in ways that were just becoming clear even in her drunken haze—pressed down on her and she started to cry. Really cry.

For some reason, the passed-out director could hear her crying when he'd been unable to hear her speaking. And he didn't like it.

"Shaddap!" he yelled.

Viveca suddenly hated him. He had a wife and kids back in Ireland yet here he was, snoring in his car with his hand on the lap of the lead actress in his movie. How typical. She hated herself even more for getting into the car with him. She had done a stupid thing. Why hadn't she gone home when she wanted to go home? Why had she gotten so irritated when Sidney had saluted her with his glass of Coke? She couldn't answer any of these questions now because she needed to get herself back to the hotel and get rid of this man and his car.

Viveca managed to execute a three-point turn in a driveway on the left side of the road and begin the downhill drive back to civilization. She hoped she was headed back to civilization. She made a few more turns—trying to reverse the way she'd come—and found herself on a steeper descent than she remembered climbing. Her mind wasn't clear. She should not have had that last margarita. She could not wait to get on a plane and get out of this place tomorrow. To put this film and its director far behind her.

Just then, Liam stirred, stretched, and reached for her as though she were his wife in bed. Viveca instinctively pulled back to get away from him. But of course there was no place to go other than to "hell in a handbasket," as her mother would have said so many years ago in Royal Oak. And to hell in a handbasket is exactly where Viveca took them both when she lost control of the car and wrapped it around a tree.

* * *

When she opened her eyes, when she saw the flashing blue lights of the cruisers that surrounded her, she did not remember Liam at first. She did not, if she were to be totally honest, remember Viveca. The person she'd become post-Ingrid. Instead, her mind did a pleasant dance of happy memories of *The Streets of Old Detroit*. Of Emilia and Mrs. Waldron. Of cookies and shadow boxes. Of her own mother and even her father. And then it collided with thoughts of Sebastian, the director and his car, and the trouble she was going to be in.

When Liam moaned next to her, when she knew that he wasn't dead and she hadn't killed him, her relief was so great she started to cry. She still hadn't talked to the cops, but she ignored the searing pain in her left arm and used her right to rummage for her phone and press in a number.

"Cowgirl?" the voice answered.

"Sidney," she said with a sob. "I need your help."

9

INGRID 1998

"I'll take these," Ingrid said as she placed—let's be honest, slammed—a box of size-nine gladiator sandals on the counter. The Payless salesgirl, Tiffani, glowered.

"Cash or charge?" Tiffani mumbled.

Tiffani knew Ingrid would pay cash. She was the one who'd refused her request to put the shoes on layaway a month before. How would Ingrid have materialized a credit card in the intervening weeks? Now Ingrid was back to pay for the sandals in full after having squirreled them under a back shelf in the store for weeks. She had decided to wear these for Halloween even before she knew about Kelly's party. And she had periodically returned to make sure they were still there. They obviously never cleaned this Payless because the box never moved.

What Tiffani did not know was exactly what type of cash Ingrid intended to pay with. As a line formed behind her on this busy Saturday morning, Ingrid took her sweet time counting out quarters and dollars—several weeks' worth of babysitting money—to pay for the Posh Spice knockoffs.

"Can you just..." Tiffani began, gesturing at the waiting buyers.

"Just a sec," Ingrid said. She fished around in her purse for the final fifty cents, which she counted out in pennies.

Tiffani swept the change into the register and shoved a plastic bag at Ingrid.

Ingrid didn't care. She'd wanted these shoes since August. She had seen the photo of Posh Spice wearing them in an issue of *People* magazine in her doctor's office. She'd ripped out the page and tucked it inside a notebook. And now they were hers. Admittedly, hers were made of pleather while Posh's were probably the real thing. But who cared? For once, Ingrid's skinny legs would show to advantage with the snaking straps wound around them.

Next stop was Party City, where she'd engaged in a similar maneuver of hiding the costume she intended to buy once she could afford it. Ingrid unlocked her bike from the rack in front of Payless and stuffed her bag into the basket. It was a mild morning. The trees lining Main Street glowed golden.

Party City was a little way out of town. Too far to walk but perfect for a bike ride on an October day. Later the temperature would drop and she'd recall how her mom had encouraged her to bring a coat with her that morning. But at the time, Ingrid hadn't paid any attention. She'd been lulled by the sun and the excitement of the outfit she was putting together.

"*How do you, pretty lady*?" Em materialized next to Ingrid, walking her bike by the handlebars.

"Hey!" Ingrid gave her a one-armed hug, keeping her other hand on her own bike. "*How do you*?"

"*I do just fine*!" Em finished their joking routine, which poked gentle fun at Mrs. Waldron's obsession with Shakespeare.

"Wanna come with me to Party City?" Ingrid asked.

"Can we get some coffee first at Starbucks?"

"Sure."

The girls walked their bikes through the Saturday-morning crowds.

"So the plan is afoot," Em said. "We'll go to Kelly Roush's party a little late. I think, since we don't really know her, it's best not to be one of the first ones there."

"You don't think we should show up before anyone else with like a Tupperware Jello mold? My grandmother always made green. With marshmallows and cubed fruit."

"Yeah, no." Em laughed. "Here, watch my bike and I'll go in. What do you want?"

"Emilia! You've forgotten my Starbucks order? I'm cut to the quick."

"I was hoping you'd come to your senses. Those mocha Frappuccinos are disgusting."

"At least you remembered," Ingrid said and handed Em a five-dollar bill.

"I've got it." Em pushed it back. "And I always remember. Unlike some people I know."

"I remember your order. Double espresso, no sugar."

"You forget other stuff."

"Sheesh," Ingrid said, forcing a laugh. "Are we gonna go there on this perfect day?"

Em said nothing and walked into the store.

Ingrid stood with the two bikes, facing the sun. She closed her eyes for a moment, letting the warmth soak in and pondering Em's comment. It wasn't like she really forgot things. Maybe if she had a migraine she'd lose a couple minutes, but it wasn't a memory problem. It was a migraine problem.

"Here," Em said. "Let's go sit down for a sec."

Emilia grabbed her bike and walked over to an empty bench. Ingrid followed.

"Sebastian wants to come tonight," Em said. "I don't know. I mean, why not?"

"Does he know anyone?"

"Do we?" asked Em.

"Point taken," said Ingrid. "Put that in your cup holder and let's go. I'm afraid I'm going to lose that costume if I wait too long."

Em hopped up. "Last one to Party City is a rotten egg!"

Later, when they'd completed their mission and were pulling up to Em's house, Ingrid felt the first symptoms of an ocular migraine as the shade pulled down before her eyes.

"Shit," she said. "I think I need to go lie down."

"You're having a migraine?"

"Maybe," Ingrid said, as the prisms of color emerged. "Yeah, I think I am."

"Wanna come inside my house? You can rest on my bed. I need to practice flute."

"I can't. The noise—" Ingrid began, then jumped off her bike to vomit, mocha Frappuccino spewing on the lawn.

"Gross," Em said. "C'mon. Let me help you."

Emilia took hold of Ingrid's bike alongside her own and tipped them over on the grass. "I'll come back for those."

Ingrid felt Emilia's strong hand on her arm. Then the world went black.

10

VIVECA 2018

"Viveca, are you all right?" Henry asked, bending down to her. He kissed her forehead and held a hand against her cheek. "I got your message and came as fast as I could. You're ice cold."

"Henry," she whispered. "Would you bring me my pills?"

"Of course." He stood up and turned to the cops. "Officers, what's going on?"

"You wanna get your wife her medication?" asked Detective Kopple. "I'll walk with you and you can answer *me* a few questions."

There was a pause before Henry went off in the direction of Viveca's bathroom in the company of the detective. After several minutes—longer than it would take to shake out a couple tablets—he was back by her side.

"Thank you," she said, swallowing the pills and handing the glass back to him. She was at the stage of the headache now that shifted away from the visual blank that her migraines always began with. The vivid dancing lights that arced over one eye or the other had begun. Tonight it was her left. But she could see Henry a little better now, even though his face was breaking into prisms of color.

"Are you okay?" he asked.

"I think so," she said. It didn't seem like the pain would materialize. "I think I'm okay."

"Listen," said Detective Gleason. "We need to take statements from both of you. Anyone else in this house?"

"We have a son who's almost ten," Henry said. "Viveca, where's Theo?"

"He's at a sleepover. At Dixon's."

"Anyone else?" Gleason asked.

"We have a housekeeper," Viveca said. "But she lives elsewhere."

"Is there somewhere we all can sit?" Kopple asked.

"Let's go downstairs," suggested Henry.

"Yes," Viveca said, taking his arm, still clutching Daphne to one side. "I'd like to get out of this room."

They trundled out of the bedroom in a group, Viveca holding onto her husband and dog. Instinctively, she and Henry turned to the central staircase.

"We need to go this way," said Gleason. "The front stairs are operational—I mean, you're not going to fall through them. But our team isn't finished with them yet."

Viveca shuddered and, together, they trooped the long hallway, passing the bedrooms in reverse order from their earlier march.

"Jesus," Henry said at the bottom of the back stairs. He stared at the family photos that had been knocked to the floor, shards of glass radiating in a series of menacing rainbows. "What a bunch of thugs."

Neither detective responded. They passed other cops wandering around the house, photographing and dusting for fingerprints. But Kopple and Gleason seemed to have been assigned as their handlers. Again in the kitchen, both Henry and Viveca moved toward the door leading to the front hall.

"How about the living room?" Viveca said.

"Can't get through that way." Kopple led them away from the door that was blocked by the broken staircase.

They made their way through the dining room doors instead. In the living room, Henry pointed to the pair of facing sofas in front of the fireplace. "Here?"

"Fine," said Kopple.

The cops took one sofa. Henry and Viveca the other. Daphne squirmed out of Viveca's arms, stretched, and ambled to the corner of the couch. Henry sat bouncing his leg.

"All right," began Detective Gleason. "Let's revisit what happened tonight. First, was there anything else that occurred leading up to it that was unusual or caught your attention in any way?"

"No," Viveca responded. "Nothing unusual."

"Mr. Stephenson? Anything off lately? Anyone lurking around? A change in people who work here? Cleaners? Gardeners?"

"I don't think so," Henry said. "I mean, not that I noticed."

"Mrs. Stephenson, you said you didn't set the alarm?"

"No."

"You know," interjected Kopple, "alarms are a strong deterrent to home invasions."

"Why didn't you set the alarm, Viveca?" Henry swiveled to face her and Viveca noticed that he was still in his tux. Of course he would be. He came straight from his board dinner. His bow tie was hanging in two straight strips from the collar that he had unbuttoned. He was unusually pale.

"I don't know. The weather was nice and I just thought we could have fresh air."

"You could have had fresh air on the second floor," continued her husband. "Then you could have set the alarm."

"Actually, Henry," Viveca began. She didn't know why Henry was pushing this point. "I think houses in Greenwich get broken into through ladders up to second-floor windows for precisely that reason."

"Are you interested in the topic of house robberies, Mrs. Stephenson?"

Viveca turned to Detective Gleason. She was roughly her own age, give or take a few years. She was attractive enough, though it was hard to tell in that awful uniform. "Not particularly. I just read that in the *Greenwich Time*."

"And you had some sort of lightning strike that took out your gates? When was that?" Gleason consulted her notes. "A month ago?"

"How do you know that?" Viveca blanched. "Are you suggesting that's why this happened?"

"Your husband mentioned it. And no ma'am. We're not making any suggestions. That episode you had up there…" Gleason looked at her notes then pointed to the ceiling. "That happen often?"

Was he referencing her migraine? Viveca did not answer and turned to her husband. "Henry? Why did you bring up the gates?"

"Seemed pertinent," he said. "I mean, the house was totally exposed."

"Why don't you walk us through the evening again?" asked Gleason.

Viveca took a deep breath and worked to collect her thoughts.

"I took our son, Theo, to the house of his school friend," she began. "Dixon Aguila. His parents are Katherine and Hector. Way up in back-country. They don't have school tomorrow. Professional development day for the teachers."

She had no idea why she was adding these stupid, extraneous details. It made her sound nervous and afraid. Well. She *was* nervous and afraid. Her house had just been broken into by people strong enough to muscle a five-hundred-pound safe out of its bolts in the floor, down the stairs, and out the door. Clearly these were people to fear.

"And did you return home immediately after that?" Gleason asked.

"No. I went to an AA meeting in New Canaan." She would not with-hold that detail as though it were something to be ashamed of.

"What time did that end? Did you come straight home?"

"It ended around nine. I drove home and stopped to get some food along the way."

"Where did you go?"

"Um." This was all so intensely personal. "Taco Bell."

"You're kidding," Henry said with a small laugh.

Viveca did not respond.

"Okay, so you got home around…?"

"Around nine thirty or so," she answered. "I didn't actually look at my phone."

"Walk us through everything that happened."

So Viveca told the tale of all that she saw and all that she misread. Of the strange disconnect between what she was looking at and what her mind understood. Of her mental efforts to add order to a disordered scene by making up a story to explain it all. Until, of course, she actually *saw* what she had previously just been looking at. A home invasion and a robbery.

11

VIVECA 2006

"Viveca?" Rachel called at eleven on Christmas morning. "Wanna see a movie and get Chinese?"

She'd caught her at home, still in bed, staring at *Home Alone* on the TV with no sound.

Viveca sat up, the phone pressed to her ear. "On Christmas?"

The concept bordered on scandalous. The idea of skipping church and a family meal ranked at the same level as the seven deadly sins. But what church did she go to now? What family was there to cook a meal? She hadn't had either of those things in years.

"What else are you doing today that's so important?" Rachel interrupted her thoughts.

Point taken. It was raining nonstop. The leaves on the sycamore trees that lined the streets had turned brown. Some of them had fallen off, but others were still clinging to branches like soldiers who'd died on the field but hadn't tipped over.

"Okay," Viveca finally said as she threw back the covers to get up and get dressed. "Why not?"

Rachel arrived within the hour. Feeling nostalgic, Viveca persuaded her to drive them into Hollywood where *The Polar Express* was playing at the old Vista.

"Are you kidding?" Rachel asked. "A children's movie? And an actual Christmas movie? I think I might throw up."

"You're the one who had the movie-on-Christmas idea. At least we should try to be on theme?"

"Fine," Rachel conceded. "But I pick at the Chinese restaurant."

"Deal."

After the movie and the meal, they lingered over tea and their fortune cookies.

"You are wise beyond your years," Viveca read from the small slip of paper, and laughed. "I don't know about that."

"You are!" Rachel said. "Well, kind of. You know, I'm not usually friends with my clients. Must be that kind-of-wisdom you have."

"Very funny. What's yours say?"

"Hang on," Rachel said as she touched every cookie on the plate. She had asked the waitress for extras and she had grudgingly brought four. "Here. I'll go with this one."

Rachel pulled it out and stared at it.

"I want another one," she said.

"Wait. What does it say?" Viveca grabbed the paper from her hand and read, "A closed mouth gathers no feet."

She paused and then they both burst into laughter.

"I mean," said Rachel. "What the fuck does that even mean?"

Viveca was grateful for the presence of Rachel. As an agent, of course. But really as a friend. In many ways, her only true friend.

* * *

In the quiet week that followed between Christmas and New Year, apart from a few more meals with Rachel, she'd spent her time alone. Catching up on sleep and books and movies. She'd walked early mornings in Runyon Canyon. She loved that hilly tract that had once, long ago, belonged to grocery store heir Huntington Hartford. The buildings were all gone, their footprints leaving a surreal impression of abandonment in the middle of the city. It fit with the equally surreal atmosphere of

Christmas in Los Angeles. It put her in mind of *The Streets of Old Detroit*. It made her feel separate from the rest of the world and it was a sensation she didn't mind. Like hiding in plain sight.

In January it continued to rain. Two weeks in, Viveca met up with a gang of colleagues at the Formosa Café. These were the actors she'd worked with on location the autumn before. They had bonded, the way actors do, and had vowed to stay close forever. Forever wouldn't last—it never did since they would go on to new movies, new locations, new friends—but they remained, for the moment, in the rosy glow of their private jokes and shared memories.

Five minutes after they'd been served a round, their waiter Josh appeared with an extra drink—a cosmo that he handed to Viveca. "From the guy at the table in the corner. Meant for the lady in white," he said, nodding in the direction of the other table.

Viveca looked down at the loose white sweater she'd worn against the chill. Then she looked over at the table Josh indicated. It was full of men. Men in suits.

"Viveca!" said Winnie, teasing. She'd played Viveca's best friend in the recently wrapped movie.

"Man slayer!" added Brandon, who'd played her dad.

"Is there something you're not telling us?" asked Marco.

He'd played Viveca's boyfriend in the film. In fact, she and Marco had had a little thing on the side, inspired by their onscreen chemistry. Or perhaps that thing had ignited the onscreen chemistry. Chicken and egg. Hard to tell.

General merriment continued from the group regarding the cosmo, the guy who sent it, and his table of serious-looking men.

"Stop!" Viveca said, laughing. "And no," she said to Josh as she slid the glass toward him. "Please send it back. Tell him the lady doesn't drink."

"Listen, Viv…" Josh leaned in. They knew each other well. He was an actor just like the rest of them, but it had been a while since he'd had a gig. "The guy said he'd tip me fifty bucks to give you the drink. I need the money. Can you just…"

"Give that to me," she said, standing.

"Watch out, bud. Here comes trouble!" More hubbub from her peanut gallery of pals.

Viveca turned, squared her shoulders, and walked purposefully to the corner table. Her energy briefly flagged when she realized she'd neglected to ask Josh precisely which guy at this table had sent the drink.

"Excuse me?" she said, clearing her throat when she got there and hoping to be heard above the crowd.

All eyes rose to her. Close up, Viveca could see that the men were actually wearing tuxedos. At this hour of the evening, however, most of them had draped their jackets over the backs of their chairs, rolled up their shirt sleeves, and loosened their ties.

"Did one of you send me this drink?" Viveca asked, holding up the cosmo.

She saw them squint to hear her.

"It was me," one of them said. A very handsome one. He stood up and made his way around the table toward her, smiling in a way that revealed perfect white teeth and a dimple. He never took his eyes off her. It reminded her of a wrangler approaching a wild colt. She—the colt—felt locked into his mesmerizing stare. When he got closer, she saw the startling clarity of his pale blue eyes.

"I'm Henry Stephenson," he said. "I couldn't help noticing you across the room and...well...I thought it might be a more graceful way to introduce myself than simply barging over to your table."

"Right," Viveca said, softening slightly. "That was nice of you. But I can't accept it. I mean, I don't drink."

"Sorry," he said, taking another step closer and taking the drink from her hand. "I hope I didn't offend you."

"No," she said, backing away from him. Not that she wasn't attracted. She'd have to be blind not to be attracted to this guy. "But will you still give my friend the tip for delivering it?"

"I admire loyalty to a friend," he said, laughing as he set the drink on the table. "And I will give your friend that tip. Give me your number and I'll double it."

By this point his friends—Henry's friends—were turning their heads between the two of them like the conversation was a tennis match. Viveca could imagine her own friends doing the same behind her.

Her first instinct was to turn on her heel and walk away, leaving the men to watch her disappear. Across the room. Out of the bar. Away from any possibility of further conversation or relationship with this handsome Henry in a tux.

"Do you have a pen?" she asked instead. And, against any instinct to the contrary, she wrote her number on a napkin.

Henry was handsome, yes. The ice-blue eyes. The chiseled bones. The dimple. But it was more than that. He looked real. Substantial in a way that her actor friends and lovers never had. He looked like the kind of person who could control his world. The kind of person who could send a drink and drop a fifty and get a girl to cross a room to *him*. Which implied—in ways that Viveca could not articulate or perhaps even recognize as cogent thoughts—stability. And Viveca had not known anyone stable, with the exception of Rachel, in a very long time.

And it turned out—in a way she hadn't realized until this very moment—that stability was the one thing that Viveca Anders wanted and did not think she could get on her own, no matter how successful she was. As an actor, she was always one screen test, one birthday, one fuck-up away from joblessness. It was the farthest thing from stable.

Three nights later, Henry picked her up and took her to dinner at The Ivy. She had mentioned on the phone that it was her favorite restaurant and he had actually paid attention. They were steered to a quiet table in a corner of the terrace and Henry took the seat facing out, leaving Viveca to face only him across the tumble of colorful roses.

"So tell me about yourself," he asked when they'd each been served a drink. Henry had chosen a white Burgundy. Viveca had chosen a Pellegrino with a slice of lemon. She had already told him—right when she met him—that she didn't drink, so she decided not to mention it again. Henry did not mention it either.

"Myself?" Viveca said. "Not much to tell. Simple background. Midwest. A farm. Homeschooled then Hollywood. Typical American dream pursued by a typical American girl."

"Hardly typical," Henry said with a smile. He looked at her closely but didn't pry. Maybe it was his age; he was twenty years older than her. He'd already been married, she knew, because he had mentioned it in the car. He had lived life already and probably understood something of what people said and did not say. And why.

"Where did you grow up?" she asked.

"A town called Mamaroneck. Outside of New York."

"Are your parents still alive?"

"My mom is."

"I'm sorry," she said. "I know how that is."

"My father and I weren't close."

"I wasn't close with my dad either," she said. "Do you have children?"

"Yes," he said, smiling. "Margo and John. They're teenagers. Remind me, once they turn twenty-one, to avoid teenagers until I'm the grandfather of one."

Viveca laughed. "Don't you want any more children?"

Any fool could see why she'd ask a question like that. And Henry was no fool. "I would consider having another child," he said as he twirled the stem of his wine glass, etching little circles around the crisp white tablecloth. "If the right woman came along."

It was the right answer.

"How about you?" he asked. "Do you want children?"

"I do," Viveca said.

"That's nice," he replied and took another long sip of his wine. It looked so deliciously good to Viveca that she knew she'd have to call her sponsor later.

"Do you get along with your ex-wife?" she blurted. "What did you say her name was? I mean, is?"

At this, Henry's smile stiffened. Just a little.

"Her name is Deirdre. We've been divorced for longer than we were married and we share custody of the kids. That's all I'm going to say,"

Henry answered, startling Viveca with his curtness. Then, true to his word, he changed the subject completely. "Tell me one thing about yourself you've never told anyone."

"Um. Well. I suffer from migraines and sometimes I kind of black out. Not for long. But it's scary when it happens."

"And that's something no one knows?"

"My mom, of course. And my best friend growing up."

"Are you still friends?"

Viveca took a big gulp of Pellegrino. Henry was treading into subjects she would rather avoid.

"We've lost touch," she said, pasting a smile on her face. Nothing near as suave and polished as Henry's returned smile.

"Tell me about your work," she said. "You look like a banker."

Henry laughed. "I actually invest in restaurants. Not quite a banker."

"You own them?"

"My partners and I find restaurants we like. We find funds to back them. That's the general idea. That's who I was with the night we met. We do these black-tie board dinners," he said. "How about you? How did you get into acting?"

"I always liked stories. All kinds of stories. There was a museum in Detroit that had this basement that was like an old town. With shops. Cobblestone streets. Lampposts. And it just made me feel, I don't know… safe. Protected, I guess."

"Well, Viveca." Henry looked long and hard at her and landed his shot perfectly. "I'm a protective kind of guy."

Was it true? Was he a safe harbor in the storm? Was there any such thing? These were questions she might have brought to a therapist. Or even to Rachel. But she didn't. She asked these questions of herself. And she answered herself yes. Yes to Henry. Yes to safety. Yes to the world he had to offer that she did not understand. She ignored her misgivings about his evasiveness. She was evasive herself. Didn't he deserve the right to his own secrets the way she deserved the right to hers?

She also ignored the fact that she didn't understand what he did for a living. She did not understand that it was not any more real or stable than the world she inhabited. It was all sort of make-believe and vulnerable to a host of exterior forces. Vagaries that blew like the wind. But she was not seeing clearly and she was won over by Henry and his square jaw and his blue eyes and his promises and the patina of security that clung to him like a layer of gold leaf.

12

VIVECA 2006

"Will you marry me, Viveca Anders? Will you spend the rest of your life with me?"

Henry proposed properly, down on one knee, nine months after they'd first met. It was like a gestation period, the time it took them to fully commit to each other.

They were walking in Runyon Canyon early one October morning with Daphne, the little Frenchie puppy she'd adopted the year before she met him. The heat from the Santa Anas had recently broken. The sun peeked through a low mist over the eastern hills. They were both wearing exercise gear. Viveca was in yoga pants and a celery-green fleece that complemented her green eyes. Henry was in gray sweats and a navy zip-up.

He produced a small gray box with the initials H and W engraved in gold on the top of it. For a moment, Viveca misread it and thought it was their initials.

"Harry Winston," Henry said as he opened the box. "Emerald cut."

Viveca was stunned by the size of it. A veritable skating rink. She wanted this. This man and all that he offered. And she loved him. She definitely loved him.

"Yes," she said, smiling. "Yes, I will marry you, Henry Stephenson."

He stood up and slid the ring on her finger. The weight of the stone made it drop to the side, around to the inside of her palm.

"We'll have to get that sized," he said. "Your fingers are so delicate."

Henry kissed her fingers, her wrist, her lips. She kissed him back hungrily. She wanted him now more than she had even five minutes before. It was as though a finish line was in sight, but a tiny panic had surfaced that she might not be able to reach it.

"How about a December wedding?" he broke away from kissing her long enough to ask.

"So soon?" She laughed. "There'll be so much to do!"

"What? What really is there to do but love each other?"

Viveca thought about it. Despite all the Disney films she'd watched as a child, Henry was right. *What* was *there to do?*

"December it is," she said. And he kissed her again, long and deep.

Then he took her hand to walk down the hill. "I've already alerted my lawyer to begin preparing the prenup. Just a formality, but something that will make us both comfortable."

This was the first little splash of cold water in Viveca's naive face. "Prenup?" she asked dumbly.

"I've been married before, as you know," he said as he kept them moving, side by side, facing the road in front of them. She wished they were facing each other so she could see his eyes.

"I have children," he continued. "We—together—well I think we hope to have a child. I want to do this the right way. As much for you as for me. You'll see that this will protect you."

Protection *was* what she wanted. Safety, security, protection.

"Is this about Deirdre?" Viveca couldn't help asking that question.

"Viveca, look," Henry said. "You are nothing like Deirdre. What we have is nothing like what Deirdre and I—what we never had. Can you just leave it at that?"

Could she? Could she trust this man, believing in what he had shown her for close to a year?

"What do I need to do?" she finally asked.

"Well," Henry said, turning to her and beaming his icy blue glow upon her. She felt better already. "It's really up to you at this point. Once you receive the papers, all you'll need to do is sign them. Have your lawyer review them, of course."

"Of course," Viveca echoed. But she did not have that kind of lawyer. She didn't even know where to find one. But Rachel would.

And Rachel did. It wasn't smooth. It wasn't easy. Rachel counseled Viveca not to do it. At least not under the terms that were written. The lawyer Rachel recommended agreed.

But what did she have to lose? Being married to Henry, even under the terms of the prenup his attorney had crafted, was better than not being with him at all. And how could she reasonably decline to agree to what he was asking? Fidelity was really it. Henry wanted fidelity. The wording in the prenup that Viveca's new lawyer objected to was all to do with that.

"This infidelity clause," said Marvin Lefkowitz, the lawyer. "It can come back and bite you in the ass."

Leave it to Rachel to find an attorney as blunt as she was.

"But how?" Viveca asked. "I don't intend to be unfaithful to Henry. And I would hope he intends to be faithful to me. Isn't that what we're already pledging when we take wedding vows? How does this prenup change any of that?"

"In a manner of speaking, yes," he said.

Rachel sat next to Viveca because she'd insisted on accompanying her to his office. Surprisingly, she said nothing.

"But there's wiggle room," he went on. "Even in *'til death do us part*. Naturally, I don't mean to disabuse you of your notions of happily ever after. But factor in for a moment, if you will, the march of time. Time can be long. It can be unkind. Life happens. Shit happens."

Marvin waved a hand around his office. The leaning piles of papers, the overstuffed shelves of books, the mismatched coffee cups scattered about—all of it illustrated the point. Shit did happen.

"Will you cut to the chase, Marvin, and stop pontificating?" Rachel finally piped in.

"Okay. Imagine, in time, that something happens. And you stray. Or you don't stray but you get accused of straying. The terms of this contract will leave you with nothing. At least nothing from Henry Stephenson." Marvin paused. For dramatic effect, it seemed. To let the import of the word "nothing" sink into Viveca's thick skull. "Do you understand? You could be married for years and be accused of infidelity and, through some slippery slope of reality or fiction or any combination thereof, end up destitute."

"But doesn't it cut both ways?" Viveca asked.

"Well, yes," he said. "Technically yes. He would have nothing from you, in turn, if he were the one to commit adultery."

"Well then," Viveca said. "It's decided. I'll sign."

"I advise you not to sign this. Can we at least mark it up for revisions?"

"No." Viveca was resolute. Fair was fair. And Henry was being fair. He wasn't holding her to any standard he was not holding himself. Henry was divorced. He had already seen one marriage blow up—a marriage he chose not to talk about. His ex-wife, Deirdre, must have been unfaithful. As a virile and masculine man, Henry must have been ashamed to talk about it. And as a woman who carried her own fair share of shame, Viveca could easily fill in those blanks without resorting to questioning him. Just as she did not wish to be questioned herself.

On Friday, December 15, 2006, Viveca and Henry drove downtown to City Hall to get married in front of a judge. Henry wore a navy suit with an aqua tie to match his eyes. Viveca had splurged on a gauzy navy Carolina Herrera skirt and a white silk blouse. She wore strappy peep-toe heels and carried a small clutch that had belonged to her mom in the '70s. It was her borrowed; it was her blue. It was her old and—she hoped—the promise of her new. It was the secret bit of Ingrid still with her that she would carry into her marriage with Henry.

Rachel was one of the witnesses. To her credit, once the prenup was signed she did not mention it again. No one would have known her misgivings, least of all Henry. Mason, one of Henry's business partners, was the other witness. He dutifully snapped photos of the happy couple. Viveca had forgotten a bouquet, so she clutched her mother's purse in its place.

They drove directly to their reception at The Ivy, which was already decked out with twinkling lights for the holidays. The flowers, the chintz, the coziness of the rooms and the terrace did not need any extra embellishment from them.

Besides Mason, Henry's other business partner, Ed, was there, along with a handful of his friends. His mother did not fly in from New York and Deirdre would not let the children attend. Viveca's actor friends were there, all still in town before going home to see their families for the holidays.

As she scanned the room, Viveca thought of Em. She thought of Sebastian. She thought of her mother. Mr. and Mrs. Waldron. Even her dad. But it was only for a moment. Then she shook her head and gave her mom's purse a little squeeze. She turned to her friends, her brand-new husband, and joined the party. They feasted on caviar and smoked salmon, the signature chopped salad, lobster and steak, and profiteroles instead of cake.

Their little band of friends clinked their glasses and Henry kissed Viveca long and hard and blindingly and all memories were pushed to the side. The next morning, they flew off to Hawaii for two weeks of newlywedded bliss.

There, they slept, made love, and lazed in the sun. Every morning Henry got up first and fetched them both coffee.

"Awake, awake, my sleeping one," he said their final morning in the hotel. Not quite Shakespeare. Not quite Mrs. Waldron or even Em. But romantic and sweet.

"Thank you," Viveca said, sipping the coffee and patting the bed to find the nightgown that had been tossed aside the night before. "You make me feel like a princess."

"Don't," Henry said, taking the coffee and the nightgown from her hand. "Not yet. This is our last morning."

"But the coffee's hot," she protested. Weakly, she knew, but still. She preferred her coffee hot.

"I'll go get more," Henry said. "Let's savor this final morning. Before we go back to all of it."

She couldn't protest against that. So she closed her eyes, if only to reduce the intensity of Henry's gaze for a moment. She allowed herself to fall back on the pillows, back into this cocoon, for a little while longer. She kept her eyes closed to revel in the sensation of safety. Of security. Of stability. Here she was—safe, secure, stable. Safe with Henry. Made safe by Henry. Safe from the past. His past and hers. Especially hers.

And she loved him. She did.

13

VIVECA 2018

Viveca opened her eyes and stared at the yellow wallpaper. It was one of her favorites: Schumacher's Saranda, a take on Indian hand-block prints. She loved the deep marigold of the blooms contrasted with the green of the leaves, all of it sparely set against a plain white background. She had chosen it for their guest room, which was evidently where she was lying in bed right now.

And then the memory of why she was sleeping in the guest room hit her like a gut punch. Thoughts of the robbery made her sit up with a start, causing Henry to groan and little Daphne to sigh and roll over.

"What time is it?" Viveca asked.

"Mmm…" Henry mumbled. "Not sure."

But that was not Viveca's real question. As she sat with a sick *morning after* sense, what she really wanted to know was: *morning after* what? *Morning after their house had been broken into, ransacked, and robbed by burglars of unknown origin?*

How could it have happened? Why *did it happen?*

"You okay?" Henry asked, reaching out for her. "Come here. Let me try to make you feel better."

Sex would not make Viveca feel better.

"I need to get Theo at Dixon's house."

"Now?" Henry picked up his phone from the bedside table. "It's five thirty."

"I can't sleep."

"No one's asking you to sleep," he said as he fondled her breasts.

"I'm going to get some coffee." Viveca squirmed loose and grabbed her terry cloth robe. She vaguely remembered brushing her teeth and washing her face—going through the normal bedtime rituals as though it had been a normal night.

"Damn it," she said.

"What?" Henry asked.

"Nothing," she said, tying the robe and sliding her feet into slippers. "I just remembered we're out of the coffee I like. No big deal."

Henry was already asleep again. And Daphne hadn't stirred. Viveca grabbed her phone and glasses off the bedside table. She had just begun to need non-prescription readers. She made her way down the back staircase and crunched on a piece of broken glass as she traversed the hall to the kitchen. She stooped to pick it up.

The sun did not reach the kitchen in the morning, facing west as it did over the river. Plus, at this late date in September, the sun didn't even rise until six thirty or so. Viveca flipped on a few lights. She noticed that the windows had all been closed and the damaged screen had been neatly propped against a wall. It must have been the cops who did all that, because Viveca had no memory of it herself. After the hour or so of questioning, she barely remembered walking upstairs.

She brewed a pot of coffee, poured out a cup, and added oat milk. She took the mug and her phone over to one of the two George Smith Kilim chairs—her Rachel Geller Memorial Chairs, she called them—that flanked the fireplace. Feeling the chill, she threw on a few logs and got a fire started.

Settling into the expansiveness of the chair, Viveca tucked her feet under her. Rachel had been right: These chairs were pretty much indestructible. They'd survived life with a dog and a child with nary a stain.

They actually looked as good as they did on the day she'd bought them so many years before.

Nowadays, people said antiques were dead. Brown furniture, they called it. But Viveca remembered her parents' Danish modern living room that looked so hopelessly dated when she was a child. Most of her friends' houses—certainly the Waldrons—had come under the influence of Laura Ashley in the '80s and '90s. The Waldrons had mixed their furniture with a unique collection of African art, lending an air of freestyle eclecticism. But at the Linds', the furniture had been austere. She found it boring as a kid and wished they'd had something similar to their neighbors. All this was a long way of saying that tastes in décor were cyclical. If you held onto something long enough, it would come back in fashion again.

Viveca sipped her coffee and stared at the fire. Her life had been a series of episodes. Her girlhood and teenage years, the years as a young actress, then marriage and motherhood. Life with Theo was something she would not trade for anything. Even if she had achieved the film stardom she seemed on the verge of, it would not have compared to this. Anyway, there was no way of knowing if her star would have continued to rise. She'd known plenty of actresses who also seemed destined for something big and she hadn't heard of them in years. Theo was the most precious part of her world.

Viveca's marriage with Henry had been mostly good. True, it had not transpired exactly as she had once imagined. He had not turned out to be the rock of stability she'd once believed him to be. But it had been her own youth and immaturity that had ascribed those qualities to him. She had naively assumed that, given his age and profession, he inhabited a universe that protected him—and would protect her by extension—from the vagaries of the world. She recognized now that Henry had been her fantasy father figure, someone she'd hoped to plug-and-play in replacement of the disappointing original. And she had loved him. She loved him still.

But Henry had been no stranger to vagaries. His career rode a roller coaster of ups and downs. They'd had to make decisions based on moments of failure—or at least setback—for him. Which was normal. It happened in the course of every human life. Viveca had just stupidly never expected it. In fact, of all the things she had worried about back at the moment of their marriage—primarily the specter of infidelity that had loomed so large at the signing of the prenup—financial instability had not been one of them.

Her thoughts returned to the present moment. Their house *had* been broken into. Their safe *had* been stolen. Their front staircase was currently in a state of complete disrepair. Which meant that Viveca would be unable to hide the story from Theo. The thought of telling Theo horrified her. Theo was now nearly ten—and a mature ten at that—but the concept of his own house being violated by intruders was not something Viveca wanted to saddle him with.

She had another sip of coffee, which had cooled too much for her liking. She grabbed her phone and went over to the microwave to give the coffee a blast. She scrolled through her messages while she waited. The detectives might have found something, she reasoned. They had taken her number before leaving.

There was only a message from Rachel.

Hey, it read, *I'm coming east. Can I stay with you? It's been a minute and we need a good catch-up. Plus, I'd love to be there for my godson's birthday.*

I'd love that, Viveca typed. *Be prepared though. The house was robbed!*

What the actual fuck?

Yeah, last night. Wait. You're up early.

Yep. Crisis on a set in Australia. Hold that thought. Gotta pop.

K. Can't wait to see you.

Me too you. Seriously, tho. WTF???

I actually have no idea.

And that was the absolute truth of it. Viveca had no idea how such a thing could have happened right here at home in Riverside.

14

VIVECA 2007

Viveca's phone vibrated from her jeans pocket as she stood atop a ladder, paint roller in hand. She and Henry had recently moved into a charming little house in West Hollywood: Spanish stucco with a terra-cotta roof. They'd chosen it because Henry said money was tight. *Temporarily*, he'd stressed, and added a couple quips about the demands of his ex. But Viveca didn't mind. She adored the little cottage and could see them being happy there for a long time.

She'd been surprised by how much she loved nesting. She bought wallpaper and planted roses and painted the walls by herself. Like today. Farrow & Ball's Green Smoke was the color she'd chosen for the living room. She had never heard of Farrow & Ball back in Royal Oak. Maybe it didn't exist then or maybe her world and the world of Green Smoke had not overlapped. Had not even passed each other at a shouting distance.

She questioned whether she'd ever want to work as an actress again. Life, as far as she could tell, was heavenly. And this tiny cottage was its epicenter. During the day she worked hard on the house. At night she was with Henry. Mostly they were alone together.

Viveca was learning to cook. She'd mastered a decent carbonara and an excellent roast chicken. Other items were still hit-or-miss. Henry was a talented cook himself. He was very good at grilling—a typical male, she teased. But he also made a mean omelet and a surprisingly good paella.

The phone stopped vibrating, then it started all over again. Only Rachel would be that persistent.

Viveca placed the roller back in the pan, retrieved the phone with only a small smudge of paint, and brought it up to her ear. "Hello?"

"You're not going to believe it!"

"What won't I believe, Rachel?"

"Monica Spironi, that's what. You know who she is?"

"Um, a French director?"

"Viveca, she is not a French director. She is *the* French director of the moment. She went to AFI and through the wonders of connections—and let's not discount *my* connections—she wants to see you for her next film."

"Shooting in France?"

"Well, that's the funny part. The film is called *Misty* and it's some sort of vague, or not-so-vague, homage to *Breathless*. But she wants to shoot it in Detroit of all places!"

Viveca thought she might fall off the ladder. Her foot slid and she set the phone on a step so she could climb down. When she'd gotten to the bottom, taken a few deep breaths, and picked up the phone again, all she could think to say was, "My Detroit?"

As it turned out, it was her Detroit. This young, edgy, French director thought there was no edgier place than Detroit. And, also as it turned out, Viveca was the actress she wanted.

Well…she had initially wanted Scarlett Johansson. Everyone that year wanted Scarlett Johansson. But Scarlett had not been available and Rachel Geller had worked her magic—or her cudgel, depending on your point of view—and secured a screen test for Viveca. Maybe it was the fact that Viveca, like Johansson, had Scandinavian roots. Maybe it was the fact that, on a lark, she'd recently cut her blond hair short, which exaggerated a resemblance to Jean Seberg. Maybe it was the fact that she was from Michigan and Monica Spironi liked that synchronicity. Whatever the reason, the part became hers. Viveca did not mind taking what

Scarlett Johansson had rejected. Careers could be—often *had* been—built on leftovers.

Thus Viveca turned away from nesting when she had barely begun.

She decided to host a little farewell dinner before she left, hoping to show off what she'd accomplished in the house and to try her hand at entertaining. And maybe, to be honest, in an effort to root herself in her new married life before going back to her old one.

Rachel would be there, of course, as would Margo and John, Henry's teenagers. Viveca was surprised their mother was going to let them come. Deirdre rarely said yes when they asked to see the kids. Viveca did not understand the bad blood between them. But for the most part she did not probe.

Yet it was clear to Viveca that the children bore the brunt of their parents' enmity. They were at the height of their adolescent surliness. Margo, at sixteen, had the sullen disposition that went with the age. Viveca had tried to reach out to her, to bond in some way, but the girl was a stone wall. It was as though she knew—at a gut level—that if she were nice to Viveca it could be seen as a betrayal of her mother. At least Viveca had not broken up that marriage. She hadn't even met Henry until long after their divorce. She wished she could reassure Margo of that fact, but she suspected it wouldn't make a difference.

John was easier. At fourteen, he was simply silent. He said nothing at all. Not *thank you for dinner,* not *pass the peas,* not *fuck you*. Oddly, to Viveca at least, John upset Henry more than Margo did. Viveca found Margo tiring with her sarcastic and snide remarks. But Henry was rendered apoplectic by John's silences. Each kid knew with the precision of a surgeon how to wield the sharpest scalpel against the adult he or she most wished to wound. In John's case it was, of course, his father. The one who had left him behind and the one he resembled most closely. And in Margo's case it was her young stepmom who was way too close to her own age for comfort.

In the year-plus since she'd been with Henry, Viveca had barely exchanged a word with Deirdre. Henry's ex maintained layers between them. The principal layers took the form of John and Margo—exacerbating the strains in their relationship with their dad and Viveca. The poor kids had to carry messages along the lines of *Mom says*, or *Mom needs,* or *Mom wants*. These missives were always delivered to Henry and there was usually an element of exigency to them.

Viveca set the table with her most colorful linens and plates and placed camellias from her garden into a cluster of bud vases. She'd decided on roast chicken, salad, and rice. She hoped the teenagers would eat it. She'd bought ice cream and really good hot fudge sauce. She knew the kids would eat that. When everything was almost ready, she popped down the hall to finish dressing.

She chose a loose, flowy caftan she'd found at a little boutique on Robertson. She intended to pair it with chunky beads she'd bought at an artisan fair. As she was fishing around in her jewelry box, she heard Henry's voice coming from the little study next door.

"Goddamn it, Margo, you tell your mother I've had enough," Henry's voice rang out. "She's bled me dry and I simply can't do it anymore. A deal's a deal."

"Daddy," Margo began in her teenage whine, "Mom said you owed her this."

"Your mother is a fucking cunt. You tell her that, you hear me?"

Viveca dropped the jewelry box to the tile floor. Beads and bangles rolled across the pavers. She was flabbergasted by Henry's choice of words in describing the mother of his two children to one of those very same kids. More than flabbergasted—she was horrified.

"Viveca?" Henry called out. "Are you in the bedroom?"

Viveca hesitated.

"Um, yes!" she finally called back with as bright a tone as her vocal cords could manage. "It's me!"

She sounded like an idiot. She looked around at the scattered jewelry and dropped to her knees to retrieve the pieces. She hoped, at the very least, to buy some time before her husband walked into the room and confronted her with her eavesdropping. But why was she feeling guilty, as though she'd done something wrong? This was her house, too.

She had simply come into her—their—bedroom to fetch a necklace before dinner.

But she was, in fact, overcome with a tainted feeling after overhearing that conversation. It was as though she'd witnessed a murder. She couldn't make sense of whatever it was she *had* witnessed. She knew that Henry and Deirdre were at odds. But to say that to his own daughter about her mother was taking it to another level.

Reaching under the dresser to grab a little pearl stud, Viveca stretched herself out on the floor, extending her right arm. She could just feel the earring with the tip of her middle finger. If she tapped it the right way, it might roll back in her direction. Then she could put the jewelry box away and get the hell out of the bedroom before this weird evening started. She stretched another inch when she felt a hand on the small of her back.

"Darling," Henry said in the most normal tone imaginable. As though nothing at all had happened in the next room that he should be the least bit ashamed of. "Can I help?"

Should she say something about what she just overheard? It would be weird if she didn't.

"Um…" Viveca tried to wriggle out from under the dresser and stand up. "Is everything okay?"

"Yeah," Henry said with a sigh. "Just the usual with Deirdre."

"That didn't sound usual, Henry. I actually can't believe what you said."

"Okay, my wording was harsh. I'll apologize to Margo."

Viveca felt better. She was glad she had addressed the subject. She stood up with Henry's help and gave him a kiss on the cheek.

"What were you looking for under the dresser?" he asked.

"This," she said, holding up the tiny pearl earring and dropping it into the box. "I just dropped my jewelry box."

"Well, we'll just have to buy you some more jewelry, won't we? And a nice big safe to keep it in."

Which was a pretty strange non-sequitur on the heels of the poverty speech he'd just given Margo in the next room. *Something was not right*, she thought. And then she thought of her favorite children's book,

Madeline, and the nun who ran the boarding school, Miss Clavel. It was what she said when she heard the voices of the little girls down the long stairs of the old house in Paris. Only Viveca had just heard the booming voice of her husband in the next room as he bellowed vulgarities and thinly veiled threats to *his* child.

Something most certainly was not right.

15

VIVECA 2018

"Theo!" Viveca called up the back stairs, straining to make her voice carry farther than it normally did. "Meet you at the car!"

She scooted back to the kitchen to pour coffee into a travel cup. Rounding into the front hall, Viveca passed the now cleaned-up mess of her front staircase. The carpenter hadn't yet replaced the spindles and banister, but at least it no longer resembled the crime scene it was. The front staircase was even usable now, though she preferred to take the back stairs. So did Theo.

The hardest part of the break-in had been explaining it to Theo. The very idea that malevolent forces could enter their home unbidden was a concept that Viveca had not wanted to introduce to her son. But there had been no choice in the matter. Their house had been broken into. Their safe had been taken. Their staircase—in its shattered state—was a constant reminder that they were, at the most basic level, unsafe.

Viveca opened the car door and leaned in to place her cup in the holder. She looked back at the house for Theo. Since the break-in, he dawdled in the morning. It was a new habit she didn't like but didn't want to nag him about. She'd spoken to the school and gotten the recommendation of a child psychologist in town. She hadn't yet taken Theo to see her but was seriously considering it. The shock of their house robbery could affect Theo in ways that Viveca and Henry were not equipped to understand—at the very least by creating a heightened sense of vulnerability.

Immediately after the robbery, she'd called the alarm company to install more cameras around the house. The repair of the gates would begin the following month; it was the first slot they could get. It would be a laborious process involving changing the underground wiring that led from the gates to the main house. It was going to take weeks.

"Theo!" Viveca called again, knowing he wouldn't hear her from out here on the forecourt. She tapped the horn lightly.

She might as well check the mail while she waited.

Viveca walked quickly down the driveway, through the open gates, and over to the mailbox. Some of her neighbors' mailboxes were fancier. But theirs stood on a wooden post, plain, black, unremarkable. She grabbed the mail and riffled through it—the way she normally did—as an occasional car passed by. Had she looked at the cars, which she didn't, she might have noticed the one that had delivered a letter that caught her attention. It bore no cancelled stamp. Its envelope was plain white in that old-fashioned small size her mother had used. Her name had been handwritten in block letters. No address was listed. But clearly someone had known her address because that someone had come in a car or on foot to drop off this letter. It had not come through the post office. And now this letter tried to blend in with those that had been delivered by the mailman. Legitimate letters. This illegitimate one didn't belong and could not, in fact, mask that truth. *Wasn't it illegal to place an item into a sanctioned US post box?* she thought as she started to open the envelope.

"Mom!" Viveca heard Theo call, as if from another universe. A universe where houses weren't robbed and letters weren't dropped by unknown hands into mailboxes. A universe where kids and their families were safe.

She stuffed the mail into her bag and ran up the driveway. She jumped into her car and fastened the seat belt and sat there, wondering at all that was happening. *What the hell is going on*? Henry had asked after the robbery. Viveca could not put it better herself.

"Mom," Theo said. "You okay?"

"Hmm?" Viveca asked.

"Can we go?"

"Sure," she said, but she didn't move.

"Mom?"

"Right," Viveca said, starting the car and shifting the gear into reverse.

She drove her son to school. She pulled into the car pool line, said goodbye to him, and pulled back out again, turning in the direction of home. Should she go home? Where else would she go? She couldn't even say why this letter was unsettling her except for the fact of the robbery. The robbery now colored everything, even the arrival of what might be an innocuous piece of hand-delivered mail. She would wait to read it at home.

Once she returned, Viveca made her way upstairs, listening for Henry. She could not remember if he was working from home or in New York. Gently she closed the door of their bedroom, a cocoon of aqua and pink floral chintz. It was meant to be soothing.

She sat on the edge of the bed, examining the envelope for clues. Its whiteness was dingy and yellowed at the edges. The block letters used the nickname she disliked. "VIV" was spelled out in black ink that skipped as if written with a dying pen. She extracted the letter and unfolded the typewritten page—for this part the sender had used a computer—and read:

Viv,

Remember me? It's been a while. Ten years since I was your best boy on "Misty." Remember how you used to call me YOUR best boy? I always liked that. You were different from other actresses.

Remember that party in Detroit when we talked for hours? I'll admit I was surprised when you confided in me. You were so mad at your husband you told me things you shouldn't have. But I've never said a word to anyone.

Last time I saw you was Cannes in May 2009. Do you remember? You waved at me and you were holding a baby and I wondered for a moment if the child was mine. Haha, right?

I'm sad to see you gave up acting. You had something special. But you always knew that, didn't you.

Funny how the years go by. We need to talk.

I'll be in touch.

Mark (Remington if your memory fails you)

Viveca sat with the letter on her lap, questions firing in her brain. Who was Mark Remington? Why didn't she remember him if they'd spent time together? And why did he keep asking her if she remembered things as though he expected that she wouldn't? Which she didn't, but that was not the point.

Her hands started shaking because it actually *was* the point. She did not remember talking with a man in Detroit when she made that film and was mad at Henry. She did not remember seeing a man at the Cannes Film Festival who might remotely construe that Theo was his baby. And *this* man who was reaching out to her now—this Mark Remington—seemed to know that she would not.

16

VIVECA 2018

Rachel. She needed to talk to Rachel.

She swiped to speed-dial her former agent.

"Rachel Geller," she answered after barely a ring.

Rachel represented some of the biggest names in Hollywood, of which Viveca had been on the cusp of becoming back in the day—the very brief day, to be honest—before she'd walked away from it all. Now Viveca, at the ripe old age of thirty-six, was a fossil, even if she and Rachel were still close. Fact was, Rachel was current in that business. Viveca most definitely was not.

"Hey Rache."

"Viveca. What's up?"

"I just have a quick question and then I've gotta run."

"Who are you kidding, you ran already. But you called me, remember?" Rachel was refreshingly thick-skinned. Rachel tangled with the biggest egos in the business and had figured out long ago that it would not benefit her to be prickly. Viveca had seen studio executives screaming in Rachel's face to the point where spittle shot out of their mouths and Rachel did not blink. She may have been a pit bull, but she was the pit bull you wanted to have in your own backyard.

"I got something weird in the mail and I wanted to run it by you."

"Separate from the robbery?"

"Yeah," Viveca said. "I mean, I think so. I have no idea."

"Shoot."

"This is a letter but it didn't come in the mail. Someone put it in my mailbox. By hand."

"So what's weird about it?"

"Do you remember anyone called Mark Remington?"

"No, should I?"

"I don't know. I mean, I don't remember him. But he says stuff in the letter that makes it seem like we knew each other well. On the set of *Misty*."

"Logging onto IMDb now," Rachel said and Viveca could hear her long fingernails clicking the keyboard. "Have you checked?"

"He's not an actor. He says he was a best boy. He says I called him *my* best boy."

"Did you…?"

"No!"

"I don't see him on IMDb."

"Are best boys listed there?"

"I don't know. I've never looked for one before. I mean, why would I? What exactly did he say?"

"Nothing much really. He referred to making that film and being at a party together at a hotel in Detroit when I was mad at Henry. Maybe the wrap party? I don't know, but he says I confided in him. He says he saw me at Cannes. When Theo was six months old. He mentions Theo."

"By name?"

"No. Just that he saw me with a baby and wondered if it was his. Then he said *haha* like it was a joke. I hope it was a joke."

Rachel paused. "Did he mention anything else? About what happened after that other wrap party?"

"No, he didn't mention that." Viveca wished Rachel hadn't brought it up either.

"Maybe it's just a fan letter."

"Maybe." Viveca considered. Was this just fan mail? Someone who'd figured out where she lived by seeing her at Whole Foods and following her home? That would explain why it was a letter instead of an email. "I guess you're right. Any fan would know when I shot *Misty* and when I went to Cannes. And when I'd given birth to Theo. It's all out there."

"So why are you worried?"

"It just seems so specific and creepy."

"Creepy maybe. Dangerous though? Hang on." Rachel held the phone only slightly away from her mouth as she boomed to someone whose name Viveca did not recognize. "Can you bring me another latte please, Kendall? Can you not wait until I ask you for something and just try to think ahead and anticipate a little? I'm sorry, Viv. I do have to run. I have a meeting with the head of Netflix for an eight-part series. You should come back. I can get you into one of those. Maybe not a lead—I mean, it's been a while. But supporting."

Viveca didn't want to hear about an eight-part series. "He said he wanted to talk. I think that's what I said before you went on that long digression."

"What did Holden Caulfield say about digressions?"

"I don't know. I'll let you go, Rachel."

"Love you. Maybe use your alarm when you're home, not just when you go out? Lock up, you know? Close the proverbial palace gates."

Rachel hung up and Viveca felt a prickle down her spine at the thought of her broken gates. But it had been good to talk to her. Rachel knew her and knew her mistakes. Most of them, anyway. Viveca tucked the letter into the pocket of her dress and went down the back stairs to get more coffee.

Making her way down the corridor that led to the kitchen, Viveca looked at the photos that had survived the night of the robbery. Half a dozen had been smashed to the ground. This was their family's gallery space, the visual record of their lives together. There were no acting pictures here, no headshots, no candids on the set. Only family.

"Hey," Henry said, popping out of his office and making Viveca jump. From behind him came the distinctive waft of the cigars he occasionally smoked, the musk of leather from the upholstered furniture, and lemon oil from polished wood. It was not unpleasant.

"I thought you went to the city!" she responded, a little too brightly.

"You okay?" he asked, but did not wait for an answer. "Listen. We need to submit a list to the insurance company of whatever was in the safe. Can you get the jewelry items to me?"

"Yeah," she said. "Sure. There were papers in there too. Important ones."

"Our passports?"

"No," she said. "I actually have those in my office."

"Well, good. Remind me what papers while you're making that list. Viveca? Are you listening?"

"Yes. I'll make a list." She started to turn away. "Wait, will you be here for dinner? Aya asked me earlier."

"I've gotta go into the city. Late dinner."

"Okay," Viveca said. "I'll let her know."

Viveca was still struggling to tamp down her heart, which was beating a little too wildly. But Henry didn't seem to notice. He kissed her perfunctorily and turned away.

Facing her again, he asked, "You'll remember the jewelry list, won't you?"

"Yes Henry, I will. Geez!"

He stared at her for a beat. "You sure you're okay?" Again he did not wait for an answer. This time when he turned, he closed the door behind him.

Viveca continued to the kitchen, straightening a few frames along the way, wondering when Henry's kiss had ceased to elicit an emotion in her. Maybe even in him.

She made herself an espresso, grateful that her favorite pods had arrived. Like most people working a program, she drank a lot of coffee. Aya was nowhere to be seen. The sun was currently streaming onto the walls, painted a deep yellow ochre. Floral curtains and striped cushions in reds, greens, and blues made the kitchen cheerful, rain or shine. Right now, though, with the low-slanting afternoon sun, the room positively glowed. Viveca's inspiration had been her favorite restaurant in all of LA, The Ivy, that bastion of the South of France in Southern California.

As Viveca added oat milk to her espresso, she focused on her backyard and the Mianus River beyond it. The blooms of blue hydrangeas and climbing pink roses were gone by now. As were the yellow blossoms of the trellised roses along the length of the terrace walls. Blues, pinks, and yellows were meant to soothe. To protect. Or at least to give the illusion of protection since Viveca knew damned well there was no such thing.

She mentally scanned for an image of Mark Remington. She came up empty. Had she had a friendship with the guy? There couldn't have been more because she was married to Henry when she shot *Misty*. Unbeknownst to her then, it would be her last film. And her best. And what would it matter if they'd had a passing friendship? She'd been an actress, after all. She knew lots of people. And lots of people thought they knew her even if she couldn't remember them.

This guy had probably been on the crew of *Misty*. They had probably chatted. Hell, maybe she'd spouted off about being mad at Henry. That sort of thing happened to actors all the time. People thought they had a relationship with them based on one or two forgettable encounters.

"You okay?"

Viveca jumped, spilling hot coffee down the front of her dress. "Geez, Aya! Way to sneak up on a person."

"I didn't sneak," Aya responded indignantly. "I called your name twice."

"I need to change out of this dress," Viveca said as she scurried upstairs.

"Bring it back so I can soak it in OxiClean!" Aya shouted after her.

Again Viveca tried to picture this guy as she put on jeans and a T-shirt, transferring his letter from dress pocket to jeans pocket. Naturally she remembered starring in *Misty*. She was proud of her work in that film and it was her most recognizable role.

And why did Rachel have to bring up the wrap party from *A Dangerous Game*? Viveca had shot that low-budget turkey back in 2002. Yes, there was that incident afterward. But how could this Mark Remington possibly know about that? It had been kept out of the press. And naturally she remembered being at the Cannes Film Festival years later—at the peak of her career—with her brand-new husband, Henry, and their baby boy, Theo.

But did she remember Mark? Did she remember working with him on *Misty*? Did she remember being at a party with him? She climbed the stairs to her third-floor office, done up in William Morris greens and deep eggplant purples. It reminded her of the forest nursery she'd created for Theo back in LA.

Across the room was the dollhouse she finally had in her life, perched on a polished oak table. She had indulged herself with a big one, complete with electric chandeliers and antique-looking furniture. All the fancy dollhouse accessories her family couldn't afford when she was a child, she had now, in her thirties. Theo seemed to think it didn't match up to her old shadowboxes. But really it surpassed them. All of it—the dollhouse, this room at the top of the house—was beyond anything she could have imagined as a child.

She settled onto the sofa and opened her laptop to google Mark Remington. It was a common enough name and—unsurprisingly—dozens of faces appeared, none of them familiar. She switched from google to Facebook. There were more than a hundred Mark Remingtons scattered across the United States and as far-flung as St. Petersburg and Cairo. Were any of these Mark Remingtons *her* Mark Remington? And then an even more chilling thought arose. What if none of them belonged to her? What if there had been no Mark Remington in her life and this was simply someone who had cobbled together a few facts from her public past and wanted something from her?

She needed another cup of coffee. She needed to call her sponsor. She slipped the letter into the left-hand drawer of the dollhouse table and headed downstairs.

17

VIVECA 2007

Viveca traveled alone to Detroit to begin *Misty*. Henry was in the middle of a stressful period in his business and couldn't spare the time away. An entire fast food chain he'd invested in had gone bankrupt. And Rachel had another client in a movie that was falling apart. That director had an addiction to uppers or downers, Viveca didn't know which. But the end result was that she got on the plane to her hometown alone, without the security blanket of Henry or Rachel beside her. This would take every ounce of her courage.

Henry promised to visit soon and often.

"It'll be like little honeymoons," he had said to her when they were entangled in the bedsheets and each other's arms the night before.

"In Detroit?" Viveca said. "Not sure it's a major honeymoon destination."

"I'll fly in and we can meet…there must be a great place to meet in Detroit?"

"It's been a long time since I've lived there. Plus, I lived in the suburbs."

"What's that museum you've talked about?" Henry asked, leaning over to kiss her. "The one with the streets."

"The Detroit Historical Museum," she said, touched and a little surprised that he remembered. "The part of it I loved when I was a kid was called *The Streets of Old Detroit*. I don't even know if it still exists."

"I'll meet you there," he said, switching on the light and sitting up.

Viveca squinted. "You're going to read?"

"For a little." Henry often had trouble sleeping and read at odd hours throughout the night. *Wait 'til you're older*, he'd ruefully say. *Sleep might elude you too*.

"My flight's early," Viveca said, pulling a pillow over her head. Fortunately, she could sleep through most anything.

The next day after a bumpy flight, Viveca was picked up at Detroit Metro Airport.

"Good afternoon, my lady," her driver greeted her at the baggage carousel. "I'm Calvin and I'll be your driver today."

"I'm Viveca," she said, extending her hand. "Hi."

"Do you have any checked bags?"

"Two," she said sheepishly. "Big ones. I'm going to be here for a while."

"That's why I'm here," Calvin said. "I'll just grab a cart and the bags, and we'll be off."

Viveca knew she'd be staying at the Townsend Hotel in suburban Birmingham. It was a village she'd always loved. She and her mother would go there to shop and for lunch, sometimes with Em and her mom.

"Hey," she leaned forward in the car to talk with Calvin. "Do you mind driving by a few places on the way to the hotel? I mean, only if you have the time."

"I have all the time you need, my lady," Calvin said like a knight in shining armor. "I'm at your service. Where would you like to go?"

"Could we drive by the Detroit Historical Museum? I kind of loved it as a child."

"The basement, right?" Calvin asked. "I loved it, too. I still do."

"Exactly!" Viveca smiled at the kinship with Calvin. "I haven't seen it in a long time."

"It would be my pleasure. I'll just pull up to the front and you can go in. Take as long as you like."

Tears sprang up in Viveca's eyes at the simple kindness.

"Thank you," she said as she got out of the car.

Inside, she went down the stairs to the recreation of old Detroit. Everything looked slightly different from the way she'd remembered it. Not enough to ruin it for her. But it was all just smaller or darker or things were in a different place from where they stood in her mind's eye. But the essence of it was the same. She found a bench on a cobblestone street and sat for a while. After several rounds of schoolchildren came through—all of them looking like the fourth graders she and Em had been so long ago—Viveca got up to leave.

When she emerged, Calvin jumped out of the car to open her door.

"Thank you," she said as she settled into the seat. "Would you mind taking me one more place?"

Viveca gave Calvin the address of her childhood home. She didn't know if Mr. and Mrs. Waldron still lived next door. Or if they were even still alive. She rummaged in her bag and pulled out her dark Chanel sunglasses. No one would recognize her, but still.

Calvin made the requisite turns into the neighborhood. The houses—like the fake ones inside the museum—looked smaller than she remembered them. The trees, in contrast, were larger. The proportions had all changed, which lent a wonky off-balance feeling to the whole street.

"Stop here," she said, about fifty yards before they got to her house.

She leaned back in her seat and looked at her old house. She looked at the Waldrons'. Theirs had been kept up. Hers had not. There were patches of snow still clinging to the grass. Dark slush lined the curbs. All of it was so much the same yet not familiar at all. Like she had entered an alternate universe.

Her phone rang, startling her. She fumbled in her bag to find it.

"Hello?"

"Babe," said Henry. "I miss you already."

"Hi!" she said, feeling lighter at the sound of his voice. "I miss you too. Hang on a sec."

Viveca leaned forward to speak to Calvin. "You can drive to the hotel now."

"Very good," Calvin replied and pulled his shiny sedan away from the dingy curb.

"What are you doing?" Henry asked. "Aren't you at the hotel yet?"

"Oh, you know. Just a little memory lane visit to old haunts."

"Well make sure you get some rest."

"I will. You sound funny, though. Is everything okay?"

"Yeah, everything's fine. I just miss you is all."

"I miss you too. What will you do tonight?"

"Work dinner at Spago."

"Very cool."

"Too cool for me."

"Henry," Viveca said. "You're the coolest guy I know."

"Well." He sounded uncharacteristically somber. "Thanks."

"Will you see your kids this weekend?" She switched to what she hoped might be a brighter topic. Though after that weird overheard conversation, maybe not. "You were going to take them to see that new *Pirates of the Caribbean* movie?"

"Yeah. I don't know. Their mother's being a pain in the ass again."

"I don't really know what the problem is." Viveca struggled for the right words. "But I'm sure you can resolve it and have that time with Margo and John. It would be good for you."

Henry was silent. Viveca feared she'd crossed some sort of never-explained Deirdre line.

"You're right, my darling," he said in an overly sunny tone. "You don't know what the problem is. I've tried to protect you from all that crap. And I'd like to keep it that way."

"I get it, but..." Another call beeped in on the line. Viveca looked at the screen. "That's Rachel calling. Do you mind if I take it?"

Henry clicked off without a word. Well, that was weird.

"Rache?" Viveca said. "Everything okay?"

"How are you settling in? Are they taking good care of you?"

"Yeah, all good."

"Okay, so Monica wants to have dinner with you tonight. Before rehearsals start. Meet her in the lobby and wear flats. You'll be walking to the restaurant. She's French and she likes to walk."

"What do I wear beyond flats?"

"She didn't say. Maybe a dress so you don't look too American?"

"Does she expect me to be French?"

"Don't think so but I'm sure you'll be fine. Sorry I didn't get more detail. I'm exhausted with that other situation going on."

"I'm sorry about that, Rache."

"Yeah. Well. Remind yourself never to be an agent. It's like being a fucking adult babysitter."

"Are you still coming to visit?"

"If all goes well. In a week."

That news filled Viveca with a whoosh of relief. She was lonelier than she had admitted. "I'll be glad to see you."

"Are you okay?" Rachel asked. "You sound off too. I can't take any more off!"

"I'm fine." Viveca laughed. "Henry's just stressed and…I don't know. He has some weird tension with his ex-wife that makes me very uncomfortable."

"He's always been weird about her. Let's talk later—that lunatic director is calling me again," Rachel said.

And with that, she was gone.

"Your palace, my lady," Calvin said as he hopped around to open Viveca's door in front of the hotel. "For the length of your stay in our fine metropolis."

"Thank you so much, Calvin." Viveca turned to him as he handed her bags to the bellman. "You've been so nice. I just want to tell you that you've made me feel really welcomed home."

"Home is home," he said as he tipped his cap to her.

But was it? Viveca didn't know. What she did know was she needed to get settled and get ready to meet Monica for dinner.

* * *

Henry did not visit for a month. Which was a horrible time to visit anyone on a movie set. By then, everyone—cast and crew alike—had formed a family. Their bond would eventually loosen when the film was finished. But, while it lasted, it served as an invisible but palpable wall that kept those who were not inside of it feeling like outsiders. Henry could not have known that. And Viveca should have found a way to tell him. But there was no way of explaining the clubby culture that evolved when a bunch of creatives spent fourteen hours a day, six days a week, together for months on end.

To make it worse, Henry got there early on a rainy March morning and was driven directly to the set. He was exhausted from the red-eye and the weather was miserable. Then he arrived to find his wife kissing a handsome Frenchman in the rain on the banks of the Detroit River. It was unfortunate timing and did not start their weekend well.

"Who the hell was that guy?" Henry asked her later in the bathroom as they were getting ready to go out for a late dinner. The hotel room that had worked just fine for Viveca alone was cramped with the two of them in it.

"He's not some guy." Viveca laughed and reached across him to grab her cosmetic bag from the shelf. "He's my costar. Gaspard Ulliel."

"Why do you do that?"

"Do what?" Viveca paused in applying her lipstick.

"Become so possessive. *My* costar. He doesn't belong to you, Viveca."

"Jesus, Henry," she said with a swiping flourish of Rouge Dior red. She loved that color and—ever since she'd had the money to buy the shade that Grace Kelly had made famous—she had made it her own. She grabbed a tissue to wipe off a smear. "It's a common expression! What am I supposed to say? *He's the costar of the film I am making*?"

"You don't have to become so pedantic, Viveca. It doesn't become you."

"Fuck you, Henry."

Viveca stomped out of the bathroom in search of her dress. She pulled the elasticized black Lycra over her head and smeared her lipstick even more. She returned to the bathroom to get more tissue. Henry did not look at her. *What the hell was wrong with him*, she wondered, as she quickly returned to the bedroom.

Leaning over to strap on her sandals—a stupid footwear choice in the freezing March rain, she knew—Viveca began to soften. What was wrong with *her*? She had never sworn at Henry, had never even responded to him in extreme anger. She knew he'd been stressed out about money. She knew he had flown all night only to arrive and find her in a lip-lock with one of France's most handsome—and eligible—movie stars. No wonder he was jealous.

"Henry?" She peeked into the bathroom where he was now brushing his teeth. As he looked over, a little spot of toothpaste dropped onto his crisp white shirt. "Oh! I'm sorry. I mean, I'm sorry I was such a bitch. Here, let me get that for you."

Viveca took a white washcloth and ran a little water over it, which she squeezed out thoroughly. Then she used a corner to lightly brush off the toothpaste from Henry's shirt.

"Thanks," he said. "I'm sorry too. It's been a rough month."

Viveca set the washcloth down on the edge of the porcelain sink and hugged her husband. "What's going on?"

"Business is bad," he said. "Really bad."

That—on top of every feeling about being back in Detroit where it all had begun or ended or however you looked at it—only served to elevate a growing sense of unease.

18

INGRID 1998

"Ingrid!" her mom yelled. Their house was a small ranch—three bedrooms and a bath and a half. This led her mom to think it was easier to shout the short distance rather than walk into a room to speak to someone. "Phone!"

Ingrid shuffled down the hall from her bedroom to grab the wall phone in the kitchen. It was still the only phone in the house, even when everyone else seemed to have added princess phones to their bedside tables. Or at least some kind of phone in the parents' bedroom. Beyond *her* parents' innate frugality, Ingrid suspected the secondary motivation was to deny their daughter any privacy.

"Ing? It's Em." Emilia always identified herself as though Ingrid wouldn't know it was her on the other end of the line. "Are your parents gonna let you go tonight?"

It was their senior year at Kimball High and tonight there would be a party. A big party, Ingrid and Em had heard, and they wanted to be there. Em was nearly eighteen but Ingrid wouldn't be seventeen until the end of November. And this party would be a first for her. Not that she intended to tell her parents about it. While they might have been distracted by work during the day, they definitely kept tabs on Ingrid at night. At least her mother did. Her dad was increasingly off in his own world.

"Yeah," Ingrid answered, pulling the cord as far as she could into the pantry, away from her mother who was sautéing hamburger for dinner. She always made Hamburger Helper on Halloween, always chili tomato flavor. Why, Ingrid had no idea. "I mean, I didn't really say where the party was. I said I was going to your house."

"That's dumb. Your mom could run into my mom."

"I highly doubt that."

"Assumptions signify a failure of the imagination." Similar to her mother, Emilia Waldron spoke poetically.

"Who said that?"

"What?"

"What you just said."

"Um, I did?"

"Never mind. Yes, I'm coming and no, I didn't really tell my mom. Or my dad." Ingrid's dad had recently taken on an extra shift at the tool and die factory, so he was unlikely to be home anyway.

"Don't forget your outfit, then," Em said.

"Yep. One Posh Spice coming up. How about you? Are we still pairing up?"

"We have so many costumes in this house I can always throw something together. Plus, Sporty Spice basically wears gym clothes. But how're you going to get out of the house?"

"I'll come in my sweats. I actually already left my costume in a bag in your bushes this afternoon. After my migraine was over."

"Genius."

"You're not the only smart one, Em."

***

Ingrid paused in recounting this story and looked around the room. It was her own living room and she was sitting here with the detective, once again, going over the events of the night. She wondered if she was giving too much extraneous detail. She'd told this story so many times to this same cop—Detective Tomasio was her name—she was amazed she'd want to hear it again.

"Should I go on?" Ingrid asked.

"What?" Tomasio looked up. "Yes, continue. Please."

So Ingrid walked the detective point to point, from the phone call through their dinner of Hamburger Helper. She recounted how often she had hopped up from the table to pass out candy to the early-bird trick-or-treaters. The little kids.

"My mom always buys what's on sale. Salted nut rolls. Stuff like that. It's pretty pathetic," she explained. "The kids just throw them away."

Detective Tomasio wrote it down.

Ingrid detailed for the detective the short walk next door to Emilia's through the gate in the cyclone fence. She almost didn't tell her about hiding her Spice Girls wardrobe in the bushes—thinking it might make her look deceitful—but decided a little honesty might help. She repeated most of the details of the girls getting dressed together. She didn't mention the bottle of vodka she'd stashed in the bushes alongside the costume. She didn't mention her father's drinking, which had escalated in recent months. She didn't mention that he had started hitting her mother. And she certainly didn't mention her own perverse need to poke at that bear. She did not have the words for any of that. Instead she went back to the story.

* * *

"Hi," Ingrid said to Mrs. Waldron when she entered their kitchen with her paper bags.

"Hi love," Em's mom replied and offered Ingrid a brownie. Waldron brownies on Halloween were as much a tradition as the Linds' Hamburger Helper.

"No thanks, Mrs. Waldron," Ingrid said, even though they were her favorite. Truth was, she planned to drink tonight. She might even try to get drunk. A brownie seemed a lot less interesting. But she did not say this to the detective.

"Hey Ingrid," said Mr. Waldron as he walked in the back door and kissed his wife. "Greetings, my love. Just shooting some baskets with Seabass out back."

"You know I hate that nickname," Mrs. Waldron said but she didn't seem mad.

Sebastian bounded in the door still carrying the basketball and made a feint of tossing it toward Ingrid with his right hand before catching it with his left.

"Very funny," Ingrid said. "I'll just pop upstairs. Em up there?"

"*What, lamb? What, ladybird?*" Mrs. Waldron responded.

"The nurse in *Romeo and Juliet*?"

"Good!" Mrs. Waldren exclaimed.

"I read it in ninth grade," Ingrid said, and moved off to take the stairs two at a time.

"Ing!" Em cried out, laughing her horsey laugh as Ingrid burst into the room. She was leaning over a small mirror on top of her dresser, brandishing a liquid eyeliner wand. "I need help!"

There were wads of black-streaked tissues all over the dresser.

"C'mere," Ingrid said. She gently pulled Emilia's eyelid and ran the eyeliner brush in a straight, neat line. "Don't fully close your eyes but look down. Relax."

She did the same with the other eye.

"How'd you do that?" Em asked as she admired herself.

"I got the touch," Ingrid said as she extracted a bottle of vodka from one of the paper bags. "I've also got the booze!"

"Ing," Em said. "You're not really gonna do this."

Ingrid ignored her and pulled out the gladiator sandals from another bag. "Aren't these amazing? The straps go up to my knees."

"They don't look comfortable," Em said as she donned her Sporty Spice sweats. In the end, she looked exactly like herself with the addition of a little eyeliner.

"Seriously though, Ingrid," Em continued. "I don't know why you want to start drinking now. It seems really stupid to me."

"Well, you're not me," snapped Ingrid, yanking off her jeans and sweater and pulling the dress over her head. She turned to look at herself in the mirror. It was perfect. Shiny black satin with the tiniest straps. And short. "Anyway, don't worry. A little vodka here and a beer or two at the party."

"I guess so," said Em, not sounding convinced.

Emilia's parents were in the living room reading when the girls bolted down the stairs. Ingrid stumbled, feeling lightheaded from the vodka. It was only her hands clenched on the banister that kept her from falling the rest of the way down.

"Oopsie daisy," she said loudly for the benefit of the Waldrons.

"Are you okay?" Mrs. Waldron asked, standing up to get a better look at her. Ingrid wondered if she suspected anything.

"Fine!" Ingrid shouted as she adjusted her skimpy dress and grabbed the door handle.

"Good night Mom and Dad," said Em.

"Good night girls. Remember, *The fool doth think he is wise, but the wise man knows himself to be a fool.*"

Emilia shut the door behind them and laughed.

"What was that?" Ingrid asked as they walked down the straight cement walkway.

"It's from *As You Like It*. It's my mom's way of telling me to be smart."

"I'm the smart one," Ingrid said as she tripped over the uneven sidewalk.

"Yeah, Ing, I'm not so sure about that."

Together, they crossed the street that was, by now, devoid of trick-or-treaters. It was very dark and getting colder by the minute. Ingrid wished she'd brought the coat her mother had tried to foist on her. The girls rounded the corner onto Shenandoah Drive when, all at once, two teenage boys jumped from the bushes in front of them. Ingrid and Em screamed in unison and took off running.

Ingrid felt the straps of her gladiator sandals slipping down her legs as she ran, which made her mad. She'd paid good money for these sandals—for the whole outfit—and she didn't intend to ruin it before the party. Precipitously she stopped and turned to face the boys. She waved her arms around, howling like an injured wolf.

The boys came to a screeching halt.

"Freak," one of them muttered before they spun off in the opposite direction.

Emilia let out one of her whooping laughs and stooped over to catch her breath. "You're crazy, Ing."

"If you only knew," Ingrid said as she howled again and lunged for her friend.

"Stop!" Emilia held up her arms. "Well, at least that warmed me up. It's freezing out here."

"C'mon," Ingrid huffed as she pulled up the straps on her sandals. Then she linked arms with Em. "We're almost there."

* * *

Ingrid would say—though not explicitly to the detective—that the night went south once she got to the party. Ingrid would say she had been in command of herself up until then. Ingrid would say that her drinking had been under control up to that point—so controlled, in fact, that she'd managed to pull off the stunt of scaring the teenage boys. But once they got to the party, tiny holes were forming in the landscape of her awareness. Not that she noticed at the time. All of these perceptions came after the fact. But she kept most of those perceptions to herself.

Ingrid definitely told the cops the name of the kid who was hosting the party. Kelly Roush. This was no big revelation. The whole town knew what had happened to Ingrid Lind in the parking lot of Kimball High after the party that had run amok. Everyone knew that Kelly's parents had left town to attend a funeral. Everyone had an opinion on Kelly Roush's judgment, along with that of her parents, who had left her home alone.

Kelly had not foreseen the tsunami that bore down upon her. She'd been surprised when liquor bottles showed up in larger numbers than the kids who were carrying them. Kelly could not have known half of them. If Ingrid lost control at that party, Kelly preceded her to it. But Kelly's night did not go—could not have possibly gone—as radically wrong as Ingrid's. Kelly ended up with smashed furniture and a living room rug that was soaked with beer and vodka, piss and puke, and in severe trouble with both her parents and the school. She would never forget it. Ingrid ended up losing her virginity and the nose she was born with, not to mention her reputation, and she could not remember it.

And yet, had it stopped there, it all might have been okay. She might have eventually gotten over it. The town might have eventually forgiven her. Her friends might have allowed her a second chance. The incident might have been filed away as a bit of bad teenage behavior—very bad, to be sure—without crossing the line into the realm of the unforgiveable.

But it was Ingrid who would not be forgiven for the thing that she did and not the guy she'd had sex with. And the sex was the very least of it.

19

VIVECA 2008

Theo was perfect. Ten fingers and toes, yes, but it was more than that. He was the baby other mothers envied. Not only did he not have colic, he barely even cried. When he was born—nearly two years after Viveca and Henry were married—they were still living in their tiny dream cottage in West Hollywood.

The house was technically four bedrooms but the smallest of those wasn't much bigger than a walk-in closet. It was this cozy space that Viveca fixed up for Theo with a crib, rocker, and dresser fitted with a changing pad. She hand-painted the walls in a forest of green trees and the ceiling sky blue, flecked with fluffy white clouds. It made her feel—when she was nestled in it with her baby boy—like they were enclosed in a protected space, the walls fitting tightly around them. Their own little life-size shadow box.

Viveca found out she was pregnant six months after *Misty* wrapped. With the exception of a couple scenes they'd reshot in LA that fall, she had not worked since then. Because the word in town was that the movie was good, Rachel did not want to be hasty in placing Viveca in her next role. She understood better than anyone the value of timing.

"They want to premiere it at Cannes," Rachel announced one day on the phone.

"This year?" Viveca was still in the grip of morning sickness and couldn't imagine getting through a festival of that magnitude. What was more, her migraines had taken a stark turn for the worse. The headaches exacerbated the nausea of the first trimester and she often found herself unable to do much more than lie in a darkened room.

"Next," Rachel said. "She may be a genius but she's not speedy in the editing room. And for whatever reason, the studio is indulging her. Early test screenings are off the charts. But since she can't make it for Cannes this year, they've agreed to hold it a full year and let her take her time."

"Wow. Okay. I mean, that works better for me."

Rachel had not been thrilled when Viveca had told her she was pregnant. On the one hand, it's hard to be negative when a married adult friend announces joyfully that she is expecting a baby. On the other hand, when you're that friend's agent, and when the work of that client is contingent on her *not* being pregnant, it's not surprising that you would feel a few qualms. Particularly when that client has a film in the can that is rumored to be a star-maker.

Theo made his arrival three weeks before his due date, on October 30, 2008. The day before Halloween. The timing, for Viveca, was not uncomplicated.

Little Theo was such a beautiful baby that the nurses at Cedars-Sinai came specially to visit him. Viveca had had trouble nursing at first. Then her breasts became engorged from too much pumping. When her milk finally came in two days later, it turned her breasts into painful rocks and Theo turned his head away.

It was one of the nurses, Laura—pronounced with an extra syllable: "La-u-ra"—a kindly beauty with olive skin and amber eyes, who saved the day. She grabbed the six-pound baby, tucked him under Viveca's arm like a football, and squeezed the nipple into his mouth. It was agonizing pain for Viveca, which quickly turned into relief as she saw her precious boy latch on. He would not starve. She would not kill him with her inability to nurture another human life. Consoled, she wept, and quickly buried memories of past sins when she most certainly destroyed the life of a different boy.

Viveca was conscious—let's be honest, cautious—of the evil eye. That corrosive effect of other people's envy. She knew she was considered lucky. She did not brag, tried not to call attention to herself, and wore her accomplishments—and those of her husband and child—humbly. She had learned this technique from Aya, who had started working with their family before Theo was born. When someone would pay Aya a compliment, she would always brush it off. *Inshallah*, *Bismillah*, and *Alhamdulillah* were the three things she said in response to everything. Viveca was not a linguist, but she knew they were all versions of *God willing* and *thank God*. Kind of like the old people back in Michigan would say, but unlike anyone she knew anymore. Certainly not another soul she knew in Hollywood.

Aya had come into their lives when Viveca was pregnant. Viveca had gone to see Aya's son, an obstetrician who specialized in high-risk pregnancies. Not that her baby was under any known risk, but Viveca's migraines had been debilitating. And she could no longer safely take the same kinds of medications.

Aya's son, Dr. Hassan Hendricks, gave Viveca nothing more than Tylenol, ice packs, and biofeedback. Well, he did give her something more than that: He gave her the phone number of his mother. A traditional healer, Aya mixed a paste of herbs to slather on Viveca's head and neck. It was the only thing that gave her any relief. Dr. Hendricks had been a product of Western medical training in Montreal and Los Angeles. Aya had been a product of traditional Moroccan methods. The old ways, for Viveca, outperformed the new.

And so life began for their family. Viveca thought it would continue much as it had since she'd married Henry, albeit with the addition of Theo. Henry went to work every day, either at his office in Century City or visiting one of the restaurants his team had funded around town. And Viveca had Aya with her, so she expected to continue to work.

When Theo was six months old, she and Henry took him to the Cannes Film Festival for the world première of *Misty*. Though it did not win the Palme d'Or, it was a crowd favorite. And when it opened in theatres the following month, it was a box-office success. Still, Viveca was reticent to go back to work. The momentum of *Misty* was strong. But, by then, she hadn't actually worked in almost two years. Truth be told, she wondered if she'd lost her stride.

Just after Theo's first birthday, Rachel called.

"There's a role I like for you. In an ensemble film so you won't have to carry the whole thing. Not that you couldn't, mind you. But I don't think you want to have to. Am I right?"

"Well hello to you, too, Rachel," Viveca said as she helped Theo stack blocks on the floor. More to the point, she stacked them and he giddily knocked them over.

"You won't have to travel, either. It'll be shot right here. Which means no Saturday work. It's perfect."

It did sound like a gentle way back in. Doing an ensemble project would keep the pressure off. Theo could sleep in his own crib at night and Viveca could see him before and after work. And on weekends. Plus, Aya had the routine down pat.

"They loved you in *Misty*," Rachel said. "But they want a screen test."

"Then they couldn't love me that much." Viveca stiffened. "I don't want to do a test."

"No, they do. But you just had a baby."

"This is a fat test?"

"No. I mean, well, sure," said Rachel. "But you're not fat. I'm fat! And they hate me but they have to work with me."

"You're not fat, Rachel. You're Rubenesque."

"Right. I'm built like a brick shithouse as my ladylike mother used to say. So does nine a.m. on Tuesday, December fifteenth, work?"

"Yeah. I mean, conceptually," said Viveca. "But it makes me nervous. It's just an opportunity for them to say no."

"They're not going to say no," said Rachel. "Unless you know something I don't. You're not pregnant again, are you?"

"No!" She couldn't imagine being pregnant again so soon. "Hey wait. I just realized that's my wedding anniversary."

"Well, it's nine o'clock in the morning. You're not going to start celebrating that early, are you?"

"Okay fine." Viveca sighed. "I'll do it."

***

Early that Tuesday morning, Viveca padded into the kitchen in her slippers and placed Theo on the rug in front of the fireplace. The kitchen fireplace was one of Viveca's favorite parts of the house. She and Henry often had small dinner parties—no more than six people—where they ate in the kitchen with a wood fire burning. It was one of the things she loved most about California, too. It got cold enough at night to need some extra warmth but most old houses did not have central heating.

In the pre-dawn hours that morning, like every morning, Theo had stood in his crib calling *mamamama* in a run-on word that pierced Viveca's heart. She never knew she could love like this—never dreamed it was possible.

Henry was still asleep. Aya had not yet arrived, though she was due in shortly to accommodate Viveca's early screen test.

She opened a bucket of oversized Legos—the kind made for little ones who still put toys in their mouths—and stepped away to make coffee for herself and oatmeal for Theo. The eastern-facing window of the kitchen burst into orange light as the sun peeked over the house next door. Theo looked up at her and smiled.

"Pretty," Viveca said, pointing at the sunrise.

"Pee-ee," Theo repeated, pointing as well.

She laughed at her own secret thought that he was an above-average child.

"Good morning!" said Aya as she opened the back door. Her voice elicited squeals of joy from Theo. He toddled toward her, with only one stumble along the way when he stepped on a Lego and lost his balance. He had only been walking for a week.

"Thanks for coming so early," said Viveca. "Do you mind if I go get dressed?"

"Of course not."

"His oatmeal is ready and cooling here in the bowl. I'll just take my coffee and get started. I don't even know where to begin…it's been so long."

"Begin with less," said Aya, who could be trusted to have an opinion on pretty much everything. "You're a beautiful woman and it is okay to look tired."

"I look tired?"

"You look like you just had a baby."

"Well I technically had a baby more than a year ago, so I hope I don't look the way I did then!"

"Of course not. But you're a mother now and motherhood is tiring."

"Not helping, Aya!" Viveca grabbed her coffee and got out of the kitchen before Aya could say anything else.

She selected a pale blue shift. While she had lost most of her baby weight, her waistline hadn't fully come back. The shape of the dress was narrow and slimming without clinging to her middle. Plus the color made her blond hair and green eyes pop. She brushed her hair until it gleamed and added just the tiniest bit of mousse to keep it from flying all over the place. Mindful of Aya's words, Viveca kept her makeup simple. Tinted sunscreen, concealer, eyeliner, mascara, and lipstick. It sounded like a lot but she applied it with restraint.

"Well?" she asked Aya when she found her on the living room floor with Theo, a pile of books spread around them. "How do I look now?"

"Perfect."

"That's a relief." Viveca laughed and bent down to kiss Theo's downy head. "Okay then. Wish me luck!"

"Mamamamama," Theo gurgled.

"That's all the luck I need!" Viveca let herself out and got into her Audi station wagon. As she turned her head to back out of the driveway, she glanced at Theo's car seat and felt a sudden stab of doubt that she was doing the right thing.

She drove east in the direction of Hollywood. Although the entire world she inhabited was known by that name, Hollywood was actually a specific place tucked inside of sprawling Los Angeles. And a pretty dingy place it could be. She swung her car into the parking lot of Sunset Gower Studios. Checking in with the guard, she gave her name and the production she was looking for.

Inside, Viveca announced herself again to the receptionist. She took her place on a couch alongside five other actresses. She knew two of them from endless rounds of auditions around town.

"Hey Taylor," Viveca said to the one next to her.

"Where've you been, Viveca," Taylor responded. "I haven't seen you for a while."

Viveca startled at Taylor's indelicate mention of the time she'd taken away from the business. Hollywood was a town with a very short memory.

"Well, I got married and had a baby," she said. "But I just had a film come out in the spring. *Misty*. Did you see it?"

Viveca knew that Taylor had screen-tested for the role *she* had played. Okay, it was a slightly bitchy move to remind her of that fact, but Taylor had just reminded Viveca of her long hiatus.

"No," Taylor responded flatly. " I didn't catch that one."

The women simultaneously turned away from each other and reached for magazines from the coffee table.

"Taylor Reese?" came a voice from the far side of the room. "You're up."

At the same moment that Taylor tossed the magazine back onto the table and collected her keys and sunglasses, Viveca looked up to see who had just called Taylor's name. It was a voice she would recognize anywhere.

Tears sprang up in Viveca's eyes as she looked into the face of Emilia Waldron, her beloved childhood friend. Em was so much the same that it stunned her. Viveca, who was not even close to the person she once had been, struggled to make sense of the familiarity of Em. Still tall and statuesque, still the same black curls—closer cropped now—finely arched eyebrows, and aquiline nose. Still the same melodious voice redolent of a lifetime of Shakespeare. It was Em, the very Em that Viveca—Ingrid—had known and loved for the first sixteen years of her life.

"You ready?" she said to Taylor. "I'm Emilia Waldron, one of the writers. The casting director and the rest of the team are inside but I wanted to walk in with you to give you a few tips on the character as I wrote her. *The play's the thing*, right?"

Viveca gasped when that little Shakespeare quotation tripped off Emilia's tongue. She was Em, for sure, but she was also so like her mother, Nan. More than Viveca would have predicted way back when. Mrs. Waldron had been right. All of her lessons had been absorbed by her beautiful daughter who stood before Viveca now and did not even see her.

But Em looked up when she heard that gasp. And she looked directly into the eyes of Viveca, a quizzical expression on her face. Viveca stared back at her, unable to look away. She could see Em trying to make sense of what was familiar in an unfamiliar face. It would be her eyes, Viveca knew—her eyes had never changed. The green of them, yes, but also the fact that they were the window into her soul. Just like Shakespeare had said.

Finally, Viveca forced herself to look down and made a great show of rummaging in her purse. She blinked hard and fast, willing the tears not to drop. She did not see it, but she heard it when Em finally shifted her weight and spoke to Taylor, the actress standing next to her. Viveca heard the door close behind them and their footsteps move down the hall, along with the murmur of Em's voice saying something which would surely have been kind and reassuring.

"Excuse me?" Viveca managed to whisper to the receptionist before she began to cry. "Where's the ladies' room?"

"You have to go back out the main door and down the hall to the left. The code is one-two-three-four." The receptionist glared at Viveca, who clearly was not listening. "Did you hear that? Just enter in one-two-three-four?"

Viveca did not thank her. She grabbed her purse and stumbled out of the office. Instinctively she turned right instead of left and made her way out of the building. She stood with both hands on the hood of her car to keep herself from falling. She had loved Em more than she had loved anyone up to that point in her life and she had expected that they would be in each other's lives forever. She had relied on Em's family as her own found family. Her family of choice. The family she aspired to be a part of. And they had welcomed her in with love in their hearts and cookies in their kitchen and sonnets and plays in their repertoires.

They had shared it all with Ingrid and she had betrayed them.

When it had happened all those years before, she'd known without a doubt that an ongoing friendship would not be possible. It was understood without question by all of them, and she had come to terms with it. Emilia was filed away in a mental compartment that Viveca rarely visited. She never thought she would see her again. And she certainly did not expect to see her here in *her* world.

Viveca knew she could not go back in that office. She could not do that screen test. She also knew she couldn't explain it to Rachel. This was the part of her story she'd never told Rachel. This had remained off limits—from that time so long ago until now. She had told Henry some of it. Most of it. Back on their honeymoon on the beach in Maui in one of those early relationship confessionals that are never revisited again.

Viveca knew, too, that it was over. This life and this career were done. Henry had been asking her to move. His business had suffered since the financial collapse last year, which they were starting to call "the Great Recession." No one knew if it would continue. No one knew if it would get worse. And he had an opportunity back East.

Viveca had resisted. She loved their little cottage and had assured Henry she didn't need anything grander. She wanted to act again. Maybe not all the time, but selectively. She wanted the stability she thought Henry offered. She wanted their life to stay the same. But all at once, today, nothing would be the same.

In fact it could not be.

20

VIVECA 2008

Viveca nosed her Audi up the driveway to the left of their cottage. It was only nine in the morning and the day that had started with such promise was over. A new film and, by extension, a new life that could meld together three different parts of herself—mother, wife, and actress—had now devolved into the most desperate sort of rerouting. The kind of steering wheel spin you're forced to do when you're careening off a highway.

She sat in the car with the radio playing some kind of new age pan flute piece on *Morning Becomes Eclectic*. The haunting tones of that instrument instilled a stab of loneliness in Viveca. She stared at the garden she had worked so hard to create. It was normally filled with fragrant roses in the colors she'd fallen in love with at The Ivy: pinks, corals, and yellows. But it was December and she had cut them back a few weeks ago. All that was left was a row of thorny stems.

Henry had been pushing her to leave, to give up their California life and move east. Not to Mamaroneck—where he'd grown up—but to Greenwich, which wasn't very far from there. Just up the road a few miles but, she was given to understand, a world away in terms of lifestyle.

Going from Mamaroneck to Greenwich was like going from Burbank to Bel Air. That was how Henry explained it.

Viveca wanted to be supportive. But if she were to be totally honest with herself she would have to admit that it was hard to reconcile this version of Henry with the person she'd thought he was when they first met. Secure. Stable. Dependable. The qualities she had ascribed to him—qualities she thought would embody her life with him—were turning out to be as illusory as anything she'd seen in her own life. The hospitality sector had just as much variability as the movie world.

And now she had run into Emilia. Her Em. Her best childhood friend. The one person in the world she could have turned to for comfort had it not become impossible to do so. Had the situation not broken them both so completely and walled them off from each other. Em and Ingrid, inseparable friends, had been separated. The thing that Ingrid did not have the foresight to imagine had happened and it had forever changed her understanding of life's possibilities.

Emilia and Ingrid had both suffered. That fact was indisputable. She imagined they both suffered still. But do people suffer differently if they caused the thing that happened? Was that worse than being the victim of it? You could make an argument in either direction about the toxic effect of guilt versus that of victimhood. Guilt rotted you from the inside out. It made you sick to look at yourself. It made you do crazy things like run away and hide.

Viveca had suffered, yes. But life had also dealt her some lucky hands. She did not know anything about Emilia's life, whether it had been a continual string of loss and sadness or if there had been brighter periods. Viveca's suffering had been mitigated over the years, softened by the feathery strokes of good fortune that had come to her more than once. She had a husband and son. She'd had a good career. Even if she were to walk away from it now, what she had accomplished could never be taken away from her. *The record of things that go well in our lives is as indelible as its opposite.* Viveca knew this. She'd had both good luck and bad. And she appreciated all the good favor she still had.

Viveca could walk in the door of her kitchen right now and pick up her beautiful and perfect baby boy and cuddle him and put him to bed in a safe and loving home. She could acquiesce to her husband's wishes and make the decision to leave.

It was a sensible moment to do it. She would be leaving her career on a high. *Misty* had come out in the spring and taken Cannes—then the world—by storm. Viveca was now seen as a serious actress with serious talent. If she left now, she would be following the model of Greta Garbo by quitting at the top of her game. She could resume her career later if she chose to, as a more mature woman. It had been done before.

She did not *need* to run now. She hadn't needed to run all those years ago. And yet she ran and was running still. That sickening feeling—the one that made her turn and turn again, away from all that happened—now grabbed her once more and gutted her.

But Emilia had seen her. Viveca knew it. Maybe Em hadn't put all the pieces together at that moment in that room. But she would. The bond that Emilia and Ingrid had shared for sixteen years was too strong to render her unrecognizable at such close range, looking eye to eye at each other.

"Hey." Viveca startled at Henry's voice just outside the car.

"Hi!" She turned to him. "What are you doing home?"

"It's only nine fifteen. I'm headed to the office now. How did it go?"

"What?"

"Viveca, are you all right?"

"You mean the audition?"

"Sweetheart, seriously?"

"Yes. I mean no. It went badly. I didn't get it."

"You know that already? Did they tell you?"

"No, but I just know it didn't go well."

"Yeah well, you're usually wrong about that." Henry laughed. "Remember the screen test for *Misty*? You met me at The Ivy in tears. And then they offered it to you."

"Yeah," Viveca conceded. "But this is different. Henry, let me get out."

Henry stepped back to allow her to open the door.

"Do you have a moment to talk before you go?" she asked, closing the car door.

"Is something wrong with Theo? I just saw him playing with Aya."

"Yes. No. Theo's fine. I just need a second to tell you something. It has to do with that thing that happened when I was in high school."

Henry stared at her and, for a moment, she was unsure if she had been right in telling him about any of her sordid past.

"Of course," he finally said.

They walked inside together and made their way to the bedroom. Viveca closed the door behind them. It was the one place in the house where Aya wouldn't disturb them.

"Henry..." Viveca sat on the edge of the bed. "I'm ready to go back East. I had a realization this morning that this is not what I want. I went to that office planning to take that screen test but it didn't feel right. I don't want this anymore. I want us—you, me, and Theo—to be in a place where you can start fresh and I can too. Just not in film. In life."

Henry sat next to her. "Are you sure?"

"Yeah, I'm sure. It took me a little bit to get here. But I'm sure."

"I don't want you to have regrets or sadness about this."

"Well," she replied, and laughed weakly. "That's a tall order. We all have regrets. We all have sadness. We're human."

"I don't want you to blame me," he clarified, "for giving up your career."

Viveca looked at him. Would she blame him? Her decision really had nothing to do with him. His presence was the reason she was able to make this decision so easily. The fact that he and Theo existed in her life meant she had somewhere to go upon leaving the world of Hollywood. But it was not his fault. It was not Theo's fault.

"I won't blame you," she said. "I ran into Emilia just now."

Henry's brow furrowed. "Your old friend from home? That girl from high school?"

"Yes. She's a writer. She was there."

"Did she see you?"

"Maybe. I don't know. I think so."

"And you didn't want to make peace?"

"That's a tough question. I mean, yes to peace. Peace is good. I just didn't…I mean, I don't know how to find that."

Henry took her face in his hands. He kissed her and she kissed him back, surprised at the passion aroused in her now, in the middle of the morning with Theo just down the hall. Viveca pulled Henry closer and they fell back onto the bed together and she cried as they kissed each other deeper and deeper. It was as though if she could only keep kissing him nothing bad could ever happen. She fumbled to unbutton his shirt and trousers. He easily slid her dress over her head and they made love in their tiny cottage as quietly as they could, knowing how thin the walls were.

Afterward Henry held her for a long while. "Don't cry, Viveca," he said. "It'll be a good life. You'll see."

Viveca wiped her teary face and sat up on the bed. "Let's go tell Aya."

And, just like that, the wheels were set in motion. Viveca had told the easy ones—Henry and Aya. Henry had wanted this so it wasn't hard for him to be enthusiastic. Aya, it turned out, was up for the change and wanted to give it a try. Rachel would be a different story. And she would not buy Viveca's explanation so easily.

21

INGRID 1998

The red Solo cup lurched—seemingly of its own volition—in the direction of Ingrid's hand. It hit her in the chest instead. Liquid splashed down the front of her, making her jump from the cold. She swiped at it in an attempt to keep from staining her satiny black dress.

It didn't seem to work.

She looked at the person handing her the drink and met the eyes of an unknown guy. Very intense dark brown eyes on a rather tall guy. Attractive maybe, but who could tell given that his face was covered entirely in a green plastic mask and he wore a hat.

"Jim Carrey?" she asked.

"*The Mask*," he answered.

She did not recognize his voice.

"Wow," he said. "Your eyes are really green. Kind of weird green."

"People say that," Ingrid said. "They match your mask."

"They actually don't." He laughed. "I got it at Party City."

"Me too," Ingrid said. "My costume, I mean."

"You're all wet," he added, reaching a hand toward her. "Let me get you some napkins or something."

"I'm okay," she said, shifting away. "I bet Kelly doesn't even have any napkins. I mean, it's not that kind of party."

"Who's Kelly?" he asked.

"Where are you from?" she asked, wondering why he wouldn't know who Kelly was.

"Troy."

"What are you doing here?" Ingrid had not realized that the party's invitation list would reach as far as the town of Troy. "I though Kelly kind of last-minute invited our school."

"Yeah, I guess. I don't know. My cousin goes to your school."

"Who's your cousin?"

"What is this? Twenty Questions?"

"Ingrid," said a voice on her left. "*How now, good friend, how farest thou this day?* Well, actually night."

Ingrid turned to face Sebastian, who was dressed in jeans and a plaid flannel shirt.

"Who are you supposed to be? Kurt Cobain?"

"*This above all*, Ingrid, *to thine own self be true*."

"So you're being yourself?"

"Always," answered Sebastian.

"So now I know your name is Ingrid," said the guy from Troy. "But who's the fag?"

"He's my friend Sebastian," said Ingrid, shocked at his vulgarity. "Who are *you*?"

"I'd like to be your friend too," he said, moving a step closer and effectively blocking Ingrid's sight line of Sebastian. Then he bent down and ran his thumb and index finger along one of the straps of her pleather sandals. "Kinky."

"Listen," Sebastian spoke to the guy's back. "You really should not be touching a lady unless the lady wants to be touched. Ingrid, am I correct?"

"Um, yes," she responded, increasingly uncomfortable with the direction this conversation was taking.

The guy slowly turned to face Sebastian. Ingrid didn't know if he moved so languidly because he was drunk or if he was doing it for dramatic purposes. Kind of like a slow-motion scene in a western when two gunslingers are about to shred up the town with bullets but, for a moment, everyone looks like they're wading through Jello. Speaking of which, she felt dizzy and wished she could sit down. She looked around the foyer for a chair but the place was so densely packed she couldn't see one.

Ingrid turned back—seemingly also in slow motion—to face Sebastian and the green guy from Troy. "Stop it," she said.

"Stop what?" Em appeared through the sea of bodies.

"They're just being weird," Ingrid said.

"Hey brother of mine," Em said, turning to Sebastian. "Why don't you come with me for a sec. There's a debate going on at the beer keg as to the merits of string theory versus particle physics. Or something like that. Anyway, they sent me to get you to clear it up."

"Well Emilia, I would go but I can't very well leave Ingrid here with this Cro-Magnon."

"Who're you calling a Cro-Magnon, bud. You're nothing but a pansy."

"Well there's a vocabulary word," Em piped in. "Why don't you try a few more? Poofter? Faggot?"

"He already used that one, Emilia," Sebastian added dryly. "His leading salvo."

"Felicitations on your expansive word choices. Your mother must be so proud."

"You guys," Ingrid said. "Just stop. It doesn't help for you to let this green guy know how much smarter you are."

For some reason, Ingrid's own words made her laugh uproariously. No one else joined in the merriment.

"Okay, listen," Ingrid said, regaining her composure. "I'm going over to the bar. This drink is almost gone and this is getting old!"

Ingrid elbowed her way through the crowd, not sure where the bar was meant to be. Maybe there was no bar, just the beer keg that Em had mentioned. In any case, she could find neither as she pushed her way from room to room. Turning a corner, she came face to face with the green guy again. This time he grabbed her arm. Hard.

"You think you're funny," he said.

"You're hurting me."

He let go of her arm and took a step back. "Sorry, you're just so pretty I didn't want you to get away."

"No I'm not." Something inside Ingrid relaxed with his compliment. "Look at how crooked my nose is."

"You're right," he said, clearly taking some satisfaction in it. "Your nose *is* crooked."

"Kids here used to call me Woodstock, like the bird from *Peanuts*."

Why had she just told him that? It was a pretty dumb thing to admit about herself.

"Want to step outside?" he asked. "It's really hot in here."

"I don't even know your name."

"Isn't that fun, though? To not know someone's name? Kind of like living on the edge."

"Yeah. No. I don't think I like the edge."

"You've been looking for a drink for a while. I know where the bar is. How about I get you a drink and you come outside with me. Deal?"

Ingrid laughed uneasily and said, "I don't want to make a deal."

He leaned in really close to her face. His breath wasn't horrible, just kind of tart like he'd chewed a piece of Juicy Fruit gum. But it was mixed with something else she didn't like. Something loamy like dirt. She wondered if that was the smell of marijuana. And then he did the strangest thing. He lifted his mask in such a way that she still couldn't see his face—it was so close to her own—and bit her lip. And he held that bite. Not hard enough to draw blood but hard enough that she was uncomfortably attached to him.

Ingrid was afraid to move. She didn't know what to do with her hands. She still clutched the sticky Solo cup. She considered dropping it and pushing him. But she feared she might tear her own lip. She had the impulse to reach up and pull his teeth apart the way you do with a dog who won't let go of a ball.

"Stop it," she tried to say, but it came out garbled.

"You like that?" he said as he released her lip from his teeth.

Oddly she did. It had felt bad and it had felt good. So Ingrid made the drunken decision to take another drink from this guy.

22

VIVECA 2018

Halloween was coming. So was Theo's tenth birthday. Each year when these two events rolled around, hand in hand like a married couple, Viveca had to talk herself off an emotional ledge. Naturally, they would throw him a party on the nearest Saturday. And, as always, Halloween would be the theme. It was pretty hard to avoid when your kid's birthday fell a day before the holiday.

Viveca had already sent out the Paperless Post invitations *before* the double debacles of the robbery and the strange letter. Not that she would have stopped the music. The robbery had unsettled all of them, but the letter had bothered only her. No one else besides Rachel even knew about it.

This year, Viveca had hired a magician, a Tarot card reader, and someone who was going to create a cornstalk maze on the back lawn. This was not the inflatable kind—Theo was too sophisticated for that—this was a guy who would set up real cornstalk bundles all over their backyard to build a complex maze. Viveca had also asked him to make a version of the Scarecrow from *The Wizard of Oz* to place at the end of it. Theo loved that movie and she wanted to surprise him with that fun—and personal—touch. Even if it rained, she would go forward with the party. Anything short of a rerun of Hurricane Sandy—which *had* ruined Theo's birthday but he was too little to remember it—would not stop the festivities.

"Theo," Viveca called upstairs. "It's time to go to school!"

He was still moving slowly in the mornings and no amount of probing on Viveca's part could get him to talk about it. She might call that child therapist after all.

"I'm going to check the mail," she added. "Meet you in the car!"

Viveca checked the mail several times a day, ever since the arrival of the letter. It had been hand-delivered at an odd hour, which introduced the concept that letters could arrive at any time, day or night, now. So she made it her business to run out there at all hours too, looking for a follow-up. In fact, she hoped there would be a follow-up. That letter had left her with so many questions and she was constantly waiting for the other shoe to drop.

Viveca had a momentary feeling—before she opened the squeaky black door of the mailbox—that something would be in there. A premonition, perhaps. Or maybe she felt that way every time she opened the mailbox these days. Sure enough, there it was: a small envelope, yellowed, like it had been sitting somewhere for years. The same block letters that spelled out VIV. The same pen used, skipping over the letters like it was about to run out of ink. The same guy had sent it. There was no doubt about that.

Once again, Viveca did not open the letter on the road. She cast a glance around in case someone was hovering in the bushes or behind a tree. Then she slammed the mailbox shut and marched back to her car. She would drive her son safely to school before she unleashed the contents of another letter from this unknown man. Mark Remington.

Theo was already in the back seat. "Mom. Where were you? I've been waiting forever."

"I told you I was running to the mailbox. Okay," she said, popping her travel mug in the cup holder and starting the ignition. "We're off!"

Oddly, Viveca was not nearly as unnerved as she'd been by the arrival of the first letter. In fact, she felt kind of engaged. As though they were playing a game and the game was afoot. As though she might be an equal player in whatever the hell game it might be.

"Bye Mom!" Theo said as he hopped out of the car with his backpack.

"Bye love," Viveca said quietly, as she watched him firmly shake hands and make eye contact with the headmaster. She did agree with Henry that such manners were important for Theo to acquire early in life.

Viveca exited the drop-off line. She made her way to a quiet little side street where she pulled over under the shade of a tree. A tree that had begun to change colors before any other tree on the block. Like a show-off, its full canopy glowed yellow against a backdrop that was still primarily green. *What kind of tree turned yellow*, she wondered as she rummaged around in her bag to find the letter she had so hastily thrust into it. *Ash? Maple?*

Her fingers met the cool texture of the paper and she let her hand rest on the letter for a moment. Whatever was being set in motion was unstoppable now. Viveca certainly had no power over the course of time and tide. She could have told anyone that back when she was Ingrid. She had not needed a lifetime of experience to garner that wisdom. She'd learned it all at once in the fall of her senior year.

She turned the letter over in her hands a couple of times. She reached down and took a sip of her still-hot coffee. She put her travel mug back in the cup holder and picked up her phone to see if she'd received any messages. She was, she knew, procrastinating.

She grabbed the letter and sliced it open with her index finger. She pulled out the same sheet of computer paper and read:

Hey Viv,

Remember me? Know why I keep asking you that? You have trouble remembering, don't you? I remember that about you because I don't have the same problem.

Do you remember when you were Ingrid? I do.

Anyway, good morning. Want to meet? How about Greenwich Point? How about now? You've probably dropped Theo off and are sitting in your car in your lululemons.

Meet me there and we can take a little walk and talk. I'll know you even if you don't remember me.

Affectionately,

Mark

Ingrid! This man had just called her Ingrid. Maybe she should meet him. Maybe she should take some sort of action rather than waiting passively for these letters to arrive. Viveca turned the car around, narrowly missing a large SUV that seemed to barrel in out of nowhere.

"Hey!" the driver shouted at Viveca. It was a mom from Theo's class. "Oh. Sorry Viveca. But watch where you're going!"

Viveca answered with a smile and a sheepish wave. Then she opened Maps on her iPhone and looked for a shortcut to Greenwich Point. One that would pass by a gas station. After all that coffee this morning, she had to pee.

As she came out of the gas station bathroom, her phone rang. She was half-expecting it to be Mark Remington, jumping the gun on their meeting. She was relieved when she saw who was calling.

"Hello?" she said.

"Viveca," began Rachel. "I just wanted to fill you in on my timing. I'll be there for Theo's party."

"Great," she said, getting into the car and starting it up again. "Hang on a sec until my phone switches over to Bluetooth."

"I'll hire a driver and come straight to you with my bags," Rachel went on. "But I'll need to head back into New York that night for a dinner. Is that okay?"

"Yeah sure," Viveca said as she pulled onto Putnam Avenue. "Wait, what day did you say?"

"I'll be there Friday. The day before the party."

"Okay," she said. "Hey Rache. I got another letter."

"From that guy?"

"Yeah. He called me Ingrid. And he wants to meet at Greenwich Point. I'm on my way there now."

"Did you fall on your head?" Rachel said. "You can't meet that guy! He could be a murderer."

"I don't think that's it. I think he wants money."

"And you have some you're giving away?"

"I just think…I don't know. I think it might help to see what he wants."

"In a park? Alone? Seriously?"

"Bad idea?"

"Yes! It's a bad idea!" Rachel practically wailed. "Go home, Viveca. Or go to the gym or the grocery or to Saks Fifth Avenue! I have no idea but do not, under any circumstances, go meet that man!"

In spite of herself, Viveca laughed. "Wanna tell me how you really feel?"

"Are you going to listen to me?"

"Sure," Viveca said. "I promise."

"Okay," Rachel said. "Share your location with me on your phone. Somehow I'm not trusting you."

Viveca rolled up to the gates of Greenwich Point. She waited while the guard examined her town pass. She wondered how this Mark Remington would get in if he wasn't a resident of Greenwich.

Rachel was right, of course. Viveca shouldn't meet him. But by the time she got off the phone, she was already so close that she decided to just drive around a little. See if she recognized anyone. Some guy lurking or waiting around. She had not shared her location with Rachel, but she would not get out of the car.

The park was enormous. She drove forward, passing cars parked in clusters as well as singly. She looked at each one. Wagons and SUVs with bike racks in back and Thules on top.

People were scattered about—hiking, biking, sliding kayaks into the still-warm water. But no one looked like the type of person who'd been dropping secret missives in Viveca's mailbox. She pulled into an angled spot and idled there, looking around some more.

And then she saw a man alone. He sat on a bench facing the water. He was ignorable in a way, but not really. He was too young, from his posture, to be the kind of retiree who would sit on a bench all morning. His back was to her but he looked tall and kind of stocky. His hair was dark—not short like a military cut but not long either. He wore jeans and a navy fleece. She couldn't tell what kind of shoes he had on.

She sat in her car watching him. He did not turn around. Maybe he was a random person and had nothing to do with letters and robberies and memories of past lives. Maybe she was losing her mind. She watched him for a little longer and then put the car in gear. She would go home like Rachel advised. No good would come of meeting anyone alone in a park.

Just then, the man stood up, turned, and looked directly at her. There was no mistaking the object of his gaze. His eyes were as dark as his hair. The word "swarthy" came to mind. But it was more than that. There was an intensity in his regard that was unpleasant. But did she recognize him?

Had she been on a witness stand, had Theo's wellbeing depended upon it—had the stakes been life or death—she would have sworn on a stack of Bibles that she had never seen this man before in her life.

Or had she?

23

INGRID 1998

"Miss Lind?"

Ingrid opened her eyes to strange tubes and poles. Sickly green walls. A curtain in a nondescript beige on a ceiling track that looped around her. Around her in a bed where she lay. She adjusted her position and felt a surge of pain in her nose, her throat, her head.

Where was she?

"Miss Lind? Ingrid?"

Then the Pandora's box of memory opened and she knew exactly where she was and why.

"What?" she rasped.

"I'm Detective Tomasio," a female cop said as she peeked around the curtain. "We met last night? Remember me?"

Did Ingrid remember her? She did. Detective Tomasio was the officer who had questioned her late into the night. The early morning, actually.

"Is there any water?" she whispered. "My throat."

Detective Tomasio advanced into the little curtained-off area of the room. She was dressed in full police attire: navy shirt, navy pants, heavy black shoes, belt, badge, gun. To Ingrid, all of a sudden, it seemed like overkill. Like this particular situation did not warrant Detective Tomasio showing up in full costume.

The thought of costumes triggered a memory of the party at Kelly Roush's house. She had taken that drink in the red Solo cup from the guy in the green mask. And Sebastian had tried to intervene.

"Sebastian?" she croaked as another memory came. Sebastian had been with her outside on the ground. He'd been trying to help her when the police arrived. They had turned their lights on them, blinding them both. The police had screamed at them to freeze. "Is Sebastian okay?"

"That's why I'm here," said Detective Tomasio as she poured out water from a plastic pitcher into a plastic cup. "Straw?"

Which would hurt less—drinking with a straw or without?

"Sure," Ingrid whispered.

Tomasio handed Ingrid the cup with the straw and stepped back. As though she did not wish to cross Ingrid's personal boundaries after those boundaries had been so utterly trounced. Even if Ingrid could not remember it. Ingrid sipped and felt a renewed stab of pain in her throat. Still, she was so very thirsty that she kept drinking. She would, she determined, master this pain with the force of her own will.

"May I?" Tomasio pointed to an orange plastic chair next to the bed that Ingrid hadn't noticed.

Ingrid nodded. Even if she planned to override the pain, she had no intention of speaking unless she had to.

"Okay," Tomasio said as she sat down and pulled a notebook and pen out of her various pockets. "Shall we begin again?"

It seemed an oddly formal question. The kind of question Sebastian would ask, with a little Shakespearean ring. *Shall we?*

"Sebastian?" Ingrid asked again.

"Why don't you tell me a little bit about him. Is he a troubled kid?"

Ingrid was surprised by this. Sebastian was odd, yes. But troubled?

"No," she whispered.

"Your friends from the party have suggested that he had some anger management issues? That he was combative with his fellow students?"

That was not exactly right. Sebastian was arrogant, yes. Convinced of his own intellectual superiority. And rightly so. *Was it conceited,* Ingrid wondered, *to think you were smarter than everyone else if it was true?*

"He was a little stuck-up," she conceded as she took another searing sip of water. "That was all."

"But he engaged in arguments with others?" Tomasio asked as she consulted her notes. "Didn't have many friends? Would you characterize those statements as true?"

"I guess so."

Detective Tomasio added to her notes and then asked, "How would you describe your relationship with Sebastian Waldron?"

Oddly, the addition of his last name alarmed Ingrid. It made it sound like this detective was narrowing her focus on Sebastian in an official way.

"I've been friends with Sebastian and Em my whole life."

"With both of them?" the detective asked, again flipping through her notes. "Emilia Waldron said that you were primarily her friend."

Ingrid's nerves were further jangled by the thought of Em—of all her friends and family—sitting up all night and talking with this cop.

"What time is it?" she asked.

"Eleven. We decided to let you sleep a little."

As Ingrid was wondering just exactly who *we* were, a nurse popped her head around the curtain.

"Morning, sugar. Just going to take some vitals," she said to Ingrid, then turned to Detective Tomasio. "Do you mind?"

"Sure. No problem," Tomasio said as she rose from the chair. "I'll just be outside."

"How'd you sleep?" the nurse asked. "I'm Donna, by the way."

"Were you here last night?" Ingrid asked in her new whisper. She did not recognize this woman's face and was hoping it wasn't another lapse in memory.

"Nope," Donna said as she plunged a thermometer in Ingrid's mouth and wrapped her arm in a blood pressure cuff. "I'm strictly a.m. I did overnights for fifteen years and can't do 'em anymore."

Ingrid remained silent with the thermometer clenched between her lips. Maybe she could keep it there for the next year and not have to talk to anyone. Not answer anyone's questions about last night. Because if this cop had a hundred questions, she knew the kids in her school would have a hundred times more. On the other hand, maybe they wouldn't ask her anything. Maybe they would just gossip behind her back. She groaned inadvertently at the thought of returning to school. A wave of shame swept over her.

"Ninety over sixty!" Donna cried, unspooling the cuff as though this was very good news, indeed. She then pulled the thermometer out of Ingrid's mouth. "Ninety-seven. Do you run a little cold, sugar? All these numbers are low and I don't want you going into shock."

"I guess so."

"Have you had a bowel movement?" Donna went to the end of the bed to read Ingrid's chart. "They gave you a stool softener about six a.m. You know, so you don't strain. Tear anything."

Ingrid eyes filled with tears. "Where's my mom?"

"I think she went to get coffee. Want me to look for her in the waiting room? I'll tell her you're okay and she can come back in. That'll make her feel better."

How immeasurably far Ingrid was from being okay could not be exaggerated.

"Sure," Ingrid said. Maybe if she said she was fine often enough, she would feel fine in the end.

"Order you lunch? Your chart says soup for now. Today's selection is chicken noodle!" Donna enthused. A lifetime dealing with sick people had clearly not dampened her ability to look on the bright side of things.

Ingrid nodded but couldn't imagine ever eating another bite of anything in her life.

Donna left and Tomasio returned.

"Where is Sebastian?" It had suddenly occurred to Ingrid to ask *where* he was since this cop never actually answered when she asked *how* he was.

"Oh," said Detective Tomasio in a nonchalant tone. "We're just holding him for a little bit. Asking him about what happened in the parking lot last night."

Ingrid sat up fully in the bed. In so doing, she was aware of how inadequately the hospital gown covered her. She pulled the thin blanket as high as she could. All of her aching parts throbbed with each movement she made.

"What about the green boy?" she rasped.

"The what?"

"The one from *The Mask*." They should not be thinking about Sebastian. They should be thinking about that guy from another town who'd come to the party in that mask. The one who had acted so predatory with Ingrid from the moment she'd first met him.

"Him. You should talk to him," she said, but she was having trouble expressing her thoughts.

"There's someone you think we should talk to?" the detective asked.

"Yes." Ingrid leaned back in relief and was overcome with a fresh round of pain. "Can you get the nurse? I need Tylenol or something."

"Of course," Tomasio said and stepped back out of the room.

Ingrid leaned forward again in an attempt to mitigate the pain. It was now making her feel nauseous and she did not want to vomit. She couldn't even imagine what that would do to her throat.

It was becoming clear that this cop thought Sebastian had something to do with what had been done to her. But Ingrid knew that would not have been possible. She knew that Sebastian was gay. He had told her so more than once. He didn't actually say the words "I am a homosexual," but he had said something that made her know what he meant. *I don't date girls*. And she knew in her gut that it was true.

Plus that kid in the mask was the suspicious one.

So why was this cop holding Sebastian? Had he said or done something—maybe been condescending to the police officers—that made them think he was the rapist? And then Ingrid wondered if Sebastian could, in fact, have been her rapist. She had heard it said that rape was not about sex. It was, more precisely, about control. And maybe aggression.

Could Sebastian have had too much to drink and taken out some kind of hostility on Ingrid?

No. That was simply not in the realm of possibility.

The nausea rose again in a tsunami and she was unable to resist it. Grabbing a plastic container that sat on the tray next to the bed, Ingrid threw up a vile liquid that scorched the insides of her throat. Surely she would never be able to speak again.

24

VIVECA 2018

"My name is…" Viveca began.

Beads of cold sweat popped out on her forehead. Her upper lip. Under her arms. She looked around the room at so many familiar faces. This had been her safe space for so long. These people had been a family of sorts, although not a family other people knew about. A secret family whose members were only known to each other. She had once gone to one of their funerals and had overheard a woman in the pew behind her say, "Who are all these people? I've known Richard for forty years and I've never laid eyes on any of them!"

"My name is…"

Now she felt dizzy. This Mark Remington had shown up out of nowhere to turn her world—her oh-so-carefully-constructed world—upside down. Viveca waved her hand and touched her throat, motioning for the next person to go ahead of her. As she sat down and grabbed her water bottle, she met the eyes of a distinguished man who had always reminded her of Sidney. Her old friend Sidney Cassin was why she was here. He had been the one who had seen her self-destructive behavior all those years ago at the afterparty for *A Dangerous Game* and had not held it against her. He was the one who had patiently waited for her to ask him what he knew. To ask him why he was so happy and self-contained without the aid of a drink. He was the one who had the wisdom to understand that Viveca would need to come to him. It would not have worked if he'd been the one to bring up the subject.

Viveca took a few sips of water and remembered when Sidney had driven her to her first meeting at St. Thomas the Apostle in Hollywood. He'd held onto her elbow as they made their way into the parish hall and led her, trembling, over to the table where two dozen people milled around a big urn of coffee and a stack of paper cups.

"We drink a lot of coffee," he'd said, then laughed as he filled a cup for each of them. "Milk? Sugar?"

"Sugar," Viveca answered.

They took their cups over to a large circle of chairs and sat together. Viveca sipped her hot coffee and watched a cadre of strangers take their places in the chairs around her.

There was a once-famous movie star who was seated directly opposite her. Now he was a venerable eminence with a thick head of silver-white hair. He was still trim and held himself with impeccable posture. He wore a tweed vest over gray woolen trousers and actually had an ascot tied at his neck. Or was that a cravat? Viveca wasn't sure what the difference was between them, but he looked like an elder statesman.

Next to him sat a young and still-quite-famous actress. Viveca wondered if the two were together. *Father and daughter? Or a May-December romance?* But as she watched them, she observed that they didn't really talk to one another. The actress, who had come in jeans and a T-shirt and not a speck of makeup—a combination which made her look like she was about twelve years old—was in a deep conversation with a young man who sat on the other side of her. The older actor sat quietly looking straight in front of him, sipping his own cup of coffee.

The other chairs were occupied by people of various ages and body types and ethnicities and genders, dressed in all manner of clothing. Some in suits like they had just come from the office. Some in overalls or painter's pants. Some in tight jeans or yoga pants. A couple of older ladies in soft floral dresses like librarians.

The thing that got Viveca was that they all looked like they were part of something that was making them happy. Or if not happy, at least serene. They all looked content and peaceful. There in that dingy room on those folding chairs clutching their paper cups, they looked glad to be there. And Viveca wanted that too.

One by one they rose. *My name is Jane. My name is Oscar. My name is Walter. My name is Lillian. My name is Peter. My name is Elaine. My name is Julia.* They each said their unique and individual name.

Then they all said the very same thing: *I am an alcoholic.*

They told their stories of hitting bottom. One of the librarians had woken up in a dry fountain at the edge of Griffith Park to find a toddler with a bright red ball watching her. A man in overalls had hit his wife and broken her arm right at the moment their son, home from college, had walked into the kitchen to witness it. The young and beautiful actress had locked herself into her running car in her closed garage until she saw that her cat was in there with her. A middle-aged man in jeans had contemplated walking into the Pacific Ocean until the moon broke through the clouds.

Each one had come to the precipice but something had brought them back. Viveca wondered if they might have all been dead had it not been for the ball or the son or the cat or the moon. Did hitting bottom require some sort of intervening presence to remind a person that life was worth living and the messes were worth cleaning up?

All of these people's stories were sad and scary and contained elements that were different from Viveca's own. And yet there was recognition. There was a thread that ran through all of them. A kernel of shame and remorse. A feeling of knowing that you've done something you should not have done. But these people seemed all right. They seemed to have somehow come to terms with the sordid pieces of themselves and been able to move on without them. Perhaps not exactly leaving those pieces behind, but relegating them to an appropriate compartment of their brains. Not a hidden compartment, for none of them was living in denial. But a compartment that contained those behaviors that had been faced and dealt with. Resolved. Many of them spoke of having made amends.

Apologized. Written that letter or made that call or knocked on that door to say they were sorry for what they had done. They owned their own pasts and no longer dwelt in lands of blame and recrimination, of self or of others.

Viveca wanted to live in the place where they lived. And she took the first step that night. She stood up when there was a lull and spoke the same words she'd heard all of them say.

"My name is Viveca. And I am an alcoholic."

At the end of the meeting they said the serenity prayer together, standing and holding hands:

God grant me the serenity to accept the things I cannot change,
the courage to change the things I can,
and the wisdom to know the difference.

She took the first step that night to deal with her drinking. She had faced the ramifications of what she had done after the wrap party of the movie in Seaside, California. Sidney had helped her do it. Rachel had given her no choice.

She could take the next step tonight. Sidney was gone now. He'd been dead for five years. Mark Remington had appeared and knew things about Viveca that she thought no one else knew. And here she was, a woman in her late thirties who'd done something so shameful in her youth that she'd never been able to face it. Something that had caused her to run not once, but twice.

Once again—like so many years before—here in the room in Connecticut, she stood.

"My name is Viveca," she said in as loud a voice as she was capable of. "And I am an alcoholic."

She cast her eyes around once more at this family who had no idea who she was. Because she had never told the truth. She cleared her throat and spoke again.

"Wait," she said. "I'm sorry. I need to say that again."

A deep breath, a clearing of the throat, a quick glance over her shoulder.

"My name is Ingrid," she finally said. "And I am a liar."

25

INGRID 1998

"Ing, wait."

Ingrid heard the voice behind her. It sounded like Sebastian but she didn't turn around. She was hot and light-headed and needed to get away from this stupid party. She had no idea where that guy in the green mask had gone. Just as well. He hadn't been nice to Sebastian. As odd as Sebastian was, he was still like family to Ingrid. She didn't like it when kids were mean to him. She elbowed her way through the crowd of sticky, smelly bodies in pursuit of an exit.

"Ow!" said another voice—female this time—and Ingrid felt a hard shove on her shoulder.

Once again, what was left of her drink sloshed and spilled down the front of her dress. She narrowed her eyes on the person who'd pushed her and came face to face with someone dressed exactly like she was.

"Hey!" Ingrid said. "Who do you think you are?"

"Who am *I*?" asked her twin. "This is *my* house. And you're totally drunk."

"Kelly?" Ingrid tried to stand up straighter, to act like a proper houseguest. She made a feeble attempt to swipe the alcohol stains from her dress. "Thank you so much for having me tonight."

"I don't even know who you are but if you throw up in my house, you're toast."

All at once, Kelly grabbed Ingrid by the arm and roughly led her out a set of French doors.

"Go home. You really are drunk and you need to get out of here. My parents are gonna kill me if this gets any worse."

Kelly precipitously let go of Ingrid's arm and Ingrid almost lost her balance. Then, just as suddenly, Kelly turned and stomped back into the house. Ingrid was alone outside.

She looked around. She seemed to be on a terrace. She tried to concentrate on what Kelly had said. Threats of being killed and being toast. Both sounded like bad ends to what was turning out to be an already bad evening. The party hadn't even been fun. All that effort to get the Posh Spice outfit, just to see Kelly in the same thing, was dispiriting. And being drunk was not as much fun as she'd thought. In fact, once Kelly had mentioned vomiting, Ingrid had begun to feel queasy. Her dress was hiking up her thighs and causing her underwear to ride up. She leaned over to yank it all back into place. Tipping her head like this turned out to be a poor choice, because dizziness joined the nausea. Ingrid barely made it to the edge of the terrace to retch up a disgusting stream of sweet and sour liquid into the grass.

When she was finished, she found an iron chair and slumped on it. It was, she realized—as much as she was able to realize anything in her current state—freezing. And the chair was wet. She had no idea where Em was. Or Sebastian. She was completely alone and miserable. She needed to get herself home.

Ingrid turned to scan her surroundings. It looked like the Roushes' backyard. Gingerly she stood, holding onto the cold arm of the chair. With her other hand, she tried to wipe any vestiges of vomit off her mouth and face. She stumbled across the terrace toward what looked like a streetlight shining between two trees. All of a sudden she lost her footing when she came to a set of steps she hadn't seen. She hit one of the steps with her knee and landed in an awkward twist on the grass. Her reflexes—in her current state of inebriation—had been so slow that she hadn't even been able to catch her fall with her hands. For a few long moments, she lay stunned and unable to get herself off the ground.

Well, Ingrid wasn't a quitter. She managed to get to her feet and reached down to pull up the straps of her gladiator sandals that had fallen down to her ankles. Once again, the act of bending over made her head swim. This time, only acrid bile came out of her mouth and nose and made her feel, for a few terrifying seconds, like she might choke on it. Even in her addled state, she vaguely remembered the story of some rock star who had choked to death on his own barf.

This time, Ingrid hoisted up her dress—what little there was of it—to wipe her face. Not only did she have puke on her mouth, but her eyes were watering from all this throwing up. She couldn't see herself but knew she must have looked a fright.

Ingrid readjusted her dress and continued toward the back of the property where she'd seen some kind of light. When she came to a tall hedge, she felt her way along it, searching for a gate. Even worse than how cold she was—not to mention wet and sore from falling—the branches were cutting the tips of her fingers. The sting of it made her even more frantic as she fumbled for a way out.

"Fuck," a voice came from behind her. Very close behind. "You're really hammered."

Ingrid froze, hoping it was Sebastian. That he and Em had come outside to look for her. But she knew it wasn't him. She knew Sebastian's voice. And Sebastian would never have used the word "hammered" any more than he would have used that other word. Ingrid turned around to look into the face of the guy in the green mask.

"You need help," he said, laughing.

"I just want to go home," she mumbled and started to cry. "I need to go home."

"At your service," he said as he took her by the arm and pulled her in the direction of the house.

"I don't want to go in there," Ingrid said, aware—albeit drunkenly—of her current state of dishevelment.

"No need," he said, gripping her arm more tightly. "We'll just slip out the side."

He pulled her roughly toward the side of Kelly Roush's house.

"And, voila!" he said, as he opened a small gate. "Off we go and no one will be the wiser."

And off, indeed, they went.

And not one soul *was* the wiser.

26

VIVECA 2018

"Hi!" Viveca said with way too much excitement when someone finally picked up the phone. "I'm just trying to confirm that a large order of corn stalks is being delivered?"

She allowed her voice to go up at the end so she'd seem less demanding. Less type-A Greenwich mother who was bulldozing her way into a perfect party for her little poppet. But she would fully bulldoze if she had to. She'd promised Theo a corn maze for his party but it seemed much harder to deliver than she'd realized. Why hadn't she promised a clown?

"I'm sorry," she continued. "My name is Viveca Stephenson. What's yours?"

"Wyatt," he said, offering no last name. "Can you pick it up?"

"The corn stalks?"

"Otherwise," Wyatt continued, "we have to charge you not only for bundling and baling the stalks—and you ordered a lot of them—but we have to charge you for delivery and set-up. We'd be driving all the way from the northeast corner of the state. Usually we sell these for cattle feed."

"I'm sorry about the cows," Viveca said. And she *was* sorry for the cows. "But I don't have a truck and I promised my son a maze."

"At your house?"

"Yes. For a party."

The man let out a long, exaggerated exhalation. Viveca wondered how he had that much air in his lungs.

"I'm willing to pay for it," she continued. "I need to have this corn maze set up so that a bunch of ten-year-old boys can get lost in it. Not actually lost. Just feel like it."

"I understand how it works," he said. "But normally you cut a corn maze into a corn field. On site. What you wanna do is drive up here with the kiddos and do it here."

"This won't be that kind of corn maze," Viveca persisted. "This'll be the kind with a bunch of big, tied-up bundles to make the maze. A fake one. I mean, can't you just take the corn you're cutting out of your fields for *your* corn maze—the extra corn stalks—and tie them up to make bundles for *my* corn maze? Are you following me?"

That was always an unwise question to ask a man.

"Yeah, I'm following you," Wyatt answered calmly. "But are you following me? It's gonna cost you."

* * *

The corn stalks arrived two days before the party. Wyatt and his team took the better part of the day to install them. They wore dungaree overalls with red kerchiefs peeking out of the pockets. Viveca wondered if these were costumes. When finished, the maze covered three quarters of the backyard and blocked all views of the water. In fact, it was tall enough for Viveca to walk through without being able to see out of it. The bundles of stalks were so thick and plentiful that it seemed like the entire state of Connecticut had been clear-cut of corn. Viveca was delighted. She dashed off to the bank when Wyatt wouldn't accept Venmo for tips.

The following day she tackled the tables, squeezing all of them onto the terrace since the maze took up the entire lawn. There was no forecast of rain all weekend, so she was setting up as much as she could in advance. Just as she was placing the last of the Indian corn centerpieces, her phone vibrated. She pulled it out of her pocket to see an unknown number.

Hey, how's party prep going? it read. *Meet me at Starbucks in Cos Cob before you get Theo.*

Viveca froze. Could this be that man? Mark Remington? How had he gotten her phone number?

More gray bubbles and then, *If you're wondering who it is, it's me. Mark Remington.*

How *had* he gotten her phone number? As if he could read Viveca's thoughts, she saw the three bouncing bubbles indicating that there was more to come.

Phone numbers aren't hard to come by. And I think you'll want to hear what I have to say.

Viveca scoffed out loud. She hadn't wanted to hear a word this man had had to say since he'd started saying them last month. As she stood there scowling at her phone, Aya popped her head out the dining room door.

"Need anything?" she asked. "I'm just going to run up to Balducci to get a few extra things for the party. They have nice-looking pumpkins and I think we need some more."

"Thanks Aya," Viveca said. "That's a great idea."

Her phone vibrated again. She turned away from Aya to look at it.

It's serious, he'd written.

"I'm going now," Aya chimed in, startling Viveca. "Do you need anything from the store?"

"What? Um, no. Thank you Aya."

Her phone buzzed again. *Ingrid.*

There was a pause, then the resumption of the typing bubbles.

Viveca. I'm not sure what you want me to call you?

NOTHING!!! she wrote. She couldn't remain silent any longer. It was maddening! *I don't want you to call me anything at all! Please leave me alone or I'm going to call the police.*

Okay, I'm going to say as much as I can in writing. It's about your husband. You're in trouble. And you need to check your mailbox before he does.

"Viveca?"

Henry's voice rang out like one of those Buddhist gongs that had been hit with a hammer. Or maybe it was just Viveca's nerves. She gasped and whirled around to face him.

"What's wrong?" he asked. "You look like you've seen a ghost."

"I…I…" Viveca stammered, shoving the phone in her pocket.

"I just wanted to tell you I'm headed into the city right now. I have a late dinner with those guys who've flown in from San Francisco. The sushi guys."

"Sure, fine," she said. "I'm just gonna check the mail and go get Theo."

"Oh here," Henry said. "I got the mail and this is for you."

She saw—why hadn't she noticed earlier?—that Henry was holding a stack of envelopes. He handed her one—large and manila. Hastily, she grabbed it and held it to her chest.

"Thanks," she said with an overly bright smile. "I'll just be off. I need to do a couple of things before pick-up."

"Okay," Henry said. "Like I said, I'll be home late."

"Bye bye," she called as she practically ran, grabbing her purse from the entry hall table along the way.

Once she was inside her car, she paused. She placed the envelope face down on the seat next to her, then put her purse on top of it. What next? Would she open the envelope and look at its contents here in the driveway?

Henry exited the house just then, jumped into his Porsche, and sped off with a jaunty wave. Viveca waited a minute or two and decided to open the envelope.

She reached over to retrieve it, turning it face up on her lap. There was the same block lettering: VIV. It had been written in the same skipping ink. Mark Remington clearly didn't even have a working pen. And the manila envelope had been used before. It was old and faded in spots; he'd had to use Scotch tape to seal it. Snidely, she wondered if Mark Remington was about to blackmail her so he could afford a run to Staples.

Viveca slid a tentative index finger under the tape and ran it along the length of the seal. Halfway along, she got a papercut. Sticking that finger in her mouth, she used her other hand to complete the job. What she pulled out was a document of about ten pages. She held it face down the way it had slid out of the envelope. She breathed in, she breathed out. She thought about the times in her life when breathing was used to gain—if not control over a situation, at least a sense of calm. She did not feel calm now. She turned the papers over and read the words printed on them:

PREMARITAL AGREEMENT

Be it known this agreement is entered into on the first day of December, 2008, by Henry James Stephenson ("Prospective Husband"), and Viveca Leigh Anders ("Prospective Wife") (collectively "the Parties").

WHEREAS the Parties contemplate legal marriage under…

It was a prenup. It was her prenup with Henry. This guy had a copy of it and Viveca could not by any stretch of her imagination come up with a reason why. What was more, this guy believed that this prenup held some sort of key as to why Viveca was, to use his words, "in trouble."

27

VIVECA 2006

"Close the door," Rachel said, covering the mouthpiece of the phone that seemed permanently attached to her ear. "Grab a seat."

She waved Viveca over to a chair and went back to her heated phone call. She wore her usual oversized jewelry: a beaded necklace, and a set of bangles in primary red, blue, and yellow. Her dress was a simple long-sleeved black that fell nearly to her ankles. Viveca suspected she had these dresses made in quantities so she'd never run out. Her look suited her perfectly and Viveca made a mental note that it would be wise, as she grew older, to develop her own signature look. Her current closet was filled with mistakes—styles that had appealed at a moment in a store but never really worked again. Dolman sleeves, for example.

Viveca walked over to one of the George Smith Kilim chairs that she'd admired so much the day she had first met Rachel. Now she had two just like them in her bungalow in the Hollywood Hills. They were probably currently being wrapped up by the movers for her move to West Hollywood with Henry.

Viveca sat and pulled out an envelope with the document she wanted Rachel to review. It was the prenup that Henry's lawyers had prepared. Viveca didn't really have a lawyer of her own. She had Rachel. As her agent, Rachel had overseen every decision that Viveca had made in the past five years. Particularly Viveca's contracts, which had grown in scope since her early days of the first word she had ever said onscreen. *Awesome*. Funny how awesomely her career had turned out. And funny the turn her life was taking now as she was about to marry Henry.

"Let me see that." Rachel hung up and came around her desk. She reached out for the prenup, which Viveca dutifully handed over.

Rachel sat in concentration for a very long time. Viveca got up to make a cup of coffee with the Nespresso machine on a side table. She plunked two sugar cubes in it—Rachel had those brown French ones—and stirred to dissolve them.

"Whose idea was this?" Rachel finally looked up at her. "This infidelity clause?"

"Oh that?" Viveca came back with her coffee. "Well, it wasn't my idea but it makes sense. Lots of actors are doing those now."

"I'm aware of that but I think it's a bad idea," said Rachel as she flipped the pages of the prenup.

"Well it might protect me if Henry ever cheated," Viveca said. "I certainly never will."

"Never say never, my dear."

"I'm sure I'll be faithful to Henry."

"Well that's just great. I'm glad you feel that way. I felt like I'd always like my big eighties hairdo but—lo and behold—I woke up one day and I didn't anymore. So I changed it! But, if that happens to you in this marriage, you forfeit any right to any monies or assets belonging to your husband."

"C'mon, Rachel, a marriage isn't like a hairstyle! And I have money of my own. Thanks to you, I'm successful."

"Viveca, listen. You have a little pile of money. And it could grow. But—let's face it, I've been in this business a long time—it could also shrink. To nothing. You really need to think about protecting yourself now before anything like that might happen in the future."

"But I don't want Henry's money if I cheat on him."

"Oh for crying out loud." Rachel stood up and walked over to the coffee maker. She opened the top of the Nespresso machine then shut it and crossed to the door.

"Lydia?" she shouted. "Can you make me a cappuccino?"

In scurried Lydia. Dropping the subject while the assistant was in the room, Viveca checked her cell phone and Rachel got on another call. This time, with some poor casting director who had had the temerity to refuse to see one of Rachel's newer clients for a role. Lydia delivered a steaming cappuccino to Rachel on the little table next to her.

"Anything for you, Miss Anders?"

"No thanks, Lydia." Viveca held up her espresso and smiled at the poor girl, who was fairly new to Rachel's office. "I'm all set."

Lydia turned to Rachel and waited for her to either get off the phone, wave her off, or give some other signal as to what was expected. When she got a hand wave, she bolted to the door and let herself out.

Rachel disconnected her call and picked up her cup. "Listen, Viveca, nobody gets married intending to cheat. Nobody. And nobody thinks their spouse will cheat on them. Well, maybe Henry does, since he's had this contract written up."

"What's that supposed to mean?"

"Just that Henry is a grown-up and can take care of himself. Which is what he's trying to do with this prenup. Frankly, my dear, I wouldn't sign it," Rachel proclaimed, and finished with a big sip of coffee.

"Seriously?" Viveca was stunned. "Henry and I are getting married next week!"

"Actually…" Rachel narrowed her eyes on Viveca. "That's a great point. I wonder if duress can be claimed should anything happen down the line. Lydia!"

Again the door opened and Lydia scurried in.

"Call Marvin Lefkowitz. Ask if there is some kind of blackout period when a prenup won't hold."

Lydia looked blank. "I'm sorry, I don't understand."

"Pick up the phone and call a lawyer by the name of Marvin Lefkowitz. He's in my contact file. If you can't find him there, look him up on the internet." Rachel lasered her eyes on the unfortunate Lydia, whose knees had begun to tremble. "Got that?"

"Yes, Rachel."

"And then ask him, if someone signs a prenup one week before a wedding, is it legal and binding, or could it be claimed to have been signed under duress? Is that clear?"

"Oh! Wait. You're getting married?" Viveca knew before the thunder rolled that the question would really piss Rachel off. It was always heedless to blurt, and it was particularly heedless for Lydia to have made the assumption that Rachel wanted this information for herself. Making any kind of assumption with Rachel was a rookie move and Viveca cringed at the coming reaction.

"Lydia," Rachel began quietly. Her quiet voice could be more frightening than her yelling. "You are here for your edification. You are not here to have an opinion. On anything. I hope you understand that. Your questions to this lawyer are abstract. Theoretical. Not literal."

Rachel stopped and took a long sip of her cappuccino. Maybe the storm was over. Maybe Lydia's cappuccino was so good—like Amelia Bedelia's lemon meringue pie—that Rachel would overlook her naivety, just like in that children's book.

"IS THAT CLEAR?" Rachel's voice boomed out so startlingly that both Viveca and the unfortunate Lydia jumped.

Lydia was struck mute.

"Rachel," Viveca said. "I think Lydia gets it. Thank you, Lydia, for making that call. It will be a big help to both of us."

Something released in Lydia at Viveca's kindness and she burst into tears, running out of the office and slamming the door behind her.

"Honestly," Rachel said as she went to work on her cell phone. "I'm surrounded by idiots. I'll just do it myself. Hello? Yes, Rachel Geller here. I'd like to speak to Marvin Lefkowitz."

28

VIVECA 2018

Viveca sat stunned in the car. Before she could consider how Mark Remington had come by this prenup, a limo pulled up the gravel drive and rolled to a stop on the forecourt, blocking her in place.

A uniformed driver exited the vehicle to open the passenger door. Viveca got out of her own car. She put the document face down on the seat and locked the door behind her. Following the driver around the limo, she peered into its open door. There sat Rachel—unmoving—her bare feet crossed on the top of the seat in front of her.

"Sofia!" Rachel bellowed. "This is the best deal you're going to get. Turn it down and you'll never match it again. In fact, I assure you that producer will blackball you around town. You might never work again."

Rachel paused to allow Sofia Whoever-She-Was to absorb the ultimatum she had just been handed. Viveca paused as well, trapped by the arrival of her friend. She was flooded with relief by her presence.

The driver popped the trunk to retrieve Rachel's bags. He extracted three of them—those hard silver suitcases that made it look like she was transporting money. As far as Viveca knew, Rachel was only staying five nights. But she had enough luggage to move in for a good, long while. Maybe she *was* carrying money.

"Where should I...?" the driver asked Viveca.

"You can just put them in the entry hall," Viveca said, climbing the stone steps to unlock the door. Watching him struggle with the weight of the bags, however, she added, "Actually, would you mind carrying them up to the guest room?"

Viveca stepped inside and held the door for the driver. The stairs had still not been fully repaired—though carpentry work had begun—but they were usable. She led him up to the yellow bedroom where she and Henry had so recently retreated on that awful night. They had slept there for several nights, in fact, but they were back in their own bedroom now.

When Viveca and the driver returned downstairs, Rachel was standing next to the limo, furiously typing on her phone.

"Can I...?" the driver began, gesturing in the direction of his car. "I have another client if it's all right to go?"

"Sure," Viveca said. "She's all set, I think. Sorry. Do you need a signature or anything? Is the tip included?"

"All good," he said, looking in the back door to check for stray belongings. He pulled out a tote bag, an *LA Times*, and a scrunched-up paper bag. He handed Viveca the tote. "Here you go. Should I throw the bag and the paper away?"

"I think you can throw them away," Viveca said. "And thank you."

"All right then. I'll just be off."

Viveca turned to her friend. "Rache. I've gotta go."

"Hey, hi," she said, still typing. "Just a sec."

"You're in the yellow room. Like before. I'll be back..." Viveca paused. "Soon."

"Wait!" Rachel finally surfaced from her phone and gave Viveca a hug. A giant Rachel-sized hug. Then she held her friend at arm's length to study her. "You look like shit."

In spite of herself, Viveca burst out laughing. "Thanks a lot. Nice to see you, too."

"Are we still acting out a Gillian Flynn novel?"

"Very funny."

"Well, there's more drama around here than on Netflix." Rachel scooped up her tote bag and headed for the front door. "Which room did you say? I'm going to freshen up and head into the city for dinner. That idiot actress Sofia Mankowitz needs convincing. She thinks because she has a famous last name that doors will fly open all over town. Let me ask you a question. You're young…ish. Do you remember who Joe Mankowitz, her great-uncle, was?"

"Um no," Viveca conceded.

"See!" Rachel said in triumph. "May I use you as my source?"

"Certainly not!" Viveca called back as she returned to her car. Mark Remington may have left the Starbucks by now. "And you're in the yellow bedroom. Do you remember it?"

"Of course I remember it, Viveca. I don't have trouble with my memory."

"Easy," Viveca said. "It's been a shitshow lately and I'm a little sensitive."

"As you should be."

"Yeah," Viveca said. "Hey, c'mere for one sec. I need to show you something."

Viveca unlocked the car and picked up the document. She turned it over and handed it to Rachel. "This just came from that guy, Mark Remington."

Rachel stared at the cover page of Viveca and Henry's prenup. Then she flipped through each and every page with a hard snap of the paper. It was as though she might—through the sheer force of her fingertips—solve the riddle of just exactly how this document had come into this man's possession.

"What the actual fuck?" were the exact words that came out of Rachel's mouth when she finished.

"I know," Viveca said. "I mean, I don't know. I don't understand any of it."

"Where did you say you were going right now?"

"I was going to meet him. To find out what's going on."

"Seriously, babe. That's a bad idea. Something strange *is* going on here."

"You think I should tell the police?"

"Viveca," Rachel spoke sharply. "The police most certainly need to know about this man who has shown up in your life and behaved in a manner that might be considered extortionary. He has delivered letters directly into your mailbox. Isn't that illegal, for starters?"

"I wondered that too!"

"And secondly, he has information about your life that makes no sense. From what you've told me, you don't remember him."

"No." Viveca deflated at the mention of this particular point. Her memory—or occasional lack thereof—was something she didn't like to talk about. With anyone. She had the horrified fear that she might have told Mark Remington things she hadn't told anyone else on that night in Detroit. He knew her birth name. How on earth would he have known that if she hadn't blurted it out in some now forgotten screed?

Still, it would not explain this prenup. The fact that this man had a copy of this document was chilling. Not just the fact that he had it, but that he was letting her know in this threatening manner. This was a document that no one would have access to unless…

"The safe," she said to Rachel. "What if he stole the safe?"

"Okay, that confirms it. You absolutely *cannot* meet him!"

29

INGRID 1998

She couldn't breathe. Something was blocking her airflow but she couldn't tell what it was. She couldn't move, either. Something was on top of her, weighing her down. She gasped and twisted her head to the side, attempting to get out from under whatever it was. She gulped in air by the icy mouthful. *Why was it so cold?* Consciousness came slowly and with it, panic. Not only was it freezing, it was very dark. She couldn't see at all. Where was she? And what was on top of her that felt like a dead body?

She disengaged her arms enough to push as hard as she could to dislodge whatever—whoever—it was. As her eyes adjusted to the blackness and she got some traction in freeing herself, the weight on her—a person, it seemed—moaned.

"Ing," the voice said. It was a male voice, which ratcheted up her alarm. Suddenly the person scooted himself to the side, off of Ingrid's body. This left her colder but still unable to move.

She—they—were on the ground. Ingrid could make out leafless trees nearby and glimpses of a slivered moon between scuttling clouds. She felt so frozen she didn't know if she could sit up. She still couldn't breathe through her nose and there was a coppery taste in her mouth. Blood.

"What..." she began. Her throat hurt worse than having strep. It stung fiercely when she swallowed. Frightened, she struggled to turn herself in such a way that would enable her to rise. There was a pulsing pressure in her head that confused her. Was it coming from her nose? Her throat? It felt like a migraine coming on. Had she passed out? She had no memory of how she got here or who was with her. If she *had* passed out, the migraine would be over already—not just beginning. Nothing was making sense.

"I had to hold you, Ing," the voice said, and all at once she recognized it.

"Sebastian?" she rasped. Her voice wasn't working properly and stabbing pain sliced her throat again.

"You didn't have all your clothes."

Ingrid reached down wildly to touch, to feel, to see if he was telling the truth, to find some meaning in this madhouse moment. She had something on. A bra and some scraps of...was that her dress?

"What's going on?" Ingrid's fingers skittered on the pavement—desperate to find her clothes. Unsuccessful, she clutched her middle to cover herself. She tried to lean forward but the throb of her head stopped her.

"I couldn't wake you. So I gave you my sweater, but it kept falling off and didn't cover you. You were so cold...I was afraid if I didn't do something you would freeze to death. So I got on top of you to keep you warm."

"You what?"

"I was trying to save you!"

"From what, Sebastian?" Ingrid was now hyperventilating. She panted from her open mouth, which seared the lining of her throat even more. "What happened to me?"

"I'm trying to tell you! I found you here and couldn't wake you. So I had to get on top of you to keep you warm. To keep you alive."

Ingrid's mind spun like the ball in a pinball game, ricocheting indiscriminately in all directions. Her brain cells were trying to locate a cogent thought. A memory. None of which came to her. She was going to throw up and she knew she mustn't—her throat couldn't take it. She worked to control the sensation, to stop herself from vomiting.

Just then a brilliant light shone into her eyes, illuminating the tawdry scene she was a part of. A half-naked, battered teenage girl. A fully dressed teenage boy. One white. One Black.

"Police!" a voice bellowed from somewhere behind that light. "Nobody move and nobody gets hurt!"

In ways Ingrid could not yet imagine, it was already too late for that.

30

VIVECA 2018

Saturday dawned crisp and clear. Viveca walked at seven thirty with the sun just peeking over the trees. Each day now was shorter than the one before. It may have been by mere minutes, but the effect was felt. Having grown up in Michigan—where the winters were harsher and longer than in coastal Connecticut—Viveca braced in October for what was to come. She braced, in another way too, for all that had come to pass.

She hadn't slept much the night before. But she needed to pull herself together, to be fresh and present for Theo. Later today they would celebrate his birthday. The outdoor tables were already festooned with Indian corn and colorful gourds. Fabric ghosts and paper monsters hung from trees. Piles of pumpkins were scattered about. The corn maze stood tall and it actually worked. Viveca had tried it a couple of times and had struggled to find the exit. And there, at the end of it, stood an outstanding rendition of the Scarecrow from *The Wizard of Oz*. As benign as that character was, he still made you jump when you rounded the final corner.

Theo, she hoped, would be pleased. She knew he would soon outgrow these kinds of parties where parents came along with their children.

Many of his classmates already had birthday parties that were kids only. But sweet Theo still wanted the grown-ups to stick around.

There was an order in place with Garden Catering to supply chicken nuggets and fries for the boys. And Aya had been cooking for three days. Her couscous and side dishes were the reason the parents still came. Aya and Viveca had been working together, peeling grapes as "eyeballs" and boiling spaghetti as "brains" for those silly old games the boys never seemed to tire of.

Viveca had not met Mark Remington at Starbucks yesterday. Whatever he wanted, however he had come to be in possession of the Stephensons' prenup, nothing good would come of meeting him unprepared. She and Rachel were going to formulate a plan—they just needed to get through the party tonight.

Viveca was still shaken by something she'd heard last night. She had gone to bed early. After she'd read to Theo and left him to continue on his own, she had settled into bed with her own book. It was still a challenge to sleep in the bedroom that had been ransacked so recently. She felt better knowing that Rachel was just down the hall. Or would be when she returned from her dinner in New York. Viveca had walked her through the alarm system earlier and had given her an extra key.

Viveca picked up her copy of *The Witch Elm* by Tana French. She had begun it with rapt attention—*was that only a month ago?* But she had lost the thread. Since the robbery and the letters, she'd been unable to concentrate.

The front door opened, and with it came the steady ring warning that the security system was about to go off. Viveca silently counted the seconds until either Rachel or Henry punched in the code to shut the thing off. Daphne didn't hear it. She didn't hear much of anything anymore. She stayed curled up next to Viveca, sound asleep. Henry had mentioned after the robbery that they might want to consider a larger dog. At least a dog who could hear. But Viveca didn't want to disturb the peace of Daphne's old age. She didn't know how long Daphne had left, but she wanted that time to be happy.

Finally, Viveca heard the code being punched in and the alarm being reset, just like she had instructed Rachel to do. She waited, listening for footfall on the stairs.

But there was nothing.

Viveca got up and opened her door a crack. There was the sound of a voice, faint and muffled. A man's. *Was it Henry?* She hoped it was him. A mad thought that Mark Remington had somehow accessed a key to her house and its alarm code crossed her mind. He was capable of many things—why not that?

Viveca cast her eyes around the bedroom for an object to carry, something she might wield in self-defense. She grabbed a fireplace poker and tiptoed into the hall. She was wearing yoga pants and a long-sleeved T-shirt, which made her feel slightly less vulnerable. At least she wasn't wandering around like a damsel in distress in a nightgown. She paused at the top of the stairs, looking down at the blank space where the spindles and railing had been.

She stood very still.

There were no sounds coming from Theo's room or the guest room. From downstairs, however, she could definitely hear someone talking. And it was most certainly a man. Should she go get her son and flee? Call the police? Walk around the house on her own? That was always the dumb idea in horror movies: marching straight into the jaws of death.

"Fuck you, Mason!" Henry's voice rang loud and clear, instantly reorganizing Viveca's understanding of the situation she faced. It wasn't a situation at all. It was merely her husband, who'd come home and gone into his office to finish a call. A hostile call. Mason was his old partner in the restaurant fund in LA. When Henry had left—ten years before—they were not on great terms. Viveca had attributed much of that vitriol to the strained financial climate of the time. And to the fact that Henry was abandoning the company. *Were they working together again?*

Eavesdropping was beneath her. She should go back to bed and simply ask Henry, when he came upstairs, what was going on with Mason. On the other hand, it would be pretty easy—now that she was already in the hallway—to go to the top of the back stairs and listen a little more closely.

Viveca's legs carried her in that direction.

She passed Theo's room. His door was closed, no light escaping below. She hoped he was sleeping already. Rachel's door was open, which meant she had not yet returned. Viveca peeked inside. A lamp had been left on. Clothing, shoes, and dog-eared film scripts were strewn across the bed and on the floor. It looked like Viveca's bedroom after the robbery.

Viveca came to the top of the small circular stairs. Henry's voice was clearer now. He was speaking in a low tone—not shouting like he had been earlier—but from this vantage point she could hear him. She could also see into his office where he sat at his desk, his back to her. Unsure where to go next, she sat on the top step and placed the superfluous fireplace poker on her lap. The waft of smells that she associated with Henry—lemon polish and cigar smoke—rose up to her. The two of them were so close to each other now. If he turned his head he would see her. If she made a noise he would hear her.

Viveca closed her eyes for the briefest moment. In avoidance? Fear? She had not really wanted to hear what Henry was saying. In many ways, that had been true for a very long time. She had found ways of ignoring what she'd seen and heard. His outburst with his daughter that night so long ago in West Hollywood. His anger on the set of *Misty*. Snippets of conversations over the years that—if she were to be honest—she would admit to having heard. But she pretended that she didn't. She always pretended she didn't.

"Listen, Mason," he said. "You need to cut me some slack here. I'll get the money. I have a plan. It's…well, it involves extracting myself from a situation in such a way as to void any financial obligations I might have incurred. It's already in motion."

Henry paused to listen to whatever Mason was saying on the other end of the line.

Viveca leaned forward to listen as well, as though she could hear through the phone line from here.

"I said..." Henry began. And it was then that Viveca dropped the fireplace poker.

Down it went, bumping along the stairs with a series of staccato clangs that rang in her ears like a tuning fork. It hit the tile floor at the bottom with a loud crack.

"Who's there?" Henry shouted as he emerged from his office with a gun. Viveca had not known her husband possessed a gun. A small gun, but still.

"Henry!" she cried before he had the chance to shoot her. "It's me! I heard a noise and came to see what it was!"

Each one of her sentences was capped with a rising exclamation point. A gun could do that to you.

Henry just stared at her, an unreadable look on his face. He lowered the gun.

"Why do you have that?" Viveca broke the silence. "When did you get a gun?"

"I've always had it."

"You have?" Viveca racked her brain for a memory of ever seeing a firearm anywhere in their house. She could not come up with one.

"Viveca," Henry said flatly. "Go to bed. I'll be up in a minute."

Viveca started to speak, to address whatever was going on now, here, on the stairs. But she had a modicum of sense and turned to walk away. As she did, it occurred to her that Henry could shoot her right there and claim it as self-defense. Especially after the robbery. She also knew, in a way she couldn't articulate, that he might actually do just that.

31

INGRID 1998

On a leaden day in November, Ingrid came home from the hospital. Thirty-six hours had passed since she'd awakened on the cold, hard ground. She had hoped—as much as she could feel hope about anything right now—that they would keep her in the hospital longer. Allow her to close her eyes in a room that—although painted a sickening green—held no associations for her. Not with family. Not with friends. Not with a lifetime of memories she'd created and stored in the form of her shadow boxes.

The nurses said she'd heal better at home, but Ingrid knew they were wrong.

Her mother picked her up, having taken the day off from work. She brought a paper bag filled with clothing that Ingrid hadn't worn in years. There was a stretched-out pair of sweatpants, dark green with splotches from bleach. The sweatshirt she'd chosen was equally baggy and bore the crest of the Detroit Tigers. Ingrid wondered where her mother had found these items and—more to the point—why.

Her father did not come. Ingrid had not seen him since the incident. Her mom mumbled something about an increase in his shifts at the factory.

Their street was empty that Monday afternoon, with just a few scattered cars parked along the curb. Her mother pulled far up their driveway to the edge of the rusted fence that separated front yard from back. She darted around the car to open Ingrid's door, as though Ingrid could no longer perform such a task on her own. Then she put an arm around her daughter's shoulder and hurried her into the house, through the side door and into the kitchen. Thereby reducing the chance for any neighbor, Ingrid presumed, to see her in her current state.

On this point, Ingrid was in full agreement with her mother. She did not wish to be seen. She wished to lie down on the first surface she found—which happened to be the sofa—and stay there indefinitely. Forever. Until she died and melded into the dull orange fabric of the Danish modern couch.

"Sweetie!" her mom called out brightly from the kitchen door. "How about I make you something to eat?"

Ingrid did not respond. She didn't know whether or not she was hungry. It would be one thing to say she had no appetite, but she couldn't even determine that.

"Ingrid?" her mother continued. "That nice detective is coming over in a little bit. She wanted to interview you again once you got comfortable at home."

Ingrid could not imagine getting comfortable anywhere.

"Would you like to watch a little TV? It's..." Her mom consulted her watch. "Well, it's two o'clock. The stories are still on."

Ingrid's mom watched the ABC line-up whenever she had a day off work. *All My Children. One Life to Live. General Hospital.* Three full hours of them. As far as Ingrid could tell, it didn't matter if you missed them for years at a time—you could pick up right where you left off. Endless threads of marriages, divorces, remarriages—sometimes to the same person and sometimes more than once—unspooled on a loop. She didn't know how her mother could stand them.

"Honey, answer me." Ingrid was startled when her mother began to cry. Deep, wracking sobs rose up from her chest and mottled her face. "Please answer me."

"Mom," Ingrid said, hauling herself up from the sofa. She approach her mother, about to hug her, but a horror at such close contact seized her. Instead, she reached out a hand to touch her mother's shoulder. "Mom. It's okay. It'll be okay."

Ingrid didn't believe it, but what else could she say?

Ingrid's touch unleashed a further layer of despair in her mother, who grabbed onto her as tightly as she could. There was no escape from it. Like the other night in the parking lot, she had no agency over her own body.

"I'm sorry, baby," her mother keened. "I'm so sorry. I'm sorry."

Ingrid patted her mother's back like an infant's as she said those words over and over again. And, though she had never been a mother herself, Ingrid recognized something primal in them. The mourning of a mother who had failed to protect her child. Ingrid began to see that it might always be worse for her mom. Ingrid had suffered pain and shame, no doubt, but her mother had other layers mixed into it. Ingrid may not have fully understood those layers, but they were plain to see.

"I'm just gonna go in my room for a little bit," Ingrid said as she pulled away from her mother. "Okay?"

"Sure, baby," said her mom, wiping at her tears. "I'm here. I'm not going anywhere."

"Thanks, Mom," Ingrid said. "That means a lot."

It was the first time she'd been in her room since leaving to get ready for the party. It all looked different now. Yellow had been her color of choice. Yellow made her feel brighter in a Michigan winter. Yellow was the backdrop for many of her shadow boxes and—even when she turned off the lights to act out her little scenes—she felt the glow of those sunny walls surrounding her. She had tried to tell her mom the exact shade of yellow she wanted that would mimic the golden light of *The Streets of Old Detroit*. Ingrid loved the yellow she'd found after trying a dozen little sample jars in various corners of the room. Now the color looked insipid. The light coming in the window was such a deep shade of slate that no amount of yellow could warm it. The gray had won.

Ingrid heard voices in the living room. It had to be the cops because—after all—what neighbor would actually pop by for a visit after a kid had been raped? What could they say? It wasn't as simple as death.

"Ingrid?" Her mom knocked softly at her door. She didn't wait long before turning the knob and poking her head in. "Honey, Detective Tomasio is here. And another nice female detective. They need to talk with you about..."

Ingrid looked at her mother and realized she could not say it. Could not pronounce the word of what had actually happened to her daughter.

"The rape?" Ingrid asked sharply. "They're here to talk with me about the rape?"

Her mom flinched but did not turn away. Instead, she held out her hand to Ingrid and they walked into the living room together.

"Thank you for the coffee, Mrs. Lind," said Detective Tomasio, who sat by the window.

"Call me Betsy, please," her mom said.

The two cops sipped the coffee. They both wore their dark blue uniforms coupled with holstered guns. Ingrid idly wondered how long it would take one of them to set down that coffee and shoot her if she acted erratically. Or would they just tackle her to the ground and bundle her off to the psych ward? How did a cop determine when to use lethal force? How bizarre would her actions have to be to warrant it?

"Ingrid?" Tomasio spoke. "It's good to see you at home. Your mom was just telling us how happy you are to be here."

Was she? Ingrid looked at her mother's face and saw an expression of such pure hope—hope that her broken daughter did take some comfort from this house, from the presence of her mother, and, she imagined, eventually her father—that she didn't have the heart to contradict her. "Yes. I'm happy to be home."

"Won't you sit down?" Tomasio said. "This is my partner, Detective Angle. We'd like to spend some time with you, to talk about the other night and what you might remember. We're hoping you'll remember more than you did yesterday."

Since Detectives Tomasio and Angle had each sat in an armchair, Ingrid took her place on the couch next to her mother.

"Miss Lind," said Detective Angle. She was taller and thinner than Tomasio and—if it could be said about anyone in such an outfit—looked more elegant in her uniform. "Would you like more ice for your nose or anything before we begin? A glass of water?"

Ingrid wondered why, exactly, these cops were acting like they were hosting her in her own home. They were nice enough but it was weird. She also wondered why her mother had abdicated the role of hostess to them.

"Would you like coffee?" Angle asked. "Your mom makes a mean cup of Joe."

"Water's fine." Ingrid looked at her mother. "May I have a glass of water?"

"Of course," her mom said as she dashed off to the kitchen.

Tomasio spoke softly while Ingrid's mom was out of the room. "Ingrid, would you like your mother to be present for our conversation? Or would you like it to just be the three of us?"

"Absolutely not," her mom said as she appeared with the water and sat down again on the sofa. "Too much has happened to my daughter when I wasn't around."

Ingrid was touched by her mother's show of backbone.

"It's fine," she said to the officers. "We can talk with my mother here."

"Okay then, Ingrid," Tomasio began. "Let's go back to Saturday night. Please walk us through everything you remember from that evening."

So Ingrid did. From her mother's Hamburger Helper to distributing candy to trick-or-treaters to dressing in Emilia's room, Ingrid led them through her motions on Saturday night. She did not mention her drinking. She considered it. She thought it might have been better had she been honest about that. It might have provided a sensible reason for her faulty memory. But in the end, she needn't have worried so much about keeping it a secret.

"Hospital records indicate that you had a blood alcohol level of .20. That is legally intoxicated for a female of your size." Angle paused and cast a glance at Mrs. Lind, seeming to consider whether to say more. Which she apparently decided to do. "In fact," she continued, "it's black-out drunk."

"Yes, well," said Tomasio, attempting to rein it in. "It is concerning."

Ingrid had no choice but to confess. "Yes, there was alcohol at the party. Someone served me a drink. More than one."

"Was that Sebastian Waldron who gave you the alcohol?" asked Tomasio.

"No, it was the other guy. The one in a green mask. From the movie *The Mask*. I don't know who he was."

"Someone from your school that you don't know?" asked Tomasio again.

Angle was the notetaker today and, like Tomasio had done, wrote down everything Ingrid said.

"He was from another school. I don't know which one. In Troy. He said he was visiting his cousin. I mentioned him before. In the hospital."

"Yes," Tomasio said. "So this fellow gave you the alcohol? And you never saw his face?"

"Yes. And no. I mean, no, I never saw his face."

Ingrid hesitated to admit that she had started drinking at the Waldrons' house. But she realized it was probably worse to lie.

"And I also had something to drink earlier," she said. "When I was getting ready at Emilia's."

"And where did you get that alcohol? And what was it?"

"Um, it was vodka. I took it from my dad."

"And did Emilia and Sebastian join you in drinking?"

"No, it was just me," Ingrid said. "Am I in trouble?"

"Well, Ingrid, for you to *not* be in trouble, we need you to tell us more. More about what really happened that night. You say you don't remember. But, see, just sitting here, your memory has improved already. Hasn't it? We think you might be able to remember a lot more if you try."

32

VIVECA 2018

"Rachel?"

Viveca tapped on the guest room door. She carried a tray with cappuccinos, croissants, and a vase of purple asters, her favorite fall flower.

Henry had taken Theo to his chess lesson at the club. Since the party planning was in such good shape, Viveca decided not to postpone her talk with Rachel any longer. She wanted to discuss what was going on now, while the house was empty. Aya would arrive at one. Theo and Henry would be back around the same time, after they'd had lunch together.

Other than Henry, it was only Rachel who knew everything—almost everything—about the past. She knew what had been *done to* Viveca. That she had been sexually assaulted. That her nose had been broken and later remade. That her vocal cords had been damaged by strangulation. What Rachel did not know was what Viveca herself had done. The part she had played in the events of that awful night and their aftermath.

"Hey," Rachel said, opening the door. She wore the most extraordinary caftan, swirled with blocks of bold blues, yellows, and oranges. "Come in!"

"Nice caftan," Viveca said as she carried the tray over to the little table and chairs near the window.

"Walker and Wade. I think the designer is from around here."

"Really? I'll google it." Viveca set the tray down. "Come sit with me for a minute. I need to tell you something."

"Before coffee? Hang on." Rachel sat opposite her and took a swig of the cappuccino. "Is it going to be bad? You look bad."

"Yeah. No," Viveca waffled. "It's a lot. Some of it you know. But there are things you don't."

Rachel downed her coffee. "I'm gonna go get another one of these. Hold that thought."

"Let me do it," Viveca said. "It'll be faster."

Viveca went downstairs and made two more cappuccinos, one for each of them. While she was at it, she grabbed Daphne and tucked her under one arm and held the tray in the other.

"Hey," she said, entering through Rachel's open door. "Here you go. I brought Miss Daphne along."

"Well, how could you leave her out," Rachel said, biting into a croissant. "I hope you have a dust buster handy. I can't eat a croissant without it exploding."

"I have Daphne," said Viveca, placing her on the floor where all the crumbs were dropping. "Even better."

"I remember when you got her. You flew where to pick her up?"

"San Francisco. There was a breeder of French bulldogs who had an eight-week-old lilac puppy available. And that was you." Viveca leaned down to kiss Daphne on the top of her head.

"How old is she now? Ten?"

"Twelve. We're on borrowed time."

"Speaking of which?" Rachel asked.

"Yeah, I know," Viveca said. "I don't even know where to begin."

"Let me start with a question. Does Henry know what you're about to tell me?"

"Mostly, yes. In the early days of our marriage we talked a lot. Then, I don't know.... We just didn't."

33

INGRID 1998

"Miss Lind." Detective Angle put down her pen and looked at Ingrid. "May I call you Ingrid?"

"Um, sure."

"Thank you, Ingrid. So, we keep coming back to a sticking point. You seem to think that Sebastian Waldron didn't have problems. That he wasn't aggressive with other students. But that's not what we're hearing from everyone else."

Ingrid shifted on the couch. "It wasn't that he didn't have problems. I mean, everyone has problems, right? It's just that he's so smart and just kind of…odd."

"Odd?" asked Angle. "What do you mean?"

"I mean that he…I don't know. He's just on another wavelength." Ingrid couldn't think of a better way to describe Sebastian. He was different from everyone else. He inhabited another universe. He could see things that other people couldn't, yet he couldn't see things in the same way that regular people did.

"Several students and teachers have suggested that Sebastian was aggressive with his classmates. Confrontational and argumentative."

"He's so much smarter. He finds us all pretty stupid."

"And you don't find that type of thinking aggressive?" asked Angle.

"Why are we talking so much about Sebastian?" Ingrid asked. "I mean, if you're trying to figure out what happened to me on Saturday night, why aren't we talking about that kid in the green mask?"

"No one else remembers anyone who matches the description you gave, Ingrid."

Detective Tomasio hadn't spoken for a while so Ingrid was a little surprised when she piped in with this.

"What do you mean? I was talking to him for a long time. Sebastian came over to try to get me away from him."

"Because Sebastian wanted you all to himself?" Angle asked.

"No! That's not…"

Ingrid didn't know if she should tell the cops that she believed Sebastian was gay. It wasn't really anything they'd ever openly discussed. The most he'd said to her was that he didn't like girls. But was she meant to share that information? Wasn't it actually Sebastian's to tell?

"Look," said Ingrid's mom, squeezing her daughter's hand. "I think you need to tone this down or maybe we need to take a break."

"Ingrid," said Tomasio, taking a deep breath and continuing in a voice so incongruously gentle she could have been reading a bedtime story. "Do you understand the nature of sexual assault? It isn't always about sexual attraction. Sometimes it's about dominance. Aggression, if you will. Whoever did what was done to you is an aggressive person. We would like to catch that person. You say you have no memory of the events of that evening after a certain point. Why don't we start again and walk through the evening, step by step."

"I've already told you. I don't remember. I really don't."

"Okay," said Angle, also in a calming voice. "I get that. But I think if we go slowly, little details might come back to you. Let's start when you walked in the door of the party."

So Ingrid began again, blinking back tears. The throbbing in her nose was worse than ever and her throat felt raw. She picked up the glass and took a sip of water. And, again, she went—step by step—through every part of the evening that she could remember.

"Who walked outside with you?" Detective Angle asked.

"Sebastian *said* he would walk outside with me," Ingrid began. "Wait. Maybe it was that guy in the mask. I'm not sure. One of them offered to go with me. Or maybe I went outside alone."

"Kelly Roush, your host for the evening," Detective Angle said, as if Ingrid might not remember who she was, "said she saw you in the company of Sebastian Waldron walking outside of her house later in the evening."

"She did?"

"Yes, Ingrid, she did," said Angle. "When you think back, does that information change your memories?"

"I..." she began. "I guess. Maybe Sebastian was trying to get me away from that guy. He'd said something mean, I remember now."

"To you?"

"No, to Sebastian. He called him a name but I don't remember what."

"Was it in reference to Sebastian's race?" Tomasio asked.

"No," Ingrid said. "I think it was in reference to him, um...not being masculine."

"I see," said Angle. "And might it have been the sort of derogatory comment that could have angered Sebastian?"

"Well, yes, I'm sure. It angered me!"

"And what was Sebastian's reaction?"

"Shakespeare?"

"What?"

"The Waldrons quote Shakespeare all the time. Maybe Sebastian quoted him."

"That seems like a pretty tepid reaction to a perceived slur. Several of the party guests have suggested that Sebastian was in a state of high agitation that evening. Particularly when he was in your company."

Ingrid didn't know who these party guests were. The cops had mentioned Kelly Roush.

"Was it Kelly?"

"And a few others."

"I didn't think Kelly even knew who I was."

"She knows who you are. She said you were wearing the same costume that night."

"Oh my god, that's right."

"Look, Ingrid," said Tomasio. "We understand your lifelong friendship with the Waldron family. We also understand that your relationship with Sebastian has been strained. Is it possible that Sebastian accompanied you out of the house that night? Is it possible that he felt insulted by the mystery man in the mask? Is it possible that Sebastian—who has a known history of hostile and aggressive behavior with other students in your school—acted out an aggressive scenario with you in the school parking lot that night? Is it possible that Sebastian later regretted his actions and stayed with you on the ground until the police arrived? To keep you alive? To atone for what he did? To try to undo an evening that had spiraled out of control…to make it right again?"

Ingrid's head was spinning. Every injured part of her was throbbing. Was it possible that Sebastian had done this to her? She had always tried to avoid him. He *was* odd. He *was* aggressive and sometimes hostile to other people. He *did* possess the kind of intelligence that felt like a coiled spring. Like he was about to leap in your direction. But was he violent? She hadn't seen that. But was it possible?

No, she really did not think it was.

But she had seen her own father strike her mother. It did not happen often and never in view of the outside world. But it happened and Ingrid had seen it, even if her parents didn't think so. Her father's excesses—his nightly disappearances and dark moods—had been chalked up by her mother to his drinking. *What was this substance that changed the nature of a human being into something so alien? Had Sebastian been drinking that night too?* Ingrid didn't know. She didn't remember.

"Ingrid?" asked Tomasio in a softer tone than before.

"Can I see Em? Can I talk to Emilia?" Ingrid looked back and forth from one cop to another. She turned her head to her mother. "Mom, I wanna talk to Em."

Her mother turned to the detectives. "Officers? May my daughter speak with her friend?"

"Not right now, Mrs. Lind," Angle said, and then turned to Ingrid. "You will be able to, but not just yet."

"Listen," said Tomasio, "we know this is hard. Really hard. And we're not asking you if you can say beyond the shadow of a doubt that Sebastian Waldron was your attacker on the night of October 31. But is there doubt? Could it be possible? Think about it, Ingrid. Is it even in the realm of possibility that Sebastian did this to you?"

Ingrid considered what she knew about human nature, and realized that it was nothing. She did not understand her father or her mother or anyone. Least of all herself. How could she claim to understand what Sebastian was capable of?

"Ingrid?" Tomasio lowered her voice to a near whisper. "Is doesn't have to be definitive. You just need to say if it's possible."

"I guess so," she finally said. "Yes."

It was a three-letter word that would echo in her head for the rest of her life. It was a word that would seal the fates of all of them and set them against each other forever. It was a word she said under coercion or pressure or suggestion or even just under the influence of a pulsing nose and aching throat. It was a word she uttered too easily, too cheaply, too readily. But she said it. And Ingrid began to cry in huge gulping sobs.

"I think you need to leave," Mrs. Lind said, standing up. "This has gone far enough."

But Ingrid's mother was wrong. "Far enough" implied it was still containable. "Far enough" was that point at which you could still stop a train from hurtling off the tracks. But this—because of Ingrid—had gone farther than that. It had gone utterly, inescapably, and tragically too far.

And it was unstoppable now.

34

VIVECA 2018

"Mom!" Theo shouted as he bounded up the stairs. "Where are you? I won!"

Viveca struggled to compose herself and answer her son. Rachel, who had been silently listening to her unspool the tangled threads of her distant past, spoke first.

"In here, Theo!" she called out as she opened the door. "Your mom is with me. Come see your Auntie Rachel."

Theo barreled down the hall and into the guest room. "Mom! I won the final chess match! I got a trophy!"

Viveca stood up to hug him. "Oh Theo! I'm so proud of you!"

"Wanna see it? Dad has it in the kitchen," Theo said, beaming. "It's big."

"Of course it's big!" said Rachel. "It'd better be the size of the house! Bigger. The size of a plane!"

"A building!" Theo laughed.

"A mountain!" countered Rachel.

Viveca was comforted by this reminder of life and love in the presence of her beautiful boy and her dear friend. She may have ruined the life of one boy so long ago, but she had been given a second chance with this one. She did not deserve it but it had been given to her. And she mustn't waste it.

"C'mon," she said. "Let's go downstairs and admire your trophy."

"They let me bring it home but I have to give it back," Theo chattered breathlessly as they descended the front stairs. Viveca had tied orange and black ribbons across the area of missing railings for the party. It was her attempt to make the carnage look intentional. Or, if not intentional, at least recognized. She didn't want to call too much attention to it, but she figured it would attract less attention decorated.

"What do you mean you have to give it back?" Rachel asked. "Maybe you can hide it somewhere they'll never find it?"

"No, Aunt Rachel! They keep these trophies at the club for like, ever," Theo explained. "They have them in a case and everybody who wins gets their name engraved on them. You get to keep it for like a day, and then it goes back. But your name is there!"

"Is that how it works?" Rachel asked patiently. Viveca knew that Rachel knew exactly how these types of trophies worked. It wasn't like an Oscar that you got to keep on your mantle. Rachel had grown up on the East Coast where she'd been in plenty of clubs with shelves filled with silver cups and bowls, all solemnly displaying the names of past champions in sailing, golf, tennis, and chess.

"Dad!" Theo called as they entered the kitchen. "Show Mom! Show Aunt Rachel!"

Henry sat at the kitchen table with a cup of coffee and the weekend edition of *The Wall Street Journal*. He looked normal. He did not at all resemble the man she had glimpsed on the stairs last night when she'd dropped the fireplace poker and he'd emerged from his office brandishing a gun.

"Hey champ," Henry said as he tousled their son's hair. Not only did he look normal, he was acting normal as well. "It's right over here where you asked me to hide it. Okay everyone, how about a drumroll?"

Rachel quickly jumped in, banging on the kitchen table with her hands like it was a set of bongo drums. Viveca, who was feeling increasingly like she was in *The Twilight Zone*, followed suit.

"Close your eyes!" Theo commanded, and Rachel and Viveca complied.

Rustling footsteps were heard, then Theo shouted, "Okay now!"

Viveca opened her eyes to see a very large silver urn with handles on both sides. It was ornately tooled with a plaque that bore a list of names and years.

"Oh Theo!" she said. "It's beautiful. I can't wait to see your name on this list. I can't wait to see it every time we go to the club! I'm really proud of you."

"I won against a guy who's old," Theo added. "He was twenty or maybe your age. I couldn't tell."

"Yes, well," said Rachel. "We all start to look alike after a certain point. Personally, I chose to freeze my looks at thirty and I'll just stay there, thank you very much. Can I make another cappuccino?"

"Of course. And how about a grilled cheese for anyone?"

"Not for me," said Rachel. "If I intend to remain thirty forever, grilled cheese is not going to help me achieve it."

"I'll have one," said Theo.

"Didn't you have lunch already?"

"I'm still hungry."

"A growing boy is a growing boy." Viveca laughed as she opened the refrigerator to get the cheese. She turned to her husband. "What about you, Henry?"

It was the first thing she'd said to him since that bizarre moment on the stairs. She looked hard, taking the measure of him as if for the first time.

"Sure," he said. "Sounds great."

Every aspect of his demeanor was normal.

* * *

Aya arrived at one and final preparations for the party began in earnest. Kids and their parents had been invited for four. Her closest mom friends, Devon, Max, and Greta, would come an hour earlier with their boys to pitch in on last-minute details. Then, together, they would help the four boys get ready for the party.

Viveca had kept Theo in juvenile costumes for as long as she could. He'd always been the sweetest little lion or giraffe. But those days were over and he was feeling the pull of popular culture. *Star Wars*, *Black Panther*, and *Incredibles 2* were hot-ticket costumes this year. But Viveca managed to talk Theo into something a little more artistic. She bought a makeup kit to turn him into a scary skeleton, complete with a railroad track scar that would run down his cheek. Black sweatpants, a black sweatshirt, and a million little strips of fluorescent white tape would fill in the skeleton and complete the look. The idea was for him to look like an actual skeleton running around in the dark. Viveca hoped it would work.

In all, thirty children and their parents had accepted. You never knew in Greenwich, though, if parents would accompany their kids or send the au pair. Viveca always counted two adults per child and had Aya cook for as many. There would be mountains of leftovers.

The cop they had hired to stand at the gates and direct folks to park on the street would arrive at 3:30. As would the magician, the fortune teller, and Garden Catering with a giant truck. The maze was in place. The tables had been set.

It was a costume party for both adults and children and, every year, the parents outdid themselves. When the boys were smaller, there were plenty of family group costumes. The *Winnie the Pooh* characters were a perpetual favorite with mom, dad, and kiddos showing up as Winnie, Eeyore, Tigger, and the gang. Others went with Aslan, the White Witch, and the children from *The Lion, the Witch and the Wardrobe*. Some went Hollywood with the Cowardly Lion, the Tin Man, and the Scarecrow from *The Wizard of Oz*. Since most of their little guests were boys, the only Dorothy in that grouping would be one of the mothers.

Viveca had her own standard costume of street clothes paired with a witch hat. Henry always sported jeans and an overcoat that evoked the White Rabbit from *Alice in Wonderland*. Or, as Viveca preferred to think, George Harrison from the *Sgt. Pepper* album.

By 3:45, everyone was dressed and ready. The boys were bouncing around, agitated for the party to start. Viveca had chosen to pair her witch hat with black jeans and an orange sweater with fringe at the hips. She was going for the relaxed-mom-on-Halloween vibe.

The doorbell rang at exactly four. Viveca opened the door to an unrecognizable little *Star Wars* character. The parents, Katherine and Hector Aguila, wore their usual gaucho attire in honor of Hector's Uruguayan roots. So the little boy had to be Dixon. Viveca hadn't seen Katherine since the morning after the robbery when she'd gone to pick up Theo. She hadn't told her what had happened and hoped Katherine didn't ask about the damaged staircase now. It was such a long story and it would seem odd that Viveca hadn't mentioned it at the time.

"Viveca!" Katherine trilled. "You look marvelous. As always."

"And you, Katherine," Viveca said as they kissed each other on the cheek. "You are one sexy gaucho."

"Gaucha," corrected Hector.

"Gotcha," teased Viveca. No one else laughed at her joke.

"Say hello to Mrs. Stephenson, Dixon," said Katherine with a little nudge on Dixon's shoulder. "And give her the birthday gift for Theo. Or, I'm assuming you have a table for gifts? We can drop it there ourselves if that's easier."

"No, it's fine," Viveca said. "Thank you, Dixon."

"You're welcome, Mrs. Stephenson." Dixon handed her the gift with his left hand and held out his right for shaking. "And good afternoon. Thank you for having me."

Like all the boys from Theo's school, Dixon had impeccable manners with adults. Boy on boy, they could be a bit savage. But with adults they behaved like little princes.

The Aguilas were followed by a stream of boys and their companions—some parents, some nannies, just like Viveca had thought—that waxed and waned for about forty minutes. The pile of gifts on the hall table grew. Viveca maintained her post at the door but she let Theo go and enjoy his party. She valued manners, but she also wanted Theo to be a kid.

When the arrivals stopped, Viveca decided to join the party and allow any stragglers to let themselves in. She reached down to click the little button on the side of the doorknob to unlock it. Just as she was closing it again, she hit a hard object and the door was pushed back toward her.

"Oh, sorry!" Viveca said and yanked on the door handle.

When the door was fully open, Viveca looked up into the face of a man. He was medium height with hazel eyes. But the eyes were all she could see of his face. Because there at her door in Riverside in 2018 stood someone in the green mask from the movie *The Mask*. Exactly like someone at the Halloween party in Royal Oak in 1998.

Viveca gasped and felt herself slump until the hands of the man in the mask reached out and grabbed her by the shoulders. Her reaction was so primal, so utterly visceral, that she screamed and struggled to pull herself away.

"Viveca?" Henry rushed up from behind. "You okay?"

She was speechless in horror that her husband was asking such a banal question when this man had her by the arms. This man, who appeared to be the reincarnation of the boy who had raped her twenty years before.

"Hey Henry," the guy in the mask said. "You wanna take hold of your wife? She looks like she's gonna pass out."

Viveca spun her head from one to the other—the man in the mask and her husband. She feared she might have a migraine right here and now at the start of the party.

"Who goes there?" Henry asked jauntily.

Viveca stared.

"It's Larry, my man," the masked man said as he removed his hands from Viveca's arms, gingerly testing to make sure she wasn't about to drop to the floor. "Larry Keenan."

"Oh, hey Larry," said Henry. "How're you doing?"

Viveca took hold of her own body. She willed herself to stand up straight, to breathe, even to smile at Larry Keenan.

"Hi Larry," she said. "Sorry I didn't recognize you and I…I just felt a little dizzy for a minute."

"You okay? You look like you've seen a ghost."

"Yeah," she said. "No. It was nothing. Just low blood sugar."

"Great costume," Henry said. "It really takes me back."

"Right?" Larry laughed. "That's why I got it. It takes me back too!"

Larry would have no idea just how much it took Viveca back. She was surprised Henry didn't seem to either. But she had to return to the here and now. This was Theo's Halloween birthday party and she had created it. She was in charge. She was ready to go back there and mix and mingle and be part of her son's special day.

As she started to walk out to the terrace, Viveca took one last look at Larry Keenan. His resemblance to that kid from all those years ago was uncanny.

35

INGRID 1998

The last time Ingrid spoke to any of the Waldrons was on a blank November day sometime before Thanksgiving. She did not know what day it was. All days blended together now. There wasn't much to distinguish day from night either. Ingrid stayed at home. Her mother increasingly did the same. Her father had ceased to appear. Except for the three hours of soap operas each afternoon—and the meals her mother painstakingly prepared and begged her daughter to eat—there was little to orient her in time.

Ingrid had spoken to the two detectives—Tomasio and Angle—endlessly since the incident. They had asked her the same questions over and over again. And they had done the same thing with all sorts of people around town—Ingrid's teachers, her friends, their parents. The picture that emerged was of a troubled neighbor boy who had difficulty controlling his impulses. A bright boy but one who was disengaged from—antipathetic toward—others. A boy who might, under the right circumstances, do a terrible thing.

Ingrid's mental picture of a boy who wore a green mask was ignored. Ingrid had tried to draw attention to that boy—the cruel and unkind boy with no name—but no one was looking for him. No one else, it seemed, even remembered seeing him. And, little by little, she looked away from that picture herself. She listened to the suggestions she was hearing. She erased—or blocked out—a mental picture of a hostile and aggressive stranger in a green mask. She came to see the possibility of another picture. That of her best friend's brother as an aggressor. That of Sebastian, a boy she'd known all her life, as her attacker. That of Sebastian—an annoying boy to be sure, a pompous and arrogant boy who was prone to mocking his intellectual inferiors—as an assaulter. That of a brilliant, artistic, gay boy as Ingrid's rapist.

What of it that the boy happened to have been Black and the girl happened to have been white? Did this play into the thinking, the mental predispositions of the Monday morning quarterbacks who were analyzing events that none of them had seen or been a part of? Did it play into the thinking of the girl who had been there but could not remember any of it?

It would be hard to imagine that it did not.

In large part, Ingrid's mind had been turned by the detectives. By their ceaseless questions and implications. Their suggestions, both covert and more obvious. But turn she did. She found herself wondering if Sebastian had done those horrible things to her.

But was it even fair to blame it on the cops? Hadn't she had those thoughts on her own in the hospital? Hadn't she considered the possibility that Sebastian had been next to her when she woke up on the ground because Sebastian had been the one who raped her? Hadn't she mentally explored the possibilities that rape was not a sexual act as much as it was an act of domination?

She had. She knew she had. And she also knew she had no moral high ground to claim. She could not lay blame on the detectives or the other kids at school or anyone. It was her, Ingrid Lind, who had pointed the finger of suspicion at Sebastian Waldron.

Ingrid lay on her yellow bed and stared at the ceiling. She remembered lying on Emilia's purple bed not long ago, doing the same thing. But it was not the same at all. She could not muster the will to get out of bed. It was afternoon. Her mom had brought her lunch on a tray, but she couldn't eat it. She could hear the stories playing from the living room so she knew it was sometime between noon and three. The day stretched out before her. The cops weren't scheduled to come. Even they had grown tired of the same old questions.

Ingrid knew they had questioned Sebastian multiple times. She knew they'd questioned Emilia and both of their parents. At least they hadn't held Sebastian in the police station—the cops had assured her of that. She wondered if he had gone back to school. She wondered the same about Em. She also wondered, without caring much, what the kids at school were saying. She got the feeling that they all thought it was Sebastian. She didn't know what she thought anymore.

All of a sudden, the kitchen door flew open, banging hard against the wall. A thin trickle of icy air crept under Ingrid's door.

"Ingrid!" a voice bellowed.

It sounded like Mrs. Waldron. What was Mrs. Waldron doing in their kitchen?

"Ingrid!" she screamed again.

Ingrid sat up on the bed. The change in position made her dizzy and her bandaged nose throbbed.

"What's going on?" came the voice of Ingrid's mother, also from the kitchen. She must have left her seat in front of the television to see what the commotion was about.

"Your..." Mrs. Waldron began, and then promptly stopped.

Ingrid heard some kind of shuffling. She couldn't tell what it was. She slid herself to the edge of the bed and placed her feet on the cold floor. Her feet were one of the few parts of her that were not in pain. She crept barefooted down the short hall. She came around the corner and found her mother holding Mrs. Waldron on the floor. Ingrid had seen a picture in an art book of a statue in a similar position. The Pietà. Ingrid's mom was holding Em's mom just like Mary had held Jesus. Mrs. Waldron seemed boneless and collapsed, like she was dead. But Ingrid knew she wasn't.

"You," she said, looking straight at Ingrid, a sob catching in her throat. "Why?"

Ingrid felt the word like a knife. She wished it was a knife. A knife would have been more welcome.

"My boy," she choked out. "My beautiful boy. My best boy."

Ingrid turned her head to run, to flee from what she was about to learn. She did not wish to hear what Emilia's mother was about to tell her. Sebastian's mother. For it was in the capacity of *his* mother that she now appeared on the floor of the Lind kitchen, dangling from her own mother's arms.

Suddenly Mrs. Waldron recomposed her body from the rubber it had just been back into bone and muscle. She pressed her hands on the floor and wrenched herself away from Betsy Lind with a force that indicated how vile she found them all. She hoisted herself up from the floor.

"Ingrid," she said, leaning in Ingrid's direction but not actually taking a step toward her. "How could you? I treated you like a daughter! I welcomed you into our home, we all did. We..."

She stopped. She looked around their kitchen which was, Ingrid knew, so different from her own. It was not the warm and welcoming kitchen of the Waldrons just next door. There was no smell of brownies. Of cookies. There was no laughter. No noise at all except the drone of the television from the next room. Ingrid saw her mother shrink under Mrs. Waldron's gaze.

"We treated you as one of our own, Ingrid!" she continued, almost spitting. "How could you do that to my boy?"

Ingrid had no words. She could not tear her eyes away from the spectacle of Mrs. Waldron but she could not answer her, either. She had the feeling of sinking down a dark hole from which she did not know if she could climb out. She did not know what Mrs. Waldron was talking about. The recent weeks were dreadful, yes, but this was something else. Something new. Something worse.

"What happened?" Ingrid asked in a small voice. "What's happened to Sebastian?"

36

VIVECA 2018

The sky was darkening around the edges when Viveca stepped outside. Children and their parents were everywhere—sitting at tables, running in and out of the corn maze, queuing up for the fortune teller, the magician, and the collection of boxes for plunging hands into fake body parts. From across the Mianus River—in the direction of the Second Congregational Church, *the highest point in Greenwich*, she wryly thought—the orange ball of sun was hanging just above the tree line.

As the last rays of sun hit the maze, she thought of Stonehenge. *Wasn't there something about the way the stones lined up that was supposed to catch the sun at just the right angle on just the right day to…* she didn't know what, exactly, it was supposed to do. *Unlock a key to another world? A realm where long-buried secrets were exposed and understood?* She was becoming maudlin, she knew. She couldn't shake the unsettled state she'd been in since seeing Larry Keenan tricked out in that mask.

"Viveca," Henry said softly behind her. She could feel his breath on the back of her neck.

"Yes?" She turned to him. The setting sun caught him fully in the face. The very paleness of his blue eyes and silver-streaked hair had become like a blank canvas absorbing an orange pigment. He looked otherworldly. Devilish.

"The caterers are asking what time you want them to open the buffet." When Henry spoke, his face softened. "Hey, earth to Viveca?"

Viveca broke out in a brittle laugh and Henry raised an eyebrow.

"Are you having a migraine?"

"No, Henry," she answered sharply. "Not everything is about migraines."

"Well you're acting really weird. First you almost faint when Larry Keenan walks in the door, when you know him and his family perfectly well. Now you're laughing like a crazy woman. I'm expecting your head to spin around next."

Viveca caught a glimpse of Larry Keenan out of the corner of her eye. Henry was right—she was being ridiculous.

"Would you ask them to open up the buffet as soon as they can? The kids'll be hungry," she said as she turned to walk over to Larry.

"Hey," she said. "Sorry about earlier. You just reminded me of someone I haven't seen for a long time."

"No problem," he said, winking. "I have that effect on women."

"Hey, Viveca…" Devon was at her left elbow. She looked extraordinary in her *Lion King* costume. With the sunset glow, she was incandescent. The same sun that made Henry look like the devil made Devon look like a goddess. "I think we have a little problem with a couple of the boys. They've been feeding candy to your dog."

"Excuse me," Viveca said to Larry. "I need to go deal with this."

"You okay?" asked Devon as they walked over to the scene of the candy crime. "You look really pale."

"Do I? Yeah. No. It's just been a crazy few weeks."

"It was nice to finally meet your agent," said Devon. "She was such a legend when I was in the business. I never met her back then though. She was too senior and I was way too junior."

"Yeah," said Viveca. "Probably better that you didn't. She kind of mopped the floor with juniors."

"So I've heard."

"Are my ears burning?" Rachel piped in next to them. She was dressed as Auntie Mame at a cocktail party in New York, in a black dress and a long rope of pearls. "I did not mop the floor with anyone who didn't act like a wet rag. I like spine in a person."

"Have another drink, Rachel." Viveca laughed. "You're scaring my friends."

"Well, it's a Halloween party," she replied. "As good a time as any to get scared."

Viveca found Daphne over by the pool—an area that was fenced off and was supposed to be strictly off limits to the boys tonight—licking at a big blob of chocolate.

"Oh, geez. Whatever she ate, I think she threw up and is eating again." Viveca scooped her up and carried her back toward the house.

"I'm going to just tuck her into my office and close the door," she called back to Devon and Rachel. "No one will go up there and bother her."

"What if she shits all over the place?" asked Rachel. "I mean, look what she's ingested tonight."

"I'll put paper down and leave a bowl of water and her dog bed. I need to keep her away from these kids...they're getting a little wild. Hold down the fort!"

Halfway up the steps, Viveca realized she had to go back to the kitchen to grab the water bowl and newspapers. As she descended again, she noticed the streamers she'd so carefully woven over the gaping hole of the stair rails were coming loose.

"Hey," she said to Aya in the kitchen.

Aya was bent over an array of colorful serving bowls, arranging her Moroccan specialties.

"How's it going? I'm just getting a water bowl for Daph. The kids were feeding her candy."

"Boys," Aya said dismissively.

"I'm sure girls do similar things."

"A boy is different," Aya said, carrying platters from the counter to the table. "I've raised two."

Viveca realized that Aya was referring to her own son and to Viveca's. She'd never been jealous of Theo's bond with Aya. In fact, she was glad he had someone like her in his life. Her own mother was long gone and Henry's mom didn't remember who Theo was. Aya was the closest thing to a grandmother that he had.

"And I've loved raising Theo with you," Viveca said as she gave Aya a big hug. "He loves you very much. So do I."

"What is this?" Aya pushed her away, laughing. "Too much American emotion!"

"Seriously, Aya. I have to be able to tell you sometimes how much I appreciate all you've done for our family."

"Aaahhhh." Aya blushed crimson. "Stop it right now."

"Okay, okay!" Viveca said as she fetched a bowl from the pantry. She grabbed Daphne's bed from under the table and some newspapers from the basket. "I'll be back in a flash."

Viveca started to leave the kitchen, then turned back to take a big taste of Aya's lemon-olive spinach.

"Aya, your cooking is a gift!" she said and left the room.

In her office, she closed the door. She dropped the bed to the floor and set Daphne in it. She covered a little area with newspapers and realized she needed to go back downstairs to actually fill the water bowl.

Down she went again, just to her own bathroom sink, and back up. She let herself into the office and took a moment to sit while Daphne got settled in her bed.

"You okay, Daph?" Viveca gave her a pat. "How much chocolate did you eat?"

Daphne did some vigorous scratching of the bed then plopped herself down. She seemed fine but Viveca would check on her periodically.

Viveca waited for a while and idly checked her phone. She hadn't charged it last night—very unusual for her—so she opted to plug it in for a few minutes while she was up here. Once Daphne closed her eyes and was snoring, Viveca got up to leave the room. The food should have all been put out on the buffet table by now and she had to get back to the party.

As she stood, something caught her eye in the dollhouse. Something that was not normally there. It wasn't like she even saw it at first. It was more like she sensed it, felt it calling to her from across the room.

From across time.

Viveca took three short steps to her beloved dollhouse and came face to face with a shadow box sitting on the open balcony of the second floor. Was it one of hers? One of the boxes she had packed up into her parents' attic so many years before? How would it have gotten here? Her mother died and the house was sold. Surely her father, or the real estate agent, would have cleaned out the attic? Would have thrown away those vestiges of the girl who was gone?

Viveca picked it up. It almost looked like her King Tut box. The one whose doll went missing. She turned it over in her hands and held it up to the light. It was close. Very close. But it was not one of hers. The wallpaper was wrong. The doll. The objects. Nothing was the same as the one she had made when she was a girl. This shadow box was a copy.

But who would have made it?

Theo? He'd had an interest in that part of his mother's life. But when would he have done this? Viveca had seen no inkling of him working on anything like this. Was it Henry? Was he gaslighting her in order to end the marriage? To get rid of her? He'd always had a horrible relationship with his ex-wife. Maybe he'd done this sort of thing before. But their relationship wasn't like that…at least, she didn't think it was. But she couldn't be sure of anything anymore. Was it Mark Remington? But how had he gotten into her house?

Questions spun at a dizzying pace until Viveca saw the migraine coming. Her field of vision shaded over and she waited for the prisms of light. She moved to the sofa and pulled a throw blanket around herself. The light show started and she waited to see if it would be followed by the headache. She reached out for Daphne and kept her hand on top of her. The touch of another living being was comforting. Viveca closed her eyes. She would wait it out up here, alone in her little office. Her safe space that had now been violated just like the rest of the house.

"Mom?"

Viveca opened her eyes.

Theo stood in the doorway. She must have fallen asleep because the colored lights were gone and she did not have a headache. "I've been looking for you everywhere. We already ate. Aya said you were up here. Will you go through the maze with me?"

Viveca looked at her boy. Her beautiful boy. She held her hand out to him. "Sure, sweetie. Let's do it."

Together they left the room. As Viveca closed the door behind them, she took one last look at the shadow box sitting on top of her dollhouse.

She forgot to grab her phone.

37

INGRID 1998

"Mom!" Emilia banged open the door just like her mother had done before her. Ingrid wondered if the glass in the door would break from repeated impact. Em looked wildly around the room, although the location of her mother was quite visible. She was standing a few feet away from Ingrid in some sort of fighter's stance.

"Em," Ingrid rasped. "I…"

"Don't." Em cut her off with that one-word command. "Don't even speak to me. How could you, Ingrid? How?"

It was exactly what her mother had said, and when Mrs. Waldron heard it, her knees buckled like a push puppet doll. Em moved quickly to catch her mother before she hit the ground. The two Linds stood still as Emilia wrangled her mother onto a chair.

"Em," Ingrid said again, this time without interruption. "What's going on?"

"You don't know?" Emilia looked up at her, and it was only then that Ingrid noticed her tear-streaked face. "You really don't know?"

Ingrid moved toward the kitchen table with the intention of sitting next to her friend. She needed to find out what new thing had happened that had so deeply disturbed them both. It was then that Ingrid's mother sprang into action and stepped in front of her daughter. *To keep her from getting nearer to Em and her mom*, Ingrid wondered, *or to keep her from hearing what they were about to say?*

"Mom," Ingrid said, attempting to sidestep her. "Move. Please."

What the hell was going on with everyone? Ingrid could not perceive what her mother had already gleaned. Ingrid, despite all that had happened to her in the past weeks, was still only a girl. Her mother was not. Her mother had seen something of the world, even if she'd never let on to her daughter. Her mother stood blocking her now, trying to protect her from what was to come even if—especially since—she hadn't protected her that terrible night.

"Ingrid, no," she said.

"Why not?" Mrs. Waldron spat out the words. She hadn't said anything for a while and her voice startled Ingrid. "You think you can protect her after what she's done? She'll have to live with this the rest of her life. She won't be able to hide from it. She won't be able to hide it from anyone. *They whose guilt within their bosom lies, imagine every eye beholds their blame.*"

It was like a curse. Mrs. Waldron was damning Ingrid with some sort of Shakespearean incantation. "But why?" Ingrid asked.

All eyes turned to her. They all knew what she did not. Even her mom knew, though she'd only intuited it.

It was Emilia who spoke. She delivered the news that Ingrid would run from the rest of her life.

"My brother is dead," Em said so quietly that Ingrid almost did not hear her. Almost. But Ingrid did hear. The entire room seemed to ring like the inside of a tuning fork with the notes contained in those four short words. *"My brother is dead."*

"He hanged himself," Em went on, "with a belt from the top of his closet door. And it's your fault."

Then Em bundled her mother up like she was a sack of potatoes and pulled her out of the chair. She held onto her as she walked to the door, opened it, and slammed it closed behind them. The glass gave one more shudder—but still, it did not break.

Months would pass before the forensics team from the police station would let Detectives Tomasio and Angle know that the blood and semen specimens found at the scene of the crime bore no resemblance to those of Sebastian Waldron. They belonged to an unknown assailant. The boy, or man, who had assaulted Ingrid Lind late that Halloween night had been a stranger.

Sebastian had been exonerated.

But Sebastian was already dead.

38

VIVECA 2018

Viveca and Theo entered the corn maze holding hands, the mom in the witch hat and the scary skeleton boy. Costumed children and their parents moved in and out around them.

"I found the scarecrow end!" screamed a boy dressed as a mummy. "It's really cool."

And off he ran toward the terrace.

"Hey," said another, dressed like Black Panther. It was Devon's son, Marcello, which made it okay for him to play a Black character because he was, in fact, Black. "Let's go get our fortunes read. I heard the guy gives out prizes at the end."

Three other boys in a rainbow of costumes—a red Spider-Man, a blue Batman, and some yellow thing that Viveca didn't recognize, came from around the side of the maze.

"Wolverine!" Batman called to the yellow one. "Let's get more candy."

They bolted up to the terrace as well. Viveca could see that the kids were on an adrenaline high—from sugar, from friends, from spooky Halloween things that go bump in the night—and that this party should come to an end soon before someone got hurt.

"Theo," Henry called from behind them.

Viveca and Henry turned in unison.

"You told me to get you when the fortune teller could see you. He's just come off break and—since you're the birthday boy—he'd like to read you next."

"Cool!" Theo said. "Oh. But I asked Mom to go through the maze with me. Maybe..."

"Theo, go," Viveca said. "We can go through the maze later. I'll come with you."

"I've got him," Henry said. "Why don't you try the maze on your own? See if you can figure it out. I tried it earlier and had a hell of a time."

"That's okay," she said. "I don't need to..."

"Babe, just let me take him," Henry said, laughing. "You're so joined at the hip, I'm gonna have to hold you back from going to college with him."

Viveca was stunned—and not for the first time this week—by her husband. But she didn't want to make a big deal of it in front of Theo.

"Okay," she said instead. "Sure. I'd like to see if I can conquer the corn maze!"

She laughed really hard at her own remark in an attempt to convey to Theo what a fun night this was.

"Seriously, Viv," Henry said. "You aren't yourself these days. I think you need to see a doctor or something."

Viveca spun around without another word and plunged headlong into the corn maze. She needed a moment to collect herself and then she would find her way through to the other side. She'd practically designed it, after all. How hard could it be?

There were a few stragglers still in the maze with her. Mostly adults at this point, since all the kids had gone through it multiple times and were bored of it. A very sexy Elvira came walking the wrong way toward Viveca.

"Fuck this," the costumed woman said. "I can't find the end, and I passed all my spatial tests at the top of my quadrant back in the day."

"Greta?" said Viveca. "You look amazing. Like a dominatrix but suburban. When did you put that on? I didn't see it earlier."

"Yeah?" Greta said, adjusting her push-up bra. "Oh, I slipped into it later. Tony keeps asking if we can go home and try it out."

Viveca laughed. "Do you want to leave Ethan here to spend the night? Have the whole house to yourselves so you can swing from the chandeliers?"

"Nah," Greta said. "That kid wouldn't hear a bomb go off once he's sleeping. And my older ones are at sleepovers."

Greta gave her a kiss on the cheek, tilting her head to avoid Viveca's witch hat.

"See you out there for the cake," she said.

"I'll be right out," Viveca said. "Meantime, let's get the boys together next week?"

"Plan on it!" Greta said as she made her way out of the maze.

Viveca turned and assessed her options. She chose to go left and walked down a tunnel, sure she remembered the way. She was surprised when she reached a dead end. She turned around to laugh with whoever was behind her, but there was no one. That was weird. She had sensed someone else not far behind.

It was very quiet inside the maze. The raucous sounds of the party were muffled. Viveca idly wondered if anyone had ever considered corn stalks as stuffing for sound barriers. She turned down another avenue, glad she would soon find the end. But she hit a wall again. This time, it rattled her a little.

Maybe Henry was right. Maybe she needed to see a doctor. Maybe the whole sordid saga of what had happened all those years ago to Sebastian had finally caught up with her. Ingrid had not meant to hurt Sebastian. He was like a brother to her. He had been part of her life for as long as she could remember. Yes, he was weird. Yes, he was annoying. Yes, he was arrogant and pompous and superior to most everyone else. But he was Sebastian and she knew and trusted him. She didn't really think that Sebastian had raped her. But—in those early weeks after the incident—she was utterly confused about everything.

The questioning cops hadn't helped. The way they had probed about Sebastian, coming at it—at *him*—from multiple angles every day. The way they had advised her to stay away from him, from Em, from all of them. Maybe if they had seen each other in those early days, her suspicions would have dissipated. Ingrid had felt so alone and muddled. Her difficulty remembering much of the evening just added fuel to the fire.

Then there was her mother's clinging and her father's abandonment. Her family had never been a model one. But nothing in their past compared to what they became after that night. They no longer felt like anything even resembling a family. Just a bunch of broken birds who shared the same nest.

Then there had been her nose. Her throat. The bruises that circled her neck like a choker and dotted her body like a string of tattoos. But that was just physical damage. The psychic toll was so profound that Ingrid—Viveca—had simply turned away. She had sealed it all off. Or had tried to.

Sure, she drank. But she had overcome that. With Sidney's help, and then Henry's, she had approached her sobriety with discipline and commitment. She had slipped once. But only once. Even when she had run into Emilia ten years before, she had stayed on the wagon. True, Theo had been a baby at the time. It was hard for her to imagine drinking the way she had once done while nursing an infant. But people did. She saw it all the time in AA. She had to give herself some kind of credit for that.

Viveca turned and hit another wall. She was so preoccupied that she wasn't concentrating. She needed to stop thinking about all these ghosts from the past and concentrate on getting the hell out of this maze. She stood very still and forced herself to look around. She took a few deep breaths. She thought about her son and the fact that they would soon be singing "Happy Birthday" and cutting the chocolate cake. To the left, she felt certain now, was the exit. She would be out before she knew it.

She took a strong, confident stride around a corner and walked straight into Larry Keenan. She burst into a nervous laugh.

"Hey, Larry," she said. "You scared me. I've gotten so turned around I don't know what end is up. Maybe we can help each other..." Then she stopped and stared at the man behind the mask.

This man was taller than Larry Keenan. Stockier too. And his eyes.

They were not the eyes of Larry Keenan. But they *were* eyes she had seen before. They were the dark eyes of the man she'd seen in the park. At Greenwich Point. Mark Remington!

What was happening here?

Viveca had no idea, but she was alone with this guy in the maze and she had to get out. She tried to scream but—no surprise—her voice betrayed her. A pathetic screech came out of her mangled throat and made her cough. Before he could grab her, she turned and ran through the twists and turns of the corn maze. Through the silence she ran, trying not to make a sound herself. She turned around quietly, hoping to find a new path, when she hit one dead end after another. Apart from the distant murmur of the party, the only sound she heard above her own breathing and the beating of her heart was when the man called out from time to time.

"Ingrid?" he said. "Viveca? I just want to talk to you!"

39

INGRID 1998

Sebastian was dead.

And Ingrid had killed him.

Her weak-minded waffling had killed him. Her inability to remember anything due to her self-indulgent drinking binge had killed him. Her failure to hold steady to what she knew to be true had killed him.

What was certainly true: Sebastian was gay and had not raped Ingrid. What was also true: Sebastian had been her friend over the course of her entire sixteen years of life. What was equally true: Sebastian had not only *not* harmed her, but actually saved her life by finding her half naked on the ground and covering her against the cold. What was most dreadfully true: Ingrid had failed Sebastian at every turn and had caused his death. Ingrid had failed the entire Waldron family after all their kindness and love. And Ingrid had lost the best friend a girl could have in Emilia Waldron.

However bad things were immediately after the night of October 31, they became infinitely worse at the news of Sebastian's death. Once Em was able to scrape her mother off the kitchen chair, once the two of them left without a backward glance, darkness fell on the Lind household.

Ingrid did not leave her room other than to go to the bathroom when absolutely necessary. She did not eat for days at a time until she could no longer deny her ravenousness. Then she would rise in the middle of the night to scarf down whatever she could find—ice cream, potato chips, once it was raw hamburger—while standing at the kitchen sink.

Eating like that would fill her with shame. Shame at the very idea that she could not stop herself from utilizing food to prolong her worthless—her undeserved—life.

Her father no longer came home. Where he was, Ingrid was never told. She hadn't asked, either. She had seen him twice since Halloween and he was hardly able to look at her. While they had never been close, even the teenage Ingrid could perceive that his behavior toward his assaulted daughter was primitive and repugnant. He was acting as though his daughter was damaged goods who held no interest for him anymore. Whatever crack in the wall of Ingrid's heart that had remained open and available to her father now firmly sealed shut.

Her mother hardly left the house. Other than shopping for food, she could not tear herself away from her shattered daughter. She certainly didn't go to work anymore. In one of Ingrid's late-night forays into the kitchen, she noticed a crumpled letter at the top of the garbage pail. She pulled it out and smoothed it open to read. It was a warning from her mom's company saying she had better return to the job or she would not have a job to return to.

It snowed the day of Sebastian's funeral. No one had invited the Linds. Her mom had heard some women talking at the grocery store and came home to tell Ingrid the date. They hadn't intended to spy. They sat on the living room sofa like they did when they watched soap operas. From their usual seats, their view was a split screen of what was playing on the television side by side with what was playing on the snowy street in front of them.

People started to arrive in cars around two. The funeral had taken place at New Bethel Baptist Church in Detroit. Ingrid knew the Waldrons attended the large Christmas and Easter services there. Mr. Waldron was the one who attended Sunday services more regularly over the years. Mrs.

Waldron more often spent her Sunday mornings reading from the *other* good book, as she called it: *The Complete Works of William Shakespeare.*

Sebastian was an acknowledged agnostic. He'd told his family in Ingrid's presence that he would, for the moment, take the position of Descartes. While most people knew that Descartes said *I think, therefore I am*, Sebastian preferred his lesser-known aphorism, *We cannot doubt of our existence while we doubt.*

Ingrid wondered if Sebastian still existed. *And, if so, was he doubting that existence—wherever he was—after having it robbed from him by the girl next door? Or was there some plane on which he existed where everything was suddenly rendered all right? Were our sins—whether of commission or omission—wiped out?* That would not be the point of view taken by Ingrid's Lutheran parents. She wondered what the pastors of New Bethel would say about it. She had gone to church on a handful of occasions with the Waldrons. In contrast to the somberness of her own house of worship, she had loved the singing there. *A joyful noise*, Mr. Waldron had said, quoting Psalm 100. *God wants us to make a joyful noise.* Ingrid knew without a doubt that their noise would not be joyful today or any day to come.

She had done that to them.

The fluffy flakes of snow were turning to sleet by then, in keeping with the mood of the world closing in on them. As soon as the guests slammed their car doors, they ran toward the Waldrons' house, umbrellas or coats held over their heads. Ingrid recognized her classmates and their parents. Families she had known all her life. They were dressed more formally than she had seen them, even at school holiday concerts. Or it was a different kind of formal. At the concerts, the girls wore green or red velvet dresses. The boys wore pleated trousers and brightly colored sweaters. Now their clothes were dark and drab. She wondered where they got them. *Did parents keep mourning clothes on hand for their children? Did they switch them up to larger sizes as the children grew?* Ingrid had not seen such items in her own closet, but maybe parents kept those things hidden away so as not to cause alarm.

Kelly Roush and her family exited a red Volvo wagon. Kelly walked slowly, head held high, next to her dad. He gripped her by the elbow and held a striped umbrella over their heads. Ingrid was surprised to see Kelly looking proud and unbowed. By now it was common knowledge that she had thrown the party that had unleashed the string of events that led to today. Though Kelly's shame could never equal Ingrid's, Ingrid was surprised that their family showed up. Kelly's mom walked in front, fast, in an apparent effort to put some distance between herself and her daughter. She clamped her mouth in a thin, straight line.

The final car to arrive was the Ford Taurus wagon carrying the Waldron family. Mr. Waldron was in the driver's seat. Ingrid watched the car travel slowly, then stop in the middle of the road. She leaned forward as far as she could to see what was happening. *Were the Waldrons having an argument, and Em's dad had to stop the car to contain it?* Ingrid stood up and moved closer to the window, heedless of who might see her.

But they were not engaged in an argument. They were not doing anything at all as far as she could see. Each remaining member of that family—Julius, Nan, and Em—sat silently in his or her seat, staring at their house. It was obvious to Ingrid—for she was thinking the same thing—that they were thinking about the family member who was no longer with them. Who would not be in their house when they entered. Whose body they had just laid in the cold, hard ground. The same cold, hard ground that he had willingly occupied just weeks before when he made the valiant and gallant gesture that ended up getting him killed.

Then Ingrid knew what she had never known before, or had never had the courage or sensitivity to look at fully in the face. Sebastian was dead in large measure because he was Black. Because he was Black, the cops had doubts about his character that they might not have had if he had been white. Because he was Black, the argumentativeness that came from his need for intellectual banter was seen as something more ominous by the rest of the school. Because he was Black, had Ingrid opened her mind to questions she never would have asked? She feared she had.

As Ingrid watched the Waldrons in their ratty old Ford in the middle of the street, Mr. Waldron slowly lowered his head to the steering wheel.

It was a gesture of defeat that was almost impossible to witness. Ingrid did not want to have this image of him in her mind. Her mind was already a minefield littered with bombs—both those that had been detonated and those that were waiting to be tripped. But before Ingrid could look away, Emilia turned to face her.

Their eyes met.

If Ingrid had had any doubts before, it was now abundantly clear. Emilia would never forgive her. Mr. and Mrs. Waldron would not either. They had borne wounds that Ingrid would never be able to understand and they had borne them with grace and elegance and a liberal dose of Shakespeare. But what Ingrid had done was unbearable. And it was she who could not be borne.

Not by them.

Not by herself.

40

VIVECA 2018

The lights in the maze clicked on. The farm hands had run long extension cords from the house out to poles planted among the cornstalks. They had hooked the whole thing to a timer set to go on when the sun set. And now—all of a sudden—lurid bulbs shone down on Viveca, exposing her completely.

Now that the blanket of darkness was gone, she needed to think more strategically. She forced herself to slow down—to cease her mindless ricocheting from one tunnel to the next. There had to be a simpler way. She scanned the endless walls of cornstalks rising around her. It all looked the same. And it was ridiculous. Here she was, a thirty-six-year-old woman, unable to get herself out of a maze that a bunch of ten-year-olds had navigated in a blink.

Of course, they weren't operating under life-and-death adrenaline. They weren't being pursued by a man who knew terrifying things about them. A man who might do them grave harm. They weren't at risk of losing everything right here in their own backyard.

But she was.

Viveca looked up and down the corridor in which she now stood that looked exactly like all the other corridors. She listened for footsteps and heard none. Mark Remington must have stopped in place too. He could be standing right behind her even now, silently waiting to pounce. She spun around to find no one.

She searched her pockets for her phone. The easiest thing would be to call Henry. He could march right in here and save her. And then she remembered two things. One was that she had left her phone charging in her third-floor office. The other was that Henry might be tied up in all this. Viveca considered the tone of Henry's voice last night, which had reminded her of his voice that night—so many years ago—when he'd called his ex-wife that vile name. Was this his thing? Turning against his wife after something had happened between them? But what had happened between Viveca and Henry? Other than the normal ups and downs of marriage, she had no idea.

Viveca worked to slow her breathing. To shake off these wildly paranoid thoughts. She needed to get out of this maze first and foremost, then everything else could be sorted from there. There must be some way of proceeding more strategically so that she might recognize a trail she had already followed.

It was then that she remembered her sweater, orange knit with fringe at the hips. If she could tear off pieces of the fringe, she could tie them to the cornstalks! Like Hansel and Gretel but with something more effective than breadcrumbs. She would be able to see the orange strings and find her way out. It was possible that Mark Remington would see the tied fringe too but, really, why would he? He wouldn't be looking for it and she could tie them low and out of his eyeline.

Viveca took hold of one of the strings and began to pull. It stretched and stretched but it did not tear. This was going to be harder than she thought. Yanking up her sweater, she bit the string off. She might crack a tooth tonight but she *would* get out of this maze. She would get back to her son. She would call the cops and get this Mark Remington out of her life like she should have done weeks ago.

"Ingrid." The voice was right behind her as she stood there like a dog with her sweater in her mouth. She had not heard him at all.

Before she could run, he grabbed her. Hard. One hand on each of her arms and she was pinioned. She realized the futility of screaming with her pathetic voice.

"Can you just cool it?" he asked, spinning her around to face him. "Slow the fuck down and listen to me. Don't you think if I intended to hurt you I would have done it already? I've had every opportunity."

It made no sense.

"Who do you think hired me?"

"Hired?"

"Do you think I'm just some kind of random stalker?"

Was that a trick question?

"You're in danger, my friend. And it's not from me."

"Viveca!" Henry's voice rang out, making her head spin.

She turned to face him as Mark Remington let go of her arms.

"Where've you been? Everyone's looking for you so we can do the cake. Hey Larry," Henry added, finally noticing the man standing very close to his wife. "What's going on here?"

"Don't you think *you* should be the one to answer that question?" Mark asked Henry.

Henry stood very still, looking at the man he'd just mistaken for his friend. Viveca could not tell, for the life of her, if he recognized him. If Henry realized there were *two* men running around this maze in the same costume. And—worst of all—she wondered if Mark was telling the truth and Henry had hired him to do her harm or set her up or she had no idea what.

Henry narrowed his gaze on the man. "I'm sorry. Do we know each other?"

At that exact moment, Viveca made a dash for it. Away from her husband. Away from this masked man. And toward, she prayed, her house and help.

Miraculously, and without the aid of strings, she bolted out of the maze with just a few false turns. She ran up the dark lawn toward the illuminated terrace where the Halloween party was in full swing. Wildly, she searched for Rachel.

As Viveca dashed up the stairs to the terrace, she ran straight into Aya.

"Viveca!" Aya's tone was sharp. "Where on earth have you been? Theo's been in tears."

"Oh, I…" Viveca was deeply chagrined. "I got lost in the maze."

Aya just stared at her. "We've lit and replaced the candles on his cake twice. Can we do this? Families are about to leave."

"Yes!" she said. "Of course."

Viveca looked around for Theo. He was sitting alone at one of the tables.

"Where's Henry? He was just here," said Aya.

"He…" Viveca began.

"I'm right here, darling," he said as he put both his hands on Viveca's waist.

She shuddered and moved quickly over to Theo.

"Hi there," she said, kneeling down to talk to her son. "I'm so sorry I got lost for a bit in that silly maze!"

"Mom," Theo said, "you're acting really weird. First you disappeared to your office and I had to find you there. Then you disappeared in the maze. It's my birthday, you know?"

"I know, sweetheart! I know. I'm so sorry. It's just…" What could she say? "I just had a migraine and it threw me off. I'm sorry and I'm here now."

"Kids are going home."

"Not before we do the cake!" she said way too brightly and clapped her hands. "Cake, everyone!"

Aya appeared instantly holding the cake with ten lit candles. Henry pulled out his iPhone to memorialize the moment. Viveca stood next to Theo, having no actual function to perform. She looked at her son's wide smile and bright eyes. She watched as he took a huge gulp of air, held it for a moment, and blew with all his might, taking each and every candle in one go. *What did he wish for?* she wondered.

Everyone applauded and Theo beamed.

"Happy birthday, Theo," Viveca said into his ear. "You're still and always my best boy."

She looked up at the exact moment she said it and caught the eye of Mark Remington, standing in the shadows at the edge of the crowd.

41

INGRID 2000

Betsy Lind drove her daughter to the bus station in downtown Detroit, a dismal setting, seemingly abandoned by civilization. As though some type of event—nuclear annihilation, the Rapture—had blown its cold breath upon the place and left it desolate.

Because Ingrid's mom did not like to drive on the highway, she had taken Woodward Avenue—one of the spokes of the wheel radiating from the center that her fourth-grade teacher, Miss Haney, had loved so much—all the way from Royal Oak to get there. It was a long and bumpy ride on streets in need of repair. Ingrid wondered if Miss Haney was still teaching at her old elementary school. Then she wondered if Miss Haney had heard what had happened to her. And to Sebastian.

"Oh look!" Her mom pointed at the Detroit Historical Museum with a tone of forced gaiety. "Didn't you used to love that place? The basement part?"

Ingrid was surprised her mother remembered. More than that, she didn't know her mom had known in the first place how much she was influenced by *The Streets of Old Detroit*.

"Yeah," she answered, struggling to remember why she had ever cared. "I did."

"Maybe you could, I don't know...work there? Not move away?"

Ingrid looked at her mother—really looked at her—and saw that she had become old. She did a mental calculation of her age.

"Mom, are you forty?"

"Don't rush me baby!" her mom said, again overly brightly. "Not until next month."

Ingrid didn't know why it would matter to her mother whether she were thirty-nine or forty. They both sounded old to her. Even so, she knew instinctively that her mother looked much more ragged than a normal forty-year-old woman should. Her mom had been twenty-two when she'd had her daughter. Her father was two years older.

"Have you talked to Dad?"

"Well..." Her mother's voice flattened. "Him and I don't get along so much anymore."

"Because of me."

"No baby." Her mother reached over to pat her hand. "It goes way back. I can't take the..." She allowed her sentence to drift off.

"Drinking," Ingrid finally said, providing the word her mother had tried to avoid.

"Yes," she said.

"Yes," Ingrid echoed.

She stared out the window at the wintry city. Plastic bags littered the streets, frozen in weird shapes. Cans and bottles lined the gutters next to less identifiable refuse. Buildings sported broken windows. Some were barred. Some were left open to whoever might wish to enter by an unconventional route.

"Look at the map, would you?" asked her mom. "Where do I turn?"

Ingrid tore her gaze away from her ravaged hometown—an apt reflection of herself—and looked at the map on her lap.

"Here," she said. "Go right on Howard Street."

Her mother turned and they found the station. A man lay collapsed on a bench right next to the door, a paper bag–clad bottle clutched in his right hand, the seat of his pants pulled down to reveal his naked buttocks. It made Ingrid think of herself on Halloween night.

"Honey, you don't need to do this," her mom whispered. She started to cry as she pulled the car to the curb.

"Mom..."

"I mean, look at you! You don't even look like your old self. Except your eyes," she said, crying harder. "Your beautiful green eyes."

"Mom, there's nothing here for me." Ingrid reached out for her mother's hand. "Except for you, of course."

"You *could* work at that museum," her mother tried again, speaking rapidly. "No one would know it was you. You could change your name. We could move somewhere. Birmingham!"

"Mom, I can't. I don't want to." Ingrid was trying to be gentle but firm. "And we can't afford Birmingham."

"No. No," she said, as though the reality of their financial predicament had just now occurred to her. "Without my job, we can't."

A car pulled up next to them. It was a lowrider, dulled by rust, and blasting rap. A man emerged—at least a dozen gold chains peeking out from the open collar of his coat—grabbed a bag from the back seat, and kissed the woman driving. Ingrid considered the irony that while he may have looked like a criminal, he seemed to have a normal life where he kissed his wife goodbye before heading off on a trip. She, on the other hand, looked like a nice suburban girl. But she was, in fact, a murderer.

Ingrid opened the car door. Like the man, she reached into the back seat for her bag.

"Mom, wanna get out?" She leaned her head in. "Let me hug you goodbye?"

Her mother hesitated, as though she could forestall the moment. As if, by staying in the car, she could undo all of it.

"Please?"

Her mother shifted the car into park and turned off the ignition. She pulled the key out and put it into her purse, clicking it closed and looping the strap over her right arm. She got out of the car, then reversed her actions with the bag so she could retrieve the key and lock the car. Having stalled as long as she could, she walked slowly to the curb and stood facing her daughter.

"Ingrid, I…" she began and stopped, her eyes filling with tears.

Ingrid took her mother in her arms, feeling the slightness of the woman who had loomed so large in her own life, who had given birth to her, raised her, and taken care of her after that awful night. Her body felt like nothing to Ingrid—light as a feather, as though she might blow away in the cold wind off the Detroit River. Her mother had not only become old at forty, she had become a bag of bones.

Her mother slowly raised her arms to hug her back.

"Oh, Mommy," Ingrid whispered as the tears flowed freely down her face. Her reconstructed and newly beautiful face that looked nothing like the face her mother had given her. "I love you so much. I really do."

They clung to each other sobbing.

A voice crackled unintelligibly over a loudspeaker.

Her mother said not one word. She gave her daughter a last squeeze then let her go. She silently walked around her car, tapping it as she went, as if for balance. She unlocked the door with the key, started the engine, and pulled away without—as far as Ingrid could tell—a backward glance.

Ingrid felt a stab of aloneness. She understood why her mother had to leave first. To not be the one left behind. She also understood that she might not see her mother again.

The loudspeaker came on for the second time and Ingrid discerned the words "Los Angeles." She picked up her bag, turned, and opened the door of the bus station.

42

VIVECA 2018

The last of the guests—Max, Devon, and Greta—departed shortly after ten. Their husbands had left hours earlier with their boys. The ladies had stayed behind to help Viveca and Aya clean up. And to drain the dregs of three half-full rosé bottles.

"It won't keep," Max had said, laughing. "So, in the spirit of efficiency…"

Viveca kissed each of their cheeks and said good night at the door. She wondered if Greta's husband, Tony, would still be waiting up for her in her sexy outfit.

"Thank you guys," she called as they walked down the gravel drive to find the cars they'd parked on the street. "Love you!"

She watched them walk off through the open gates that still weren't fixed. She watched until she could no longer see them. Then she stood in the open door a bit longer, listening to their voices as they chattered in the night, blocked from her vision by the towering rhododendron bushes she still hadn't pruned. She continued to wait and listen for the slam of their car doors, their final calls of *Good night! See you Monday! I'll call you!* to each other.

After the hum of their car engines drifted off into the distance, Viveca lingered in the doorway a bit longer. The only sounds came from the rustle of the wind in the leaves that were past the peak of their color. And maybe a few remaining autumn crickets who would soon find their world frozen. She scanned the front yard, the driveway in either direction, as far as she could see all around her. There was nothing and no one. Mark Remington had disappeared shortly after the cake. Blending into the departing groups or slipping off into the bushes.

At least she wouldn't be alone. Rachel had retired to the guest room after helping the ladies polish off the rosé. Aya was staying the night. She'd gone to her room after turning off lights and closing doors and windows. Viveca had tucked a very wired Theo into bed half an hour ago, allowing him to keep his reading light on for a while. Henry was somewhere in the house. She didn't know where. Viveca locked the front door and opened the panel to set the alarm.

It would not work.

A fault showed in the system, a window or a door left open. She tried to remember which button to push to scroll the panel and find the entry point that wasn't closed. After a few attempts—which made her fear she might trip the alarm and invite the police—she found what she was looking for. The living room doors, which led to a little conservatory where she grew her plants, had been left ajar. Viveca set off through the dimly lit hallway.

The glass doors, which led from the living room to the conservatory, were wide open. She thought she'd asked Aya to make a sweep of the house after the party, but she must have missed these. Viveca grabbed hold of both doors and was just latching them when she heard a chair slide.

"Who's there?" she asked, freezing in place.

Moonlight entered the conservatory, casting it in a dark blue glow. If she were not so nervous she would find it beautiful.

"It's just me," came Henry's voice from inside.

Viveca felt a quick burst of relief, followed by a second one of fear. She hesitated, then walked into the conservatory to talk to her husband. She found him sitting in a little metal chair next to a tea table. She sat across from him. There was no sense avoiding this any longer. This man was her husband and she needed to be able to speak frankly with him. And to listen to whatever it was he had to say.

"Henry," she said. "Something is happening here and I don't know what it is. Do you?"

Henry sat quietly for a very long time. In the dim light, Viveca could not see his eyes and wondered if he'd fallen asleep. When he finally spoke he startled her.

"I'm in trouble," he said.

Viveca waited.

"I thought I could resolve it."

"What kind of trouble?" she asked.

"We borrowed some money. From bad people."

Viveca turned this news around in her mind.

"Why didn't you mention it before?" she asked. "How long have you known?"

"I thought I could…I don't know…fix it."

"How?"

Henry did not answer.

"Henry, how would you fix it?"

"It was one of my partners," he said.

"Not you? So you're not in trouble?"

"You know that old saying. *Fish rots from the head down.*"

Viveca thought with a pang of those long-ago days when one member or another of the Waldron family quoted Shakespeare all the time.

"Shakespeare?" she asked.

"What?"

"Was it Shakespeare who said that?"

"I have no idea, Viveca. But that's not really the point."

"It kind of is the point, Henry. I want to live in a world where people quote Shakespeare."

"Like your old friends from Michigan?"

"Yes," she said. "The Waldrons."

"Why didn't you ever talk with them again?"

"You know all that. I just felt such grief and..." Viveca searched for the right word. "Remorse."

"But I never thought it was your fault."

"Like you said. *Fish rots from the head down.* I may not have killed him myself. But I didn't do what I could have done to prevent him from killing himself."

"I've always felt that you need to let this go."

Viveca was silent. Finally she cleared her throat and asked, "What is your relationship with Mark Remington?"

"Who?"

"The man in the maze."

"Jesus, Viveca. That's not what we're talking about."

"Isn't it?"

Henry rose from his chair, his face still obscured in the dark room. He took two steps toward her. Once again, she felt a stab of unease in his presence.

"I'm at my wit's end," he said. "I cut you a lot of slack after the robbery, thinking it was some sort of reminder of your past. But you've become downright accusatory, Viveca."

Viveca battled her instinct to flee. Ever since that Halloween night so many years before, she had been unable to tolerate certain kinds of physical proximity. Men who moved too close too quickly. Henry knew that. Normally he was gentle and slow. Tonight, though, he was borderline threatening.

"Henry, back up a little," she said. "You're crowding me."

"Cut the crap. I'm trying to tell you about a very serious problem I have and you're going down that *I'm all triggered* path. Enough, Viveca. You need to grow up."

"How dare you take my private pain and make a mockery of it?" she retorted. "I trusted you with a shameful secret from my past. Because I trusted you to hold it—hold *me*—in a place of honor. I should have known when I heard how you spoke about Deirdre to Margo. That was vile, Henry! I never told you how much it bothered me."

"What the fuck are you talking about now?"

"You called Dierdre the C-word to her daughter. Your daughter. How could you do that?"

"Honestly, I have no idea what's going on here."

"Neither do I! You're treating me the way you've always treated her! And for no explainable reason!"

"Viveca, this isn't about you!" Henry raised his voice. "You're so wrapped up in Theo and your life in Greenwich that you just have no idea what's going on!"

"I have no idea what's going on because you haven't shared it with me! And I have no idea what you mean about Greenwich. You're the one who wanted to move here, not me."

"Could you just listen? I told you I'm in trouble! I think those guys robbed our house! The guys we borrowed money from."

Viveca paused.

"What?" she asked, trying to make sense of this new piece of the puzzle. "Who?"

"The guys we owe the money to. They're…not good people."

"And they robbed us?"

"I think so. I mean, I can't prove it, but…"

"Jesus Henry! Our house? With our kid? And these are the people you've gotten yourself involved with?"

"Viveca…"

"And where does Mark Remington fit into all this?"

Henry was silent for a good long while. She stared at him in the dim light, willing him to give her some kind of answer that would make this all make sense.

"I need some air," he finally said and walked out of the room and out of the house. Viveca heard the front door slam. She heard his car start in the forecourt, and pull off, spinning gravel as it went.

43

VIVECA 2018

Viveca flipped on the lights of her office and hesitated in the doorway. She didn't know who had gotten in here before. Frankly, from what Henry had just told her, it could have been anybody. But who would have left the shadow box on top of the dollhouse? As far as she knew, only Henry and Theo knew about her childhood shadow boxes. Then Viveca considered the concept: as far as she knew. What, really, did she know about what Henry might say to others? Or what he might do himself?

The room looked just as she'd left it. Daphne asleep on her doggy bed, stone-deaf to the world. Her phone plugged into its charger. And, yes, the random shadow box sitting atop the dollhouse.

Viveca closed the door softly behind her. Henry had made enough noise to wake the dead when he'd gone out a few minutes before. She would try to be quieter. She walked to the sofa and sat, squeezing her eyes shut. Maybe with her eyes closed she could make sense of this kaleidoscopic night. This kaleidoscopic month.

She should not have allowed herself to get into that fight with Henry. It was out of character for both of them. Viveca could count on one hand the number of blowups she'd had with him. No, their marriage wasn't perfect. No, she hadn't liked the side of him on display when it came to his ex. And sometimes, she had to admit, to herself. But for the most part they'd had a good marriage. She thought so, anyway. Hell, they still had sex, more often than not, which was more than she could say for some of their friends twelve years into marriage.

Still, there was so much unexplained. The robbery, for openers. Henry just came out and said he knew who did it. Guys he'd chosen to get involved with for money. Guys who wanted that money back. Guys who, in all likelihood, would not stop with a safe. Bad guys.

Then there were the letters, the prenup, and Mark Remington. A guy who intimated—who had practically said—he'd been hired by Henry. But how could that be? Had Viveca really worked with him eleven years before, on the set of *Misty*? Did all these threads tie together and lead up the gravel path to her safe and protected—or so she had always believed—house on the water in Riverside?

Viveca's eyes popped open. She had not set the house alarm. She'd completely forgotten after the argument. Leaving Daphne sleeping for this final chore of the night, Viveca went downstairs to secure the house. Henry would be able to get in later—whenever he returned from his late-night drive—through the garage door with a code. She would not be able to sleep in the meantime, however, if she did not set the alarm.

Not after the robbery. Not after Mark Remington.

Viveca tiptoed through the silent house. Even Rachel and Aya must have gone to sleep by now. She patted her jeans pocket to check the time on her phone and realized she hadn't taken it off the charger. She'd have to pop up to the third floor one last time to retrieve it before she went to bed. Well, she had to get Daphne anyway. The whole evening was turning out to be like a StairMaster workout.

It didn't take long to retrace her steps, close the doors to the conservatory, and go back to the front door and set the alarm. She breathed a sigh of relief when the final beep sounded, letting her know that the house was sealed.

Climbing the stairs again, Viveca took a detour to look in on Theo. When she popped her head in the doorway, her heart swelled to see him sound asleep with a book on his chest. The soft light of the bedside lamp saturated his face in a golden glow. His long eyelashes brushed his cheeks and his mouth was slightly open. He was, in every way, the picture of an angel.

She moved closer to see what he was reading. *Harry Potter*. Theo had recently started to work his way through the series. He was still on the first one, *Harry Potter and the Sorcerer's Stone*. She remembered her own youth when the books came out. She was already a teenager by then, so she wasn't the prime reading candidate. But she had loved them and secretly devoured each and every one. Even after that terrible Halloween night. Even after Sebastian's death. Even after she'd moved to LA and had become an actress—an adult—she had read them.

Viveca gently took the book from Theo's hands. She carefully marked the page with the bookmark he'd cast aside and placed it on the bedside table. She kissed him and clicked off the lamp. A plug-in nightlight switched on when the lamp went off, so the room had an ambient glow. Before she left, she touched his hair and kissed him once more.

As she turned to leave, she spotted a strange object partly hidden by the bedclothes. She reached for it and was stunned to see it was a *gun*.

"Theo!" she blurted. "What's this?"

"Hmm?" he answered sleepily. He opened his eyes and rose up on one elbow. "Oh. It's a gun. Dixon gave it to me."

"What?"

Viveca was apoplectic. *That damned Aguila family was so macho with their backcountry hunting clothes and guns and taxidermy everywhere. How dare they give her boy a gun?*

Trying to mask her rage, she asked gently, "What kind of a gun is it, Theo?"

"It's a Gamo Swarm Fusion 10X air rifle. We're gonna go target practicing next time I sleep over."

It would be a cold day in hell before that *happened.*

"Okay, honey." Viveca kissed him once more on the forehead. "I'm just going to take this right now. You could put an eye out with this. We can talk about it in the morning, okay?"

"Okay, Mom. Love you."

"I love you too, sweetie. Good night."

"Night," he said and turned over.

Stepping into the hall, Viveca noticed light under Rachel's door. She walked over and softly knocked.

"Who goes there?" came Rachel's voice from the other side. "Friend or foe?"

"Definitely friend." Viveca laughed, turning the knob and poking her head in. "Hey, how're you doing?"

"Happy to be here for my godson's birthday for the first time in years. The question is, how are *you*?"

"Well…I'm not getting along with Henry. I have a stalker. And a robber. Maybe they're one in the same. But hey!" Viveca ruefully laughed. "I'm so glad you're here."

"I am too," Rachel said.

"Wait!" Viveca held up the weapon. "Look at what one of the kids gave Theo. The dad is one of those master-of-the-universe hedge fund guys."

"Come sit on the bed." Rachel held out a bottle of tequila. "I confess I've been drinking a little."

Viveca burst out laughing. "You've actually surprised me, Rache. Of all the things I expected to see when I opened your door, an open bottle of hooch wasn't one of them."

"Always surprise 'em honey," Rachel said as she poured herself a short shot.

"You okay?" Viveca asked.

"Yeah. Just tired. Actually, I'm dealing with some health stuff. Tests. Don't wanna talk about it."

Viveca climbed up onto the bed and sat next to her friend, placing the gun on her lap. Her own life was so out of control—with stalkers and guns and safe robberies and who the hell knew what else was going on—she hadn't even asked Rachel what was happening with her.

"I love you, Rachel," Viveca said, and reached out to hold her friend's hand. "You sure you don't want to talk?"

"I love you too," Rachel said, setting her glass on the bedside table. "But give me that gun. Fucking John Birch Society around here!"

Viveca laughed in spite of herself as Rachel placed the gun next to her glass.

"Seriously, Viv," she continued. "The thing that happened when you were young. How have you kept that in for all these years?"

Viveca sat with the question.

"You said Henry knew?" Rachel asked.

"Most of it. I told him on our honeymoon. In Maui. You know how it is in those early days of a relationship where you tell absolutely everything about yourself?"

"No. I don't."

Viveca looked at her friend. "I know you've been alone a long time."

"Let's not go there," Rachel said. "I'll have to polish off the bottle!"

"Okay. We won't go there. But that's how it was in the beginning with Henry. He seemed so strong and mature.... He just felt like the person who could keep me safe from the world. I felt like I had to confess to what I'd done. I had to do it—almost as a test to see if he still would love me knowing how flawed I was. How guilty."

"Viveca, you were sixteen years old when it happened. You were brutally assaulted and raped. You lost consciousness. You lost your memory of the event. You were under pressure from those cops to point the finger at that boy, your neighbor. Your friend's brother. What young girl wouldn't have felt confused? Doubted her own perceptions?"

"You probably wouldn't have. I don't think Em would have."

"You don't know that. You're looking through a skewed crystal ball where you think the better qualities you see in a person are the sum total of who they are. And who they were. Remember that experiment in the 1960s? People thought they'd never do what average Germans did in World War Two. But when 'experts'"—Rachel made air quotes with her fingers—"ordered them to up the dose of electric shocks to the point where they thought they were killing people? They did it! Because someone they perceived to have authority told them to. They weren't monsters, Viveca. They were us."

"Then we're monsters. I'm a monster."

"No, honey, you're just a flawed and fucked-up human. Like me. Like all of us."

They sat for a moment in silence.

"But the Waldrons blamed me," Viveca finally said. "They had no space for forgiveness of me."

"Not then, no. Who can blame them? You say they were Black?"

"Yes."

"Well, that probably explains why the cops were so quick to blame him."

"Yes," Viveca sighed. "I do think the cops were more open to the possibility that Sebastian was capable of such violence because he was Black. And I just, I don't know…he had always been odd and he was, in fact, combative. But not violent like that. Plus he was gay. It wasn't so open back then, you know?"

"Did you ever try to reach out to your friend? Emilia? To apologize as an adult for the mistakes you made as a kid?"

"I…" Viveca began. "She wouldn't forgive me. She couldn't."

"Well that's a very judgmental thing to say, my dear. How do you know that she, a mature adult, is incapable of forgiveness?"

Viveca thought about it.

"Shit," Rachel said. "I think I'm tipsy."

Rachel took the bottle of tequila to the bathroom and poured it down the sink. "Should I go to a meeting with you tomorrow?"

"You need to sleep it off," Viveca said, and kissed her friend good night. "And tomorrow, please talk to me about what's going on with you, okay? Your problems are as important as mine, you know."

Viveca clicked off Rachel's bedside lamp and walked over to the door.

"Hey wait!" Rachel practically screamed as she turned the light back on and leaned over to snatch her laptop from the floor. "I can't believe I almost forgot to show you this! C'mere!"

"What?" Viveca stayed in the doorway.

"Seriously! I did a little research.... Well, I had my latest useless assistant do some research. And this one may not be so useless after all. Come here!" she said again.

"Okaaaay." Viveca came back to sit next to Rachel on the bed. "This better be good."

"Ta-da!" Rachel pointed to a photo on her laptop. A photo of a man, tall and lanky, with a dirty blond mane and bright blue eyes. He wasn't young—his tanned face definitely had its fair share of sun lines—but he was the picture of a California surfer boy.

"Who's that?" Viveca asked. "Your new boy toy? I'll admit he's cute."

"Viveca," Rachel said. "Look."

"I am looking. Am I supposed to know him?"

Rachel scrolled the screen with two fingers on the cursor.

"Look again!"

And there at the bottom of the image was the man's name. Mark Remington. For a moment Viveca was shocked. This Mark Remington bore no resemblance to the man who had followed her in the corn maze, the man she thought of as Mark Remington.

"Well, that could be anybody," Viveca said, recovering herself. "It's a common name."

"It could be," Rachel said. "But it isn't. This is the Mark Remington who worked on *Misty* with you. I'm sure of it, Viveca. I've verified. Is this the guy you saw?"

"No," Viveca answered, her head spinning. It would be unusual to have two migraines in one night, but it could happen. It might happen. "Not even close."

44

VIVECA 2007

In Detroit that spring it rained every day. The dampness seeped into everyone's bones, into their moods on set. The director would try to shoot interiors when it rained, but it rained so much that they eventually had to give up and shoot their outdoor scenes in the midst of it. The crew stood, holding gigantic golf umbrellas over the actors' heads, until Monica called *action!* Then Viveca and Gaspard played their scenes under the dripping skies.

Not for nothing, everyone joked, *that the movie was called* Misty.

On the last Saturday in April, they'd been filming for two months and had one more month to go. Henry had flown in that morning for only his second visit. Unlike his earlier promises to come often to see her in Detroit, he'd barely been able to find the time.

And now here he was, miserable on the cold, damp set. More than once, Viveca suggested he leave and meet her later in the warm hotel room. Instead, he elected to say and suffer.

It was Monica's idea to go to the club that night. A little team-building fun for her wet and weary crew. Viveca had loved working with her. She had never felt so heard by a director. Monica listened to Viveca's thoughts about her character and the story in general. Often she would change a bit of dialogue or action to reflect what Viveca had suggested. She did the same with Gaspard and the other actors. While Monica certainly had her own vision of what she wanted *Misty* to be, she wasn't hamstrung by it. She worked in tandem with the actors, the cinematographer, the crew. It was a gratifying experience that transcended Viveca's earlier movies. And, she could tell from the dailies they watched each evening, it was making *Misty* a stronger film.

They'd been working that day on Belle Isle. A rambling park that covered an entire island in the Detroit River, it sat halfway between Windsor, Ontario, to the south and Detroit to the north. As a Detroiter, Viveca already knew that bit of trivia: Detroit is the only city in the continental United States that looks south to Canada.

There, location scouts had found a stretch of tree-lined road evocative of the French countryside. Viveca and Gaspard bicycled up and down it for hours. Gaspard's bike carried a long baguette in the basket which, because of the rain, had to be changed out every hour. Viveca's basket carried a huge bouquet of wildflowers, which held up better.

There wasn't much dialogue. A little laughter and some lines called back and forth, bicycle to bicycle. The cinematographer had set up the camera on a dolly that moved quickly backward as the two actors approached. When they hit their marks, they stopped, leaned into each other, and kissed. This kiss was being filmed late in their production schedule, but it would be the first kiss that audiences would see in the film.

"Don't forget," Monica said to her actors as they sat in director's chairs, the ever-present umbrellas held over each of their heads, blankets wrapped around their legs. "When you lean in to kiss each other, I want it to be a mutual kiss, no? Not Antoine kissing Misty."

She used their character names, not their personal names, as everyone usually did on a film set.

"I'll hang back and let her come to me," Gaspard teased.

"No, no," said Monica. "You move toward one another in tandem. You kiss each other. I'm sure of it."

"No arguments from me!" he said, and winked. "I like kissing her."

At that, Viveca cast a glance at Henry, who was sitting in a chair nearby. But he never looked up from his phone.

After hours of the bicycle scene, Monica wanted to grab interior shots in a nearby building. Easier said than done. One thing Viveca knew by now was that everything in a movie took longer than you thought it would. It was late when they finished. Everyone hopped into various cars to head off to the nightclub, ready to blow off some steam.

Henry did not want to go. He'd caught a chill on set, both from the damp and from the endless kissing. Viveca didn't think her husband doubted her, but he was still a man. And it was a rare man who felt comfortable watching his wife kiss a handsome Frenchman over and over.

"C'mon, Viveca," Henry said as they were leaving the last set-up. "Let's just go back to the hotel?"

Gaspard was walking in front of them and slowed to keep pace.

"Viveca," he said. She loved the way he pronounced her name, with the accent on the second syllable. "You will join us, *chèrie*?"

Viveca looked at Henry.

"C'mon," she said. "It'll be fun! We're wrapping in less than a month and we won't have a chance to do all this stuff again."

Henry glared at her and Gaspard. She could see that his preferred timeline for doing any of this again would be never.

"Henri," Gaspard said, using the French pronunciation. "If you are fatigued, I am happy to accompany your wife for a drink and on to the hotel."

"I bet you are," Henry muttered under his breath, surprising Viveca. She looked at Gaspard, who did not react. Perhaps he hadn't heard.

"Come with me, Henry," she said, touching his face. "I want to dance with you."

They had always danced well together. It was one of their things. Early in their relationship, Henry had commented that she was an unusually good dancer for someone her age. Normally women of her generation, he said, danced while clutching a cocktail, like some kind of grown-up pacifier.

"All riiiight," Henry groaned. "One hour?"

"One hour!" she promised.

Gaspard looked briefly disappointed to have to share his costar with her husband. But he put on his most charming smile.

"*Bon. On y va*," he said, then turned to Henry and made a point of translating. "Shall we go?"

The nightclub was hard to find. It was down a back alley in a section of town near the Eastern Market. Nowhere Viveca had ever been. They parked all the cars on the street, then strolled down the alley together as a group.

Once inside, Gaspard's attention moved onto other possibilities. Viveca last spotted him on a corner sofa in conversation with a pretty actress who had a small part in the film. The two of them soon departed to continue their evening elsewhere.

"Hey," Viveca said to Henry, trying to ease the tension. "Wanna dance?"

His face was inscrutable.

"Sure," he said, and took her hand to lead her to the nearly empty dance floor.

The song quickly finished and Henry turned away.

"That's it?"

"C'mon, Viveca. I told you I didn't want to come." He turned and walked off, leaving her on the dance floor alone. "Cut me some slack."

Viveca froze, embarrassed that her colleagues might have seen this. Henry's visit was not going well at all. She had half a mind to follow him and really get into it. Yet she didn't wish to escalate the argument in front of everyone here. Instead, she wandered over to talk with the guys from the electrical department, who seemed to be deep into some shot drinking game.

"Hi," she said.

"Viv!" one of them called out. The cute surfer-looking guy. The best boy.

"What're you guys doing?" she asked.

"Shots," he said and poured an extra for her.

"No thanks," she said, pushing the glass away. "I don't drink."

"Neither do I," he said. "Normally. But we're all so fuckin' cold from all that rain. Consider it a hot toddy."

The words "hot toddy" elicited thoughts of childhood and Michigan and family. And Em. It was always Em who floated in Viveca's mind when her mind traveled back to that time and place. The place she'd come back to now.

"I'm leaving," Henry said, all at once right next to Viveca. She hadn't seen him approach. "Are you fucking coming or not?"

She spun to face him. "Henry don't. I..."

"I'm serious. I am walking out this door right now, with or without you."

Viveca felt her cheeks burn. Everyone was watching them, yet she felt utterly unable to make a decision. As it turned out, she didn't need to. Henry spun on his heel and left.

"Whoa," said the best boy. "Sure you don't want this?"

Viveca hesitated. And in her hesitation the die was cast. She took the shot and downed it, all thoughts of her sobriety floating away. It burned all the way down her throat—her damaged throat that had never recovered—and hit her belly like a warm blanket.

"Good girl," the best boy said.

"I'll have another," she said, slamming the glass on the table. "What did you say your name was?"

"Mark," he said, pouring another shot.

"Mark what?" she asked as she knocked back another. It didn't taste as good as the first. The second never did. Nor did the third, or fourth, or fifth.

"Remington," he said, smiling shyly.

It was the last word she remembered hearing before her mind became blank. And she would forget having heard it, even then, for many years to come.

45

VIVECA 2018

"Holy shit!" Viveca said. "There *was* a guy. A Mark Remington on that movie. But the guy I saw here in Greenwich is not the same guy."

"We need to call the cops," Rachel said. "Like now."

"Not tonight," Viveca said. "I can't have another all-nighter with the police. Theo's here. I don't know where Henry is. The house is locked up. We're safe. It can wait until morning."

"Okay, but *first* thing in the morning, Viveca. This is no joke."

"I had a drink that night," Viveca admitted quietly. "On the movie. More than one. It was the first—the only—slipup I've had since I've been in a program."

"Why didn't you tell me?"

"You had all kinds of other problems with that director, remember? And they were the same kind of problem. I didn't want to pile on. And I dealt with it so quickly. Went back to meetings and got on with it."

"Henry knew?"

"He actually was very kind. The next morning I was a mess. It was a Sunday. I don't know how I got back to the hotel or anything else. But he was supportive."

"Did he meet Mark Remington?"

"Yes. I mean, he must have," Viveca said and paused. "Do you think Henry has something to do with all this?"

Rachel reflected on her question for a moment. "It doesn't look good."

"But why?"

"Answer that and you answer everything."

"There was always something crazy with him and his ex."

"Could be a pattern," Rachel said.

"You always liked him, though," Viveca said, but Rachel went silent. "Didn't you?"

"Viveca, remember that story of Greta Garbo on the set of *Queen Christina*?"

Viveca did not.

"She was standing on the bow of a ship, looking out to sea. And she asked the director what she was supposed to be thinking. 'Nothing,' he said. 'Think nothing. People will assign their own thoughts and feelings to you.'" Rachel stopped, resting her case.

"What the hell is that supposed to mean?" Viveca asked. But she knew.

"Henry is Greta in this scenario," Rachel expanded. "In your entire life together. And you keep giving him thoughts and feelings that he might not actually have."

Viveca was silent.

"And that freaking prenup you signed," Rachel blurted. "Who asks for an infidelity clause?"

Viveca had no answer. Had her whole marriage been a lie? Was any part of it true?

"I'm going to say good night," she finally said. She needed desperately to go to bed. To sleep and end this nightmare. "I'm going upstairs to grab Daphne from my office. Then I guess I'll sleep...I don't know where I want to sleep."

"You can sleep in here. I don't mind sharing. It'll be like old times," Rachel said as she slid down under the covers and turned off the light. "Seriously babe. First thing in the morning you need to deal."

"Yeah. You're right." Viveca closed the door behind her, making her way down the hall and back upstairs one last time to fetch her dog and phone.

After climbing the stairs yet again, Viveca opened the door to a dark room. She hadn't remembered turning off the lights. Because there was no overhead lighting in the room, she had to feel her way to a table lamp. Just as she put her hand on the switch, a voice came from behind her.

"Yoo hoo."

It was a man's voice. The man whose name she did not actually know. The man who said he was Mark Remington but was not.

Viveca flipped the switch, illuminating the room, and turned around to face him. He was still in his costume from *The Mask*.

"What are you doing here?" she demanded.

"Hello, Viveca." He sat on her sofa with Daphne on his lap. "Or I should say, Ingrid."

"Who *are* you?"

"My dear, has your memory failed you again so soon?"

"See, I actually *do* remember Mark Remington. And you're not him."

"Sherlock Holmes lives again," he said, laughing. "Have you figured it all out?"

Viveca wanted to say that she had. But she hadn't. Not all of it.

"Why are you here?" she asked, hedging for time, trying to figure out how to get her dog and her phone and get help. Maybe she could scream for Rachel. But Rachel wouldn't hear her. No one ever did.

"Did my husband hire you?"

"You don't actually know?"

"I think he did hire you." She kept her voice low and steady. "I think he hired you to pretend you're someone I knew years ago. To make me think I'm losing my mind or I had an affair or I don't even know what. The letters, the robbery, the prenup—it was all you, wasn't it?"

"I don't know anything about a robbery," he said, then she saw his eyes dart to the doorway.

"I'm sorry, Viveca," Henry said from behind her. "I really am."

Viveca turned and looked into the eyes—the beautiful eyes—of her husband. She turned her head once more to look into the eyes of the man in costume. She stood midway between the two.

"I…" she began. It made no sense. It made every sense. "Why Henry? Why all this?"

"I need the money, love," he said. "All of it. I'm sorry. I didn't want it to come to this but I'm up against a wall."

"We could have worked it out together," she said, feeling like an idiot even as she said it. "I could have gone back to work."

"Look, Viveca, this could get ugly in ways you can't even imagine. You saw what happened when they broke into our house. And that was only for openers."

"Why didn't you just ask for a divorce?"

"I fully intend to do that."

"But you want to keep all the money." She did not say it as a question. There was no longer a question in her mind.

"This is really best for everyone. You and Theo too. And you *can* go back to work. You should."

Viveca couldn't believe he was giving her career advice right now. Life coaching! But before she could speak, she once again noticed the man on the sofa dart his eyes to the doorway behind Henry.

The man made a motion to stand but, before Viveca could turn around to look, there was a loud pop. Suddenly he pulled back, wailing.

"Fuuuuuuck!" he screamed and grabbed his thigh. "What the fuck!"

"Sit down, motherfucker," said a voice. Rachel's voice! "Or I'll put out an eye. Maybe two!"

And there was Rachel, smack-dab in the middle of the doorway. Like a domestic avenging angel, she wore a terrycloth bathrobe and pink fluffy slippers and brandished the air gun that Dixon had given Theo.

"And you!" Rachel said to Henry, waving the air gun in the direction of the sofa. "You get over there too!"

Then Aya poked her head around the corner. She was wearing a crimson caftan, her hair a blaze of wild curls. She carried a small gun and pointed it at the men.

"Is that…?" Viveca gasped.

"Henry's gun!" Aya said proudly.

"Listen to me," the nameless man began, his voice constrained by the obvious pain in his leg. "Call the cops. I'm ready to talk."

46

VIVECA 2019

The first snowfall of the year always stirred mixed feelings in Viveca. She could take it back to childhood, when there had been skating outings at the General Motors Tech Center pond in Warren. When there'd been hot chocolate at the Waldrons', and on rarer occasions, at the Linds'. Simpler times. Or she could take it back to her senior year, when she'd sat with her mother in the living room as her classmates arrived for Sebastian's funeral. When the very idea of simplicity had been punctured and made flat. Or she could take it back to highlights of winters past with Theo and Henry. When they had thrown snowballs at each other in the backyard right here in Riverside. Simple? Maybe not. But happy.

Or so she had thought.

It was always a choice what you focused on, wasn't it?

Viveca lay in bed, fully dressed, watching the snow fall over the Mianus River. The trees and church were nearly obscured in the distance. It was the middle of December. You never knew now if you'd get snow before Christmas. It wasn't like the old days. In many ways, she knew, that was good. She had spent so many years running from the darkness that had enveloped her that she had become unable to recognize darkness around her.

She had not recognized it in Henry. Her husband and the father of her child. In glimpses, yes. But she had shunted those glimpses to the side of her peripheral vision. Into the zone of the prisms of light that danced there when she had a migraine. But that's the funny thing about migraines. They consume you when you have one. But then they are gone and—if only in relief at their absence—you live as though they don't exist.

The doorbell rang. Viveca rose and slowly made her way downstairs to answer it.

"Viveca," Henry said. "Hi."

The snow swirled behind him as he stood on the porch. *The porch,* Viveca ruefully thought, *that was the scene of such drama not much more than a year before.*

"Come in," she said.

She cast a glance over his shoulder to see Paula, the court-appointed supervisor sitting in the front seat of Henry's car. He drove a Ford Focus now. His Porsche and her G-Wagon were the first to go. Items at the top of a list of assets that had to be liquidated. The house would have to go, too, in time. She hoped for a little more time. For Theo.

Henry might be going to jail. There would be a trial. Maybe more than one. Henry and his partners were accused of financial misdeeds in their restaurant empire. And the fake Mark Remington—a guy by the ridiculously fake-sounding name of Vinnie Marconi—had told the cops everything he knew about Henry's machinations to get out of his marriage to Viveca. Was any of that a crime?

Viveca did not know. She also did not know what she wished for. Conviction or exoneration for what Henry had done to her. To them. To their beautiful boy. But, for now, he was allowed to see his son for supervised visits.

"I got a job," she said, not knowing what else to talk about with this man who had become a stranger. "A small part playing a mom."

"Ah," Henry said. "From the ingenue to the mom."

"Right. That's usually how it goes."

"Will you have to travel?" he asked.

"No. It shoots in New York. My part is small so I only work five days and I'll come home every night."

"Well, that's good. For Theo, I mean."

Was it good for Theo? She had no idea.

"I'll go get him," she said.

"Hey Viveca," Henry said as she mounted the stairs. "I'd still like to explain. Maybe now that a little time has passed?"

Viveca turned around.

"Explain?" She looked at him hard, in a way she had never looked at him in their dozen-plus years together. His ice-blue eyes were the same. His square jaw, toned physique, salt-and-pepper hair—same, same, and same. But there was not a single aspect of his person that she recognized. Or perhaps, that she had ever really seen.

"I don't think there's anything you could say to make any of it make sense," she said.

"I just..." he began. "I was in trouble."

"Henry." She was still looking down at him from her elevated perch. "I'm standing on the stairs that were trashed by some thugs *you* got into bed with. How are you going to explain that? And then you hired someone to make me think I'd had an affair so you could leave me penniless? How the hell are you going to explain all that?"

"You weren't exactly who you said you were either," he said.

"What is that supposed to mean?" she snapped. "I was raped. A boy died. Yeah, I kept a low profile on that one. And I... You know what? You're a sociopath! And I'm not supposed to even be talking to you."

She was *not*, in fact, supposed to talk to him. That was one of the things her lawyer had advised. No conversation. It was too easy to get drawn into saying something she would regret. And now she'd called him a sociopath.

"Theo!" Viveca turned to run up the stairs, calling as loudly as she was able.

"I'm right here, Mom," came the small voice of her son. As she rounded the corner, she saw him sitting on the top step.

Damn. Adding to every other hell Henry had rained down upon their heads, now Theo had heard all that ugliness.

'C'mon," she said, holding out her hand. "Your dad's here and you're going to go play chess."

"I don't want to."

"Theo, you guys have a date. Your chess teacher is waiting. Then Dad's going to take you down to Mamaroneck for a Walter's hot dog. Your favorite!"

Viveca realized as she said it that her frenzied enthusiasm made her sound as crazy as Henry had been trying to make her.

"No, Mom," Theo said. "I'm quitting chess."

Viveca climbed the remaining stairs and sat next to her son. His young life was now tinged by the stain that both his parents couldn't help bleeding onto him. Whatever happened now, she had to handle this correctly. She had to help her son continue being the healthy, happy kid he was.

Had been.

"Look," she said, taking his hand. "I know there's a lot going on. Your dad and I have had some real troubles. But we both love you very much and we're both here for you."

Theo looked at her. "You don't believe that, Mom. So why are you trying to get me to believe it?"

She didn't know. She had stopped believing in her own father when she was a teenager. It had hardened her. Theo was at a similar crossroads at the tender age of eleven. And his parents' failings were exponentially magnified from those of her father. *What would this do to him?* She looked out the window at the snow, which had been falling steadily all morning. It was starting to accumulate.

"Shall we go downstairs and talk to your dad? Maybe since it's snowing so much, you guys can stay here and play chess?"

"I don't know. I think I just want to stay in my room."

"Okay," she said. "Why don't you go to your room now and—maybe in a little bit—you'll feel like going? I'll invite Dad in for a cup of coffee."

Theo silently got up and walked to his room. Viveca went downstairs.

"Henry, I think he wants us to talk."

"Well at least someone's got some sense around here."

"Don't," she said. "Really, don't."

"I am not a sociopath, Viveca. I've just made some bad decisions."

"That, I would say, is an understatement. Is this what you did to Deirdre?"

"You know what?" Henry was angry, as he always was, when his ex-wife's name came up. "I'm just going to go. Tell Theo I love him."

"Henry, I..." She stopped herself.

She had actually been about to beg him to stay, to go upstairs and talk to Theo.

How had they gotten here? How was it that Viveca was completely unable to judge the character of another human being? Or was it just the character of a man? She was better at picking her female friends. But she'd gotten it wrong with men over and over again. Sebastian was blamed for something he didn't do. Henry was excused from what he had done in the past, primarily by Viveca herself.

She had handled her marriage all wrong. In her fear of being seen for all the terrible things she had done in the past, she had allowed Henry to withhold the truth of what had gone wrong in his first marriage. And, she suspected, he had operated from the same playbook. They had each granted the other an emotional escape hatch because of how much they had wanted it for themselves. An *I won't ask you if you won't ask me* tacit agreement.

But it had all gone too far.

Viveca had a flawed memory, yes. But the Swiss cheese holes of her mind were small ones. Little blanks when she had a migraine. Larger ones back when she drank. But she hadn't had a drink in years. Henry had gone to great lengths—to travel all the way back to that time in Detroit—to make her question herself. To undermine her confidence and her belief in her own mind.

It was gaslighting of the first order.

47

VIVECA 2019

Rachel hit the curb with Viveca's newly acquired used Subaru as she tried to snag a parking spot on Central Park North. "Fuck!" she said with gusto. "I can't believe you got me to drive in New York. No one drives in New York."

"Are you sure we should be doing this?" Viveca asked. Maybe they could turn around. "I mean, should *I* be doing this?"

"You're doing the right thing," Rachel said, and patted her hand. It was an unusually intimate gesture for Rachel.

"Hey," Viveca said as she squeezed Rachel's hand, "I'm glad you're okay. Really glad."

Was she right in noticing that Rachel had softened after her health scare had proven unfounded? She thought so.

"And I'm glad you've come for the holidays," Viveca added. "To be with me and Theo."

"Well," Rachel said. "Let's not get too sentimental."

"Speaking of sentiment," Viveca said. "A little promising news. Theo's mentioned getting another dog. Which is a change. On top of everything and then Daphne dying, he's been so shut down. He'd refused to even consider a puppy."

"That is a good sign," said Rachel.

"Right?" Viveca said. "I think so too."

At least she hoped so.

Viveca squeezed Rachel's hand once more and opened the car door. She looked at her phone to confirm the address. It was a sunny December day. Christmas lights decorated windows and wreaths hung on doors. The recent snow had nearly disappeared, leaving only a few dingy mounds where it had been shoveled to the curb. "It'll be nice having you for Christmas."

"As long as you give me a Hanukkah bush!" Rachel shouted. Then she said more quietly, "Good luck. You've got this."

Viveca looked up and down the street and located the building. It was nice. Modern, all glass—not what she had expected at all. Inside, she gave the name to the doorman who sat at a large desk.

"Emilia Waldron," she said, her voice catching.

"I'm sorry?"

Viveca cleared her throat. "Emilia Waldron."

"Thank you," he said as he rang upstairs to announce her.

He waited while the person on the line—Em, she guessed—said something.

"Fifteen-O-one," he said, turning back to Viveca and motioning in the direction of the elevator bank.

She was nervous as she rode up alone. She'd brought a gift. An old edition of Shakespeare's sonnets that she had found through a rare books dealer. Em probably knew them all by heart but it was a beautiful book. Dark leather binding with swirly marbleized end papers in shades of purple. Purple that made Viveca think of Em's childhood room.

The elevator door softly whooshed open and gave a little ping. Viveca looked both ways and set off to the right. Emilia's apartment was three doors down. She rang the bell and waited, smoothing her hair, pulling her coat down in case it had ridden up in the car, running her tongue along the front of her teeth in case she had lipstick on them.

The door opened and there stood Emilia. Viveca had nearly forgotten how tall she was. If anything, she appeared to be even taller than she was as a girl. She stood in the doorway, not inviting Viveca in. She wore black pants, a black sweater, and large chunky jewelry that reminded Viveca of Rachel. Maybe that was one of the subliminal attractions of Rachel all those years ago. Maybe Viveca had sensed at a visceral level that she had tastes in common with her old friend.

"Em," Viveca spoke first.

"It's Emilia."

"Yes, of course," Viveca fumbled. "Emilia. I always liked your whole name."

Emilia still didn't move. Didn't invite her in. Viveca realized with a sense of crushing loss that this might be it. It might be all she ever got as a chance. This moment in the doorway. At any second, Em…*Emilia*… could slam the door in her face. She quickly grabbed the wrapped package in her tote and thrust it forward.

Emilia did not take it. She continued to stand with her hands at her side. After a painful beat, she lifted one hand and took the package from Viveca.

"Peace offering?" Emilia asked.

"Um…" This was not going to be easy. Not one second of it. "I don't know, Emilia. It just made me think of you. And I didn't want to come empty-handed."

"I almost wish you had. It would have been better. More honest. Because that's how you left me all those years ago. And my family. You never apologized. You never said goodbye. Nothing. Not one word after… You know what? I don't think I can do this. I'm sorry. I tried but I can't."

She started to close the door. Viveca reached out to stop it with her hand.

"Please, Em," she said, then corrected herself. "Emilia. Please let me in."

Emilia hung her head in what looked like defeat and Viveca felt a fresh wave of shame at all the pain she had caused. Emilia stepped back and swung the door open.

"Fine," she said, waving Viveca over to a furniture grouping near a wall of glass. The views swept down over the entirety of Central Park and the city beyond.

"*How do you, pretty lady*?" Viveca began.

Emilia said nothing.

Viveca turned to the windows. "This is breathtaking. Really beautiful."

"Sit down."

The furniture was modern in bright, solid colors—oranges, pinks, and greens. Not too different from the kinds of Scandinavian pieces the Linds had had back in Royal Oak. And the walls were covered with African art. Some of the pieces Viveca remembered from the Waldron home.

"Does this remind you of your house?" Emilia asked, indicating the furniture style.

For the first time the two of them laughed. Awkwardly, but they laughed.

"Kind of," Viveca admitted. "Combined with your house, too. The art, I mean. I hated all of this furniture back then."

"Well, you should have kept it," Emilia said as she sat on a hard couch, tossing the wrapped book on the glass coffee table. "It's worth a fortune now."

"I didn't keep anything," Viveca said as she sat on an equally hard chair. "Nothing."

"You kept my brother from me," Emilia said flatly.

"I…" Viveca looked out the window and then back at Emilia. "I'm sorry. I need to say that first and foremost. And I don't know how to say it in a way to convey how deeply and truly sorry I am. For the things I did. For the things I failed to do. For all of it. I am just so sorry."

The two women sat in silence, each turning her gaze away from the other.

"We took you in because we loved you. Then your family got so messed up. Your dad… My mother said you were vulnerable," Emilia said softly. "I was mad at my mother for years. Because she lied. She knew *we* were the vulnerable ones. Not you. And she didn't tell us. It was like she thought she could protect us from all that ugliness with the beauty of Shakespeare. But she knew."

"I didn't know," Viveca said. "I didn't understand any of it. And I didn't know how to fix it once it was broken. My body was trashed,

Emilia. Like it was a bag of garbage. That's how I was treated. I know I was drunk. But I didn't deserve that."

Viveca had never said that before. She had never claimed her own innocence in any of it, her own victimhood. All she had ever seen for the past twenty years was her own culpability.

Emilia's shoulders softened slightly. "I'm sorry that happened to you. And..."

She stopped. She snapped her head away from looking at her old friend and seemingly forced herself to look out the window. It was clear that she was engaged in an internal battle. She looked back at Viveca and took a very deep breath.

"And I'm sorry I didn't have more compassion for what you went through. I was so focused on my pain. My family's pain. I'm sorry, too, Ingrid."

They lapsed back into silence, staring at the view. The sky was darkening. It looked like it might even snow.

"Your parents?" Viveca asked.

"They died. First my dad, in '05. My mom lived another five years. They're both buried next to Sebastian."

"I'm glad. I mean, in as much as I can be glad of any of that."

"I know what you mean, Ingrid. I'm not an idiot."

"No," Viveca said. "You were never even remotely an idiot."

They sat in silence again.

"You've had quite a career," Viveca began, then corrected herself. "*Have*. I've watched you. Congratulations on the Emmy." Viveca pointed over Emilia's head to the golden statue on the austere fireplace mantle. "Pretty amazing."

"Yes," Emilia said. "I've worked hard but, you know, there's always luck. Good or bad. Why did you quit acting?"

"Did you know it was me that day? At that audition?"

Emilia barked out her old horsey laugh. "Of course I did. I was waiting for you to say something."

"You were?"

"Ingrid, the ball was in your court. For all the reasons we just discussed."

"I guess I'm the one who's always been an idiot."

Both of them lapsed into silence.

"How has your life gone?" Emilia asked.

"I'm still an idiot. I married the wrong man. I couldn't even see it. It was really bad but that's for another time. If we have another time. But I have an eleven-year-old son. He's a sweet boy. His name is Theo."

"I like that," said Emilia. "I like his name and I like that he's sweet. Sebastian was sweet inside. But he didn't always show it."

"He was too smart for the rest of us. He saw things we didn't."

"He was. And he did."

"I like to think I've done something right with Theo," Viveca said. "How about you?"

"I never had kids," Emilia said. "Never got married. I just couldn't ever fit it in or find a place for any of it."

"Do you ever go home?" asked Viveca.

"Of course! I have tons of cousins. Most of them have kids now. I'm their artsy auntie." She laughed.

Viveca sat with the normalcy of it all. After all that had happened, Emilia had retained her family. She had kept her ties to home.

"I never have. My mom died and my dad…I don't know. I just couldn't face anyone."

"Ingrid, I'm going to speak to you straight. You've been a coward. You've done a terrible disservice to yourself. Your family. Your old friends. Even your son. Your son deserves to know about your life. All these secrets and lies make people sick."

Viveca thought about what she said. About telling Theo. That was enough to make her sick right there.

"My husband turned out to be a bad man. I just…I don't know. He had such good in him. I thought so anyway."

Emilia sat back on the sofa. She did not speak for a while.

"Listen," she began. "I have tickets to the theater tonight so I need to get ready now. It's a play I'm considering optioning and I'm expected. This is enough for today. Okay?"

"Okay," Viveca said, disappointed at how short their time was together. She was fearful it wouldn't happen again.

Then Em tossed her an olive branch. "Do you want to have lunch one day?"

"I'd love to!" Viveca said. "Want to come up to my house? Meet my son?"

"Maybe someday, Ingrid. Don't rush it. It's a lot."

"You're right," Viveca said, rising from the chair and walking to the door.

She turned back to her old friend.

"Thank you," Viveca said. "Thank you for having a bigger heart than I could imagine."

"You always had a good imagination, Ingrid. Remember your shadow boxes?" Em asked as she walked out of the room for a moment. When she returned she held one up. The King Tut one. Viveca was stunned.

"Is that the one I made?"

"I kept it all these years. When your mom died, your dad came to the house and cleaned it out. He left a bunch of these in an open Hefty bag on the curb, so that's where I found the box. But the doll was in Sebastian's room. I don't know how he had it."

Viveca sat with the concept of her life's work—such as it was at that point—being treated like garbage by her father. And, at the same time, being treated like treasure by Emilia. Em had kept it all these years.

"We never spoke again. My dad and I."

"You've suffered too," Emilia said. "I wasn't able to see that."

Viveca leaned over to kiss Emilia's cheek, warm and soft and redolent of chocolate chip cookies. *Wait.* Was she imagining that?

"Do you bake?"

"What?"

"You smell like cookies?"

"What?" Emilia seemed a little miffed. "I'm wearing a very expensive French perfume and I distinctly do *not* smell like cookies."

"I must be imagining it," Viveca said.

And she wondered, as she rode the elevator down, if Mrs. Waldron had sent her a sign that maybe—after all these years of grief and guilt—she had forgiven her as well. But when she emerged on the street, her thoughts crystallized. It wasn't going to be as simple as that. She had apologized, yes, but it was an apology that was twenty years overdue. There was much more she would have to do to make it right. But, even if that whiff of cookies didn't mean that all was forgiven, Viveca hoped it meant there was a path to get there.

"Hey!" The bubble of Viveca's reverie was pierced by Rachel's voice. She looked up to see her friend standing next to the car with a towering stack of soft pretzels in her arms.

"Look what I bought for Theo!" Rachel said. "Does he like these?"

"Well, yeah," Viveca said as she opened the passenger door. "I mean, he'll eat *one*. Here, you get in. I'll drive."

Viveca helped Rachel into the seat and closed the door. Once she was settled in, she looked over at Rachel, buried under what must have been two dozen pretzels. "That's kind of a lot."

"You can freeze them. That's what the guy said. And I got a deal for quantity!"

"Rachel…" Viveca laughed. "For once, I think you got taken."

And she aimed her car for home.

Acknowledgments

Thanks abound for *Best Boy*. I could not have written it without a host of friends, colleagues, and even an unwitting inspirer! So why don't we start there? A few years ago, I received an email from a man with whom I'd worked years before on a movie. He—like the character in this book—reminded me of several touch points in our shared past. BIG touch points. And I—like the character in this book—did not remember them. Or him. But I googled him and found he was exactly who he said he was and we corresponded for a time. But, wow, did he inspire an idea for a book! So, thank you, Jeff Buchanan, for being the spark that ignited *Best Boy*.

On a similar note, thanks to the real Kelly Roush! Though we have never met, I was so touched when you showed up at a fundraiser for my beloved alma mater, Lake Erie College, and bought my auction donation: the right to have your name appear in my next novel! I hope you get a kick out of your fictional counterpart though I am sure she bears no resemblance to you.

Deep gratitude goes out to Beth Davey for being an agent both smart and wise; Anthony Ziccardi for being a publisher who allows this author to have a voice; Susie Stangland for her brilliance in social media and career strategy; Emi Battaglia and Kathie Bennett, the incredible PR duo that keeps my work visible in the world; and Lauren McKenna and

Rachel Paul for the masterful edits of *Best Boy*. To Aleigha Koss, Patsy Jones, Destiny William, and the team at Post Hill Press, thank you for guiding this ship. And to graphic designer, Cassandra Tai-Marcellini, profound thanks for keeping the whole package looking as beautiful as it does.

Thank you eternally to all the writers who said yes to reading this book in galley form: Joanne Leedom-Ackerman, Jeffrey Blount, Christa Carmen, Lynne Constantine, Sara DiVello, Ann Hood, Elise Hart Kipness, Angie Kim, Jean Kwok, Dara Levan, Sarah McCoy, Victoria Christopher Murray, Allison Pataki, Luanne Rice, Lisa Unger, Karen White, Lauren Willig, Lee Woodruff, and Laura Zigman. You're all busy beyond imagining with your own books and your generosity of time and spirit has touched my heart.

To Amy Scheibe and Luanne Rice, thank you for being my "deer" co-conspirators in the creation and running of the Deer Mountain Writers' Retreat. We have birthed and nurtured what we were looking for ourselves—a serene and beautiful haven where writers gather to write. Well, maybe share a little wine and conversation too! *Best Boy* was helped along its path at the DMWR.

To Lauren DiStefano, Lindsay Makowicki, Gretchen Miller, and the teams at the Ocean House, Martin House Books, and WCRI: thank you for partnering in the Ocean House Author Series. We have welcomed so many of the best and brightest to our little corner of Rhode Island and it just keeps growing and getting better every year. I could not imagine a more creative and capable team.

Thanks overflow for my family. We've lost three matriarchs in the past year: my mother, Kathy Goodrich, my daughters' other grandmother, Barbara Porter, and my son-in-law's grandmother, Ginger Newmyer. We are all a little lost and sad and yet we continue without you. Thank you for sticking around as long as you did. We so enjoyed you. You've left big shoes to fill. The best we can do is try to imbibe the best of you and maybe that is how any of us can hope to live on.

To my husband, Chuck, who has been my life companion for twenty-five incredible years—years that I could *never* have imagined before they happened—thank you. You create adventure wherever you go and you create so much for so many. To our tribe of children and grandchildren, you are a delight and it is so much fun to walk this path with all of you and watch you create your own lives.

To all my beloved independent bookstores and libraries across this continent and beyond, thank you for bringing books to your communities. You do us—writers and readers alike—the greatest service at a time when it isn't always easy to do.

And last—but never least—to my dear friends and readers, all, thank you for such foundational relationships. I rely on you and love you with my whole heart. To Ruth Terry Walden, especially—gifted teacher, Shakespeare afficionado, and encourager of the teenage mind—who was the gem of the idea of Mrs. Waldron. To Hassania Taffe, my dear Moroccan friend and inspiration for Aya. To the dear ones I work with every day—Leigh, Nimfa, Djuana, Tim, and the gang—you make everything possible and so much more fun! And to all of you who pick up a book and come to a talk and share your experiences with me, thank you. I write to connect with you and our shared humanity is everything.